OVERSIGHT

OVERSIGHT

A Novel

Steven C. Golly

PORT HOLE PUBLISHING
Florence, Oregon

OVERSIGHT

ISBN-10: 1-943119-14-7
ISBN-13: 978-1-943119-14-1

Published by:
Port Hole Publishing
179 Laurel St. - Suite D
Florence, Oregon 97439
Ph: 541-999-5725

For my lovely wife Janet.

CONTENTS

SECTION III: RESOLUTION

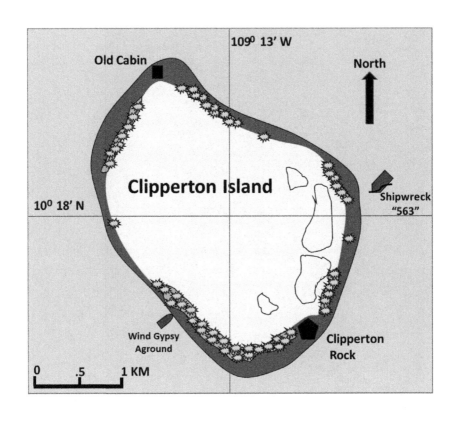

PROLOGUE

Walking rapidly along the coral sand trail that circled the island, John Finney reflected on how a coal miner like himself had ended up on this God-forsaken rock. When he took the job, he knew very little about phosphates or phosphate mining. He was, however, a quick study and the job offer was lucrative. Pacific island guano mines were the richest and most profitable source of phosphates and the demand for higher crop yields had spawned the emerging agrochemical industry. Phosphate mining companies were formed and backed by national policy to "secure the new riches of the Pacific islands." Finney saw the earning potential from the industry, and he felt the lure of the "Pacific Island Paradise".

That was 11 months ago. The lure of the Pacific island paradise had passed. Now, as he walked along the western reef of the sparsely wooded low island, he surveyed the work of its major inhabitants, goony birds. These fowl had painted the low island and all of The Rock, a 70-foot- high rock formation on the southeast reef, a slippery and generally unpleasant gray-white color with their droppings. And the stench. Well, it took a bit of getting used to.

In his short tenure as the manager of the island's mining effort, Finney had learned a considerable amount about phosphate mining, at least as it is done on *Isle de la Passion*, as the old French charts marked it, or the "armpit of the Pacific," as it was referred to by the Englishmen on his crew.

The trench mining approach, implemented by his predecessor, had worked well on the coral and shoal waters of the western reef, but the equipment used for the trenches was inappropriate for harvesting the rich content of The Rock. He needed equipment and men familiar with hard-rock mining. At the moment, he had neither. But after months of requests to his superiors in London, he had been assured that the equipment was "on the way." As for the men…"Make do with those you have."

The labor standards his father had fought for in the coal mines of Durham had not reached the Pacific islands. His crew were essentially conscripts. The work was arduous and the pay minuscule. The men remained impoverished by the company store, just as his ancestors had been. Few of his men were knowledgeable of mining. They had little free time and on this remote islet, even less to do with it. Any distraction was welcome.

And so, the rumors could be expected, the biggest of which was that there was pirate treasure buried in the caves that speckled the sheer rock face of the outcropping he now approached. Oh, yes, and the caves were haunted!

A group of men were gathered on the beach near the rock mound. Finney noticed the day crew chief entering a small cave, as he rounded a corner in the trail. The man emerged a few seconds later as Finney approached the opening.

"Ah can hear him screamin' in there, but the shaft is too tight fur me to git through," the man said. "The workers won go near it," he added, pointing at the cave.

Finney nodded to the man and continued to the mouth of the opening. It was small, perhaps two feet across and three feet high. He took the torch from the crew chief and entered.

"Polished stones," he mumbled to himself. "These people would kill themselves for a handful of polished stones."

Inside the entrance. the cave opened up to a small cavern, which provided standing room. Opposite the entrance, Finney could see a narrow tunnel that appeared to run a considerable distance into

2   *Steven C. Golly*

The Rock, disappearing into darkness. He knelt down on his hands and knees with the torch in front of him. The tunnel appeared to have been dug, unlike the natural opening at the cave entrance. Scraps of old shipping crates had been used for shoring. It looked passable. The crew chief had clearly not tried to reach the man. He was probably as frightened of the cave as the rest of the miners.

As he started down the tunnel on his hands and knees, Finney heard a scream from deep in the bowels of The Rock. It was the American, one of three people on the island with mining experience.

"Blast," he said easing his way forward as fast as he could.

At 40 feet from the opening, he came to a cave-in. The tunnel had overcut a void in the rock and collapsed. Before him a rubble-filled shaft ran precariously down and to the north. "Gas pocket," he said to himself, a chill running down his spine. He had seen the devastation that resulted from igniting a gas pocket in the coal mines. If this lower cavern was filled with gas…he instinctively pulled the torch back from the shaft opening.

As his eyes adjusted to the darkness before him, Finney noticed a faint blue glow coming from the opening at the bottom of the shaft. It was not the light of a torch flame.

"Hank," he called out the American's name.

"Help me…it's coming," was the terrified response.

The man was close, perhaps 30 feet away, at the bottom of the shaft. The faint blue light grew brighter. The American screamed.

As Finney peered down the shaft an intensely bright blue object flashed past the opening at its base. Above his head, 300 tons of rock gave way.

"Holy Mother of Jesus…" were Finney's last words.

17 September 1922 Moscow, Russia

Alexei was assigned to the People's Commissariat for Posts and Telegraphs only a short time before being transferred to Moscow to help with the installation of the large radio-wave facility near the east end of the capital. He was proud of his posting with the

Commissariat. He was there in the audience when the great party leader V. I. Lenin had said:

Every village should have radio! Every government office, as well as every club in our factories should be aware that at a certain hour, they will hear political news and major events of the day. This way, our country will lead a life of highest political awareness, constantly knowing actions of the government and views of the people.

Alexei knew that the technology of radio-waves would change the politics of the world. And he wanted to be right here at the largest radio facility in the world. He had worked for several years earlier on the development of the "Peterov" valve, which was invented by Nakita Peterov and later stolen by the Englishman, DeForest. His coworkers had succeeded in producing the two valves that were now installed in the output stage of the radio-wave generation facility's large transmitter. Alexei was responsible for ensuring that the transmitter worked properly during the three-hour broadcast. He knew the facility well and was admired for his competence by his comrades. With the valves and drive circuitry operating at peak performance, Alexei sat back at his bench and listened to the first live broadcast from Radio Moscow, titled Great Events in History:

Comrades, let me tell you today about the great cataclysmic event of the century which occurred in the Tunguska region of Siberia back in 1908 and galvanized our great leaders into action....

21 Dec 1944 USS LST-*563* Eastern Pacific

Lieutenant Jim Hockslander sat at the tiny desk, which took up a considerable portion of his sea cabin. He had taken command of LST-*563* when she was commissioned in May. The Landing Ship Tank was unnamed, not an uncommon omission for her class. His ship was referred to simply as the *Five-Sixty-Three*.

The ship had an exceptional crew, and Jim was eager to take her into action in the Western Pacific. But after a short series of sea trials, *563* was sent to San Francisco to take on a research team. The mission was Top Secret. So top secret that the War Department decided he did not have a "need to know." Now, nearly 20 days out of San Francisco, with one man badly hurt, and others possibly lost, he still didn't know the purpose of the mission in which his ship was engaged. Frustrated, he reviewed his orders for the hundredth time.

```
O 0023Z 04 DEC 44
FM CTG 36. 3
TO CTE 36. 3. 8
INFO COMTHIRDFLT; CTF 36
BT
T O P S E C R E T
SUBJ HELLFIRE {S}
1. {S} CHOP CTG 36.3. REDESIGNATED CTE 39.1.9
2. {S} PROCEED HUNTERS POINT SHIPYARD, SAN
   FRANCISCO,
3. {TS} AS DIRECTED BY COMTHIRDFLT REP. SAN
   FRANCISCO, EMBARK HELLFIRE PERSONNEL.
4. {TS} ON OR ABOUT 0100 10 DEC 44, SORTIE SAN
   FRANCISCO. PROCEED WITH ALL DUE HASTE LAT 10
   DEG 17 MIN N, LONG 109 DEG 13 MIN W.
5. {U} AWAIT FURTHER ORDERS.
```

The Hellfire Personnel (which the crew came to refer to as "the scientists") and their equipment were taken aboard and transit was made to the designated position without incident. During their passage, the ship had been "info-ed" on several messages, which referred to Hellfire. Jim did not know what Hellfire was and could glean little from the message traffic. And although he did understand the purposes of strict security, he had become increasingly uneasy with being left in the dark. Just prior to arriving at the destination further orders arrived:

```
O 0259Z 17 DEC 44
FM COMTHIRDFLT
TO CTE 39. 1. 9
INFO CINCPAC; CINCPACFLT
BT
T O P S E C R E T
SUBJ HELLFIRE {S}
REF {a} CTG 36.3 0023 04 Dec 44 {TS}
{b} COMTHIRDFLT INST 5120.1 {S}
1. {TS} UPON ARRIVAL POSITION SPECIFIED IN REF
   {a} DISEMBARK HELLFIRE PERSONNEL. PROVIDE
   APPROPRIATE SECURITY FORCES FOR SHORE PARTY.
2. {S} MAINTAIN POSITION IN VICINITY AS SPEC-
   IFIED REF {a}. SUPPORT SHORE PARTY AS
   REQUIRED.
3. {C} PROVIDE SITREP IAW REF {b}.
4. {TS} WHEN REQUESTED BY HELLFIRE PERSONNEL,
   EMBARK SHORE PARTY AND PROCEED TO HUNTERS
   POINT SHIPYARD, SAN FRANCISCO WITH ALL DUE
   HASTE.
5. {U} AWAIT FURTHER ORDERS.
BT
```

Following the Incident as it was now referred to in message traffic, he had been directed to not land any further personnel but rather to stand off the island and await further orders. Hockslander had interpreted that to mean circle the island and look for survivors, which they had been doing for the last two days. So far, Ensign Jones was the only survivor, spotted just outside the southeastern reef nearly 20 hours after the explosion.

Almost everyone that was above decks at the time had seen the blast. It reminded Jim of the explosions he had seen from shore bombardment; it was like the explosion of a 16-inch round from a battleship.

He had taken the ship to general quarters. They had been at general quarters off and on for most of the two days since the Incident. The crew now showed signs of fatigue, and the captain was becoming impatient. He had men missing on that island. They were probably lost, but he couldn't be sure, since he had not been allowed to do anything about it. And he still didn't know why they were there.

He picked up his comm handset and buzzed the bridge.

"Bridge," the quartermaster of the watch answered.

"This is the captain, put on the OOD please."

He glanced at the watch list. Ltjg. Palmer was Officer of the Deck for the current watch.

"Yes, Sir," came over the handset. It was Palmer.

"Frank, on the next pass around the southeastern side, I want to come in close on the reef and get a good look at that rock and the surrounding area with the Big Eyes." The captain was referring to the large, pedestal-mounted, binocular telescope on the signal bridge. "I'll be up in a bit, soon as I check on Mark."

"Aye aye, Skipper. I'll get us in tight, Sir."

Leaving his sea cabin, the captain walked out on deck and scanned the island with his binoculars. The small boat used by the landing party was still beached on the southwestern reef. Ensign Mark Jones had been the boat officer and shore party commander when the Hellfire team was sent in. Three other men from the ship's company, along with all five Hellfire personnel, were still on the beach.

To the south of the island, he could see one of the other boats patrolling in close to the reef. The seas had remained nearly flat since the Incident. He had decided the previous day to launch all the remaining boats, using them to search in close for survivors. Although he had been specifically directed not to land further personnel on the island, he would test the boundaries of those orders looking for his men. He had already decided he would break them if need be to recover his people.

Captain Hockslander estimated it would be an hour before the ship was back around the island and in close. He made his way down the starboard side ladder and headed for sickbay.

———————•———————

Ensign Jones was conscious enough to talk, but before their conversation could begin, the captain was waved to the back of sickbay by the corpsman.

"He's very weak and groggy from the pain medication." The corpsman said. "It's not good, Sir. I don't think he is going to make it."

The captain nodded and silently turned to Ensign Jones's bedside. He needed something, any information concerning what had happened to the rest of the shore party, anything that might help direct the search.

The young officer's memory of events on the beach was sketchy. Apparently, once ashore, the scientific team had split up into two groups, one moving north along the narrow reef, the other south and east toward the rock peak. Both teams carried one of the box-shaped instruments that had been part of the equipment brought aboard in San Francisco.

"The dial moved, and the things made kind of a clicking sound every so often," Ensign Jones said, continuing his story.

The ensign's group reached the base of the rocky outcropping rather quickly, following an old trail through the palm trees and underbrush. They remained at The Rock, investigating several caves along its base until the other group joined up with them, having traveled the circumference of the small island. At this point, the young officer's story became sketchy.

"You say the bright flash came from this…thing?" the captain asked again.

"Yes…yes…the ball…the *thing*," the ensign repeated. He had become visibly agitated.

"Can you describe this ball thing?"

"It came...it came out of the cave...the shaft," Jones began again. "The scientists seemed to know it was there. They had been looking for it the entire time, but it wasn't until the other team got there that they found it. He paused to catch his breath.

"The shaft was deep. Four of the scientists went in. I sent Chief Carson." He paused again. "The chief had his pistol. I sent him along with the scientists. They went down the shaft. I heard a shot. There was a flash of light and then screams. I fired the signal shots for the boat crew. Henry and Carter came around the southern end of the island with the .30 caliber machine gun and grenades. We went in the shaft with the other scientist. The chief and the other men were dead." He paused again, catching his breath. "I told the boat crew to go ahead with the machine gun. At about 60 yards, the shaft opened into a large cavern. There was a ball, maybe four feet in diameter suspended from the overhead. The ball was glowing blue, and it moved. It touched the scientist. The man screamed and Henry opened fire. We started out of the shaft. It followed us....The blue ball followed us." He paused again.

"Take your time, Mark," the captain said.

"We got back to where the others were lying on the ground. I was helping the scientist who touched the ball. His clothes and hands were burned. There was a turn in the shaft where the others had died. The boat crew set the machine gun up there, and I headed for the surface with the wounded man. Fifteen yards from the opening, I could hear them open fire. There was an explosion behind us--a blast!...I don't know what happened after that."

"We saw the explosion, Mark," the captain said. "It happened 20 hours before we picked you up. Did you see Carter or Henry after the explosion, or the other scientist?"

The ensign looked at him with a blank stare and shook his head. He closed his eyes and seemed to lose consciousness.

At that moment an explosion rocked the ship.

"Take care of him, Doc," said the captain, as he headed out the door and topside.

As Hockslander took the ladder three steps at a time, the blare of the Claxton came over the ship's public address system. The ship was alive with activity.

"Captain on the bridge," announced the quartermaster of the watch as Hockslander entered through the aft door.

He scanned the horizon. The island was off the starboard side, he estimated 3,000 yards away. The seas were flat. He could see no other contacts.

"We've been hit," said Palmer, still on duty as Officer of the Deck. "Unknown object. It was submerged and moving at high speed. It looked like it went right through us, Sir. It hit us starboard side forward of the #2 boat davits. It came out on the port side about frame thirty. It looked funny, Sir, like it was glowing blue."

The OOD paused, listening to the sound-powered phone he had just donned.

"Flooding forward," he said.

Both men looked forward through the thick glass windows of the bridge. Smoke was billowing from around the edges of the ramp used to transfer cargo between lower and upper decks. The ship was beginning to list slightly to starboard and becoming noticeably bow down. The *563* was sinking.

"I have the con," said the captain, assuming operational responsibility for the ship. "Helmsman, come right, new coarse 235 degrees. All ahead flank. Sound collision, boatswain. We're going to beach her before she sinks out from under us."

Five minutes later, USS LST-*563* was aground on the eastern reef of Clipperton Island.

Ensign Mark L. Jones died the following morning. The remainder of the shore party were never found.

15 Aug. 1977 Big Ear Observatory, Columbus, Ohio

The huge antenna, which formed the lens of the Big Ear Radio Telescope, was now passing out of alignment with the target region of the sky. The telescope had been used to map the frequency signature of nearly three-fourths of the heavens so far. Jerry's team was now working on the last quarter of the sky. He had to admit, it was sometimes monotonous work. That night, the big antenna had been pointed in the direction of the constellation Sagittarius. A large computer now processed the radio signals they had received and was printing out the results. The printout was formatted in columns of data with each column corresponding to a different frequency band. The data showed signal strength for each frequency band in hexadecimal format. Jerry tore the latest outputs from the printer and removed the perforated tracking strips from either side of the paper as he walked to his desk. He sat down and started scanning the printout for any obvious indications of a significant signal, absentmindedly circling any value above strength five. A string of six figures––6EQUJ5––appeared in the 1420. 5 MHz band. He unconsciously circled all six characters together, for a moment not realizing what he was looking at…and then he realized.

There it was!

What this search for extraterrestrial intelligence had been looking for all these years. As the implications of this enormous signal reached his consciousness, Jerry penciled "Wow!" in the margin of the printout.

At that moment, unbeknownst to him or any other human being on the planet, there was a rumble from the bowels of a small rock mound on an insignificant little island in the eastern Pacific Ocean. An ancient machine again came to life.

INTRODUCTION

In late April 2008, the then new French Prime Minister received a communiqué from her ambassador in Washington DC. Included with the communiqué was a letter from the U.S. Secretary of State. In the letter, the U.S. Secretary advised the French Ambassador that the United States of America has laid claim to L'ILOT CLIPPERTON, a small island approximately 1,000 kilometers off the Pacific Coast of Central America. The Secretary cited an obscure 19th century law, the *"American Guano Island Act of 1856,"* as authority for this action.

At that time, Clipperton Island was a possession of France and had been for more than 100 years. One would have thought that French sovereignty could not be questioned. However, none of the attempts at bilateral negotiations with the U.S. Administration had been successful in changing the United States' position.

In the months following the American action, it was widely held within the French government that this was little more than a clumsy attempt to use the recent global crisis as distraction for what was America's latest imperialistic venture. The new prime minister, herself, could not understand why the United States would risk the détente between the two governments that she and the previous prime minister had worked so diligently to foster.

Within days of the notification, and much to the prime minister's dismay. the U.S. had deployed a modern day "armada" to the island. A military response to this "invasion" would have been futile, and so has been their appeal to the United Nations. As of this writing, the French "Petition for Redress of Grievances" is still bogged down in the U.N. bureaucracy.

It has become clear from information released in later correspondence that the prime minister was deeply interested in what the Americans were after on the island.

She was never to know.   SCG

Discovery

1. Impact

1143 27 March 2007 11° North, 109° West

There was a cracking sound. The boat lurched to starboard, its bow lifted momentarily and then came back down some 30 degrees off the original course. The autopilot responded immediately. Teetering between sleep and consciousness, Alan could hear the muffled sound of the electric motor and worm gear of the autopilot turning the rudder in response to the disturbance. He could also hear the electric bilge pump switch on, as the boat slowly came back around to its original heading.

He had been having the dream again.

At 43, Alan Peterson was comfortable in a small boat at sea. An accomplished sailor, he had learned the ropes from his father, a lifelong fisherman by trade. Tall and a little too lean from eating his own cooking for the last six months, he was the shorter of two boys in his family and the only one of his six siblings to have embraced his father's love of the sea. At 18, he had left the family. He stayed on in Anchorage to attend the University of Alaska, while they moved on to San Diego and his father's new job on a purse-seiner, fishing tuna off the Mexican coast. He liked to think that he hadn't left the family, but, rather, the family had left him.

They had moved often while he was growing up, living on both coasts as well as Alaska––always on the ocean and always around boats. Now, a quarter of a century later, his parents had passed, and he rarely communicated with his siblings. Not because of any animosity, just inconvenience. How does one's family become inconvenient he asked himself in his half-consciousness? Was it that he hadn't been around them since college or that he had spent nine of the last 10 years overseas?

He had been dreaming about the accident again, the explosion that ended his last assignment in Indonesia. He was the site manager at the Kelian Gold Mine near the southern coast of Kalimantan Island. Were it not for the accident he would still be there. "How had it happened," he asked himself for the thousandth time, still drifting in and out of consciousness? And how is it that the explosion, which occurred in his dream, coincided with the impact to the boat? He could feel himself falling back to sleep.

Did something hit the boat?

Groggy, Alan forced himself to sit up. He had fallen asleep in the cockpit, leaning against a backrest of seat cushions propped against the cabin. Maybe it was too comfortable with the cushions, he thought, as he stretched the kink out from between his shoulder blades. Maybe it was too easy to fall into a deep sleep as opposed to the short cat naps that were the mainstay of single-handed sailors. He stretched some more and rubbed his eyes. Even with the cushions, he was stiff and sore. He decided to keep using them.

The night sky was moonless. Starlight reflected off the nearly flat ocean surface. There was just the hint of a breeze from the east. He scanned the horizon. There were no lights visible in any direction. Aft and to starboard, he could just make out a broad line of phosphorescence in the water and the wake of something traveling very fast beneath the surface. The object was on a northerly track. It must have passed directly under the boat. He watched as the wake disappeared. Whatever it was, it was moving too fast to be a whale. Maybe a submarine, but then, no. It didn't look right. "Too fast for a submarine," he said to himself.

He glanced at his wristwatch. It was 2 a.m. Stretching again, he started to relax, leaning back against the cushions. Whatever it was, it was gone now. Then he noticed that the bilge pump was still running.

He was instantly wide awake.

Initially, Alan had not been concerned when the bilge pump had turned on. In fact, the noise of the pump hadn't really registered in his consciousness when he first awoke. It was what one might call a normal occurrence. A sudden movement of the boat would cause the residual water in the bilge to slosh around enough to trip the pump's float switch and cause the pump to come on. The switch was set so that when the water in the bilge reached the level of a few gallons, the pump was turned on. The float switch would then turn the pump off when most of the water was out of the bilge. It tripped on every other day or so, as water made its way slowly through the propeller shaft packing gland into the bilge. However, the pump should have gone off by now, as it only required a few moments to discharge several gallons of bilge water overboard.

Alan got up and grasped the rails on either side of the companionway entrance, like one would parallel bars, dropping down the steps, while carrying most of his weight with his arms. At the bottom, his feet splashed into two inches of water that had flooded over the top of the cabin floor. The unthinkable was happening. Six hundred miles off the Central American coast, his boat was sinking.

———————•———————

A quick inspection of the bilge uncovered the problem. Water was flooding into the boat through a large hole under the forward bunk. The hole was roughly eight inches in width with what looked like charred edges, as if something had burned through. The damaged section of fiberglass was just a few inches forward of a corner in the cabinetry. The only access to the damage was through a small hatch underneath the bunk's mattress. Even then, the hole was partially hidden and difficult to reach. Water gushed around the cabinetry framing.

The leak was impossible to patch from inside the boat, and its location made it difficult to even slow the flooding. Alan grabbed towels from the head and stuffed them between the framing and the hull as best he could. Digging around in the forward stateroom, he found scraps of wood he had brought along for repairs as might be needed. He wedged what little of it he could use for shoring between the towels and the surrounding cabinetry, glancing aft every so often to gauge the water level in the main cabin. By the time he had finished wedging the makeshift patch into place, the water level in the boat had risen to nearly a foot above the cabin floor. He stood for a moment watching water ooze through the towels. It wasn't the prettiest job in the world, but the patch was holding. Yet, there was still a lot of water coming through the towels. Exhausted and shaking from the aftermath of adrenaline, Alan sloshed his way back to the main cabin and sat down. He leaned back against the cushions and watched as the water level slowly receded below the floorboards. The temporary patch was holding well enough that the bilge pump could stem the remainder of the flow.

Too tired to move, Alan closed his eyes and relaxed, listening as the pump did its work.

He awoke when the bilge pump went off. It's funny how sometimes a noise wakes you up, and sometimes it's the cessation of a noise that stirs you to consciousness. He lifted the access cover above the bilge pump and peered down below the cabin floor and into the bilge. There was nearly a foot of water in the keel section. The pump was nearly submerged. As he watched, the float switch tripped, and the pump came on again. After what seemed like far too much time, the water level receded several inches until the pump went off. Alan moved forward into the main cabin and lifted another access cover. Water flowed down the port side of the hull. The flow rate was significant, similar to what one might see coming out of a garden hose with the spigot wide open. The bilge pump went on again. He checked his hull patch, as he thought through what to do next.

The survival of the boat was dependent on the patch and the continued operation of the bilge pump--a pump that was working almost full time. Alan was certain the plastic cased submersible pump was not designed to be running 100% of the time. Still, if the pump gave out or the flooding got worse, there was the manual pump located under the seat in the cockpit. It required inserting a lever and forcing it up and down by hand. It was a workout he did not look forward to.

As Alan saw it, he had two options. (Well, three, but he was not yet ready to consider the third one). Option one, try repairing the hull. He didn't really have the right material aboard the boat for such a job, nothing that would adhere well to the fiberglass hull while under water anyway. He could try it with the materials he had, but then there was the issue that the work would have to be done from outside the hull. That meant going overboard in the open ocean. That was something Alan really did not want to do.

The second option was to run for land. The closest shoreline was Central America, over 600 miles northwest. At the boat's maximum speed under power, maybe eight knots, it was over three days away. Between the submersible pump and the manual pump, could he keep the boat afloat for three days if he really had to? Maybe, if the leak didn't get any worse. Maybe.

Then there was the other option. If worse came to worse, he could call the Coast Guard and get ready to abandon ship. "Not going to happen," he told himself.

———————•———————

Comfortable for the moment that the bilge pump was holding its ground with the flooding, Alan went topside to retrieve what little fiberglass repair materials he had stored. He decided to get everything he had together and see whether something might work for an at-sea repair job. Topside, he sat for a few minutes, waiting for his eyes to adjust to the darkness, then he scanned the horizon for any contacts. There were no lights visible, except for the planet Venus to the east. "The sun would be up soon," he said to himself, as he lifted the cockpit seat cover for access to the storage locker underneath. On top of several storage containers was his fishing gear. Seeing it, he remembered he'd moved the repair material into the forward state-room storage under the bunk to make room for his fishing gear. He stepped back down the companionway ladder, glancing at the chart table. He had better plot his current position before he did anything else, he thought. If all else fails, he would need it for the Coast Guard report. He sat down on the swing-out stool at the navigation table. A glance at the chart jogged his memory; there was an island south of his last fix, maybe 100 miles off his course. He studied the chart that was taped to the tabletop.

Wind Gypsy had made 38 miles the previous day. That was an average speed of just over 1½ knots. The boat was doing little more than drifting with the current. He glanced at his GPS receiver. **11° 06.8' N, 109° 05.9' W** appeared on the display. The instrument was an older model that had been on the boat when Alan purchased *Wind Gypsy* the previous summer. Position, coarse and speed were about all the functions it could perform. The newer models had video displays of navigational charts with current position, track line, course and speed displayed, as well as all other significant navigational features, soundings, land masses and navigational aids.

Alan's experience as a navigator, while in the navy, made him at ease piloting down the coast of Mexico and, now, navigating in open water. He preferred a paper chart, compass and parallels to the newfangled electronics. Even so, the instantaneous display of current position provided by this *somewhat*-more-modern equipment was handy, so, he kept the dated GPS onboard when he left San Francisco.

Reading off the position on the display, he ran his finger along latitude 11 deg. 7 min. to a point just south of his last plotted fix. It looked like he had traveled less than 10 miles in nearly 22 hours. "That can't be right," he said to himself, picking up his parallels to more accurately plot the position displayed on the GPS receiver. "We should have done better than that just drifting."

Alan's reference books indicated that the currents in this region typically flow at a rate of one to two knots to the southwest. If nothing else, they should be pushing the boat along its course at a faster rate than 10 miles in 22 hours. Without moving through the water, the boat should drift to the southwest at a rate of 24 to 48 nautical miles a day, and certainly more than 10. 6 miles in 22 hours.

Alan sat at his chart table staring at the GPS receiver for several minutes. He concluded that he could not trust that the position on the GPS was accurate. It would have to be verified. As he reached for the wooden case that held his old sextant, the bilge pump tripped back on. He had been listening to the pump turn on and off, as he plotted the boat's position. The off time was getting shorter. The leak was getting worse. He looked back at the chart and found the island he had noticed the previous day. Clipperton Island was approximately 90 miles SSW of the GPS position, which he knew was wrong. The boat should be closer to the island than that. He poked his head out of the companionway and scanned the southern horizon. The sun had risen and sunlight reflected off the ocean surface to the east. Nothing was visible. He needed a reliable position fix, but as the bilge pump turned on again, he realized he needed to slow the leak first.

———•———

After working the entire morning at decreasing the flow of water coming through the damaged hull, Alan was beginning to see some small success. Comfortable with that, at least for the moment, he had retreated to the cockpit with his sextant and watch. He had been watching the GPS receiver all morning. It was obviously locked up, its display remaining fixed at the same position, all morning, even though he had turned it on and off several times.

From his favorite navigating location, sitting on a pile of sail bags that he had lashed on the boomkin, Alan completed a local apparent noon sun sighting. He knew that he had collected enough data for a good position fix.

Below deck, he reduced his sextant sighting and plotted the position on the chart. Studying the chart for a moment, he ran his finger down the longitude line yet again to the small dot labeled Clipperton Island. Heading for this island may be the best of his options. "Option four," he said to himself.

Alan reached over the chart to a small bookshelf at the rear of the table and pulled out a tattered copy of *NOAA Publication 153* "Sailing Direction: West Coasts of Mexico and Central America (En route)." He opened it to Section-1 and read:

Ile Clipperton to Isla del Coco

1. 5 Ile Clipperton (10°17'N, 109°13'W), which is under the sovereignty of France, lies about 640 miles SSW of Cabo Corrientes (20°24'N, 105°43'W). This dangerous atoll consists of a low coral ring of varying width which encloses a lagoon filled with stagnant water. Two openings that formerly led into the lagoon are now closed.

The atoll is mostly 1.5 to 4.5m high, but Rocher Clipperton, a prominent formation, is 20m high and rises on the SE side. From a distance, this rock resembles a sail, but on closer approach it has the appearance of an immense castle. A shoal, with a depth of 9m, is reported to lie about 1-mile WSW of this formation.

A derelict hut, with a mast, was reported (1976) to stand near the middle of the NE side of the atoll. A rock lies close offshore, about 0.5-mile E of this hut.

Soundings give little warning when approaching the atoll from any direction. A high, breaking surf pounds the coral reef that encircles the atoll and, at times, completely sweeps across it into the lagoon.

Anchorage can be taken in depths of 37 to 82m about 250m from the reef at the NE side of the atoll, with Rocher Clipperton bearing between 177° and 190°. The bottom is coral with good holding ground, but heavy squalls from between N and ENE are frequent and vessels at such times should be prepared to quickly leave this anchorage.

In the vicinity of the atoll, the flood current normally sets E and the ebb current sets W, but the strength and duration of these currents depends largely upon the wind.

With no mention of any villages in the sailing directions, the island was, apparently, uninhabited. He read the entry again. Alan knew that "dangerous" meant dangerous to shipping, not necessarily to small craft. The island would probably provide some protection from the seas on its western side should the weather worsen. He would get the boat out of the water on the western reef and make repairs. He did the subtraction in his head—46 miles almost due south. It was his best chance.

2. Anomaly

Midnight 27 March 2007 Kula, Maui

The telephone struck the floor with a plastic crack, silenced in the middle of its second ring. Kate Harris fumbled for the nightstand light switch with one hand and the telephone receiver, which had apparently slid under the bed, with the other. The large glowing numbers on her dresser clock read 12:04 a.m. She found the phone. It was Phil Beckman. He sounded excited.

"…Can't be calibration." Phil was saying as she put the receiver to her ear.

"What can't be calibration?" she said.

"The elevation readings. Haven't you been paying attention?" Now, he sounded irritated.

"Tell me again, I'm awake now."

"It looks like the telescope elevation readouts are out of calibration. On the first shot tonight, the declination was off––too low. We tried several other sightings. Everything we've looked at is off to the south. Thing is, everything checks out. It can't be calibration."

Kate forced herself to concentrate on what Phil was saying. She brushed her short brown hair back from her eyes and sat up in bed. She was dead tired, having had little sleep for the last week.

"Did you check the clock?"

"No," Phil said sounding irritated again. "How could it be the clock? Right ascension is close, its declination that's off."

Steven C. Golly

"You know, Bennett has been telling the brass all week that we'll be ready on Friday." Phil changed the subject. "If it's calibration, it won't go over well. He'll be here this morning for status." He paused, probably for effect. "Are you coming in?"

Kate groaned. "I'll be there in 40 minutes," she said. "Do me a favor and check the clock."

She stood up and started for the bathroom, tripping on the textbook she had fallen asleep reading. Squinting at the mirror, she switched on the bathroom light. At 38, Katherine Harris was her father's daughter. He was tall and thin with brown hair and bad vision. Kate was tall and thin with brown hair and, if not bad, marginal vision. Looking in the mirror, she saw her blurry reflection. She returned to the bedroom and retrieved her glasses from the nightstand, tripping on the book again.

Kate's father had graduated from the University of Chicago with advanced degrees in physics and astronomy. Kate had graduated from the University of Chicago with advanced degrees in astronomy and physics. He was on the swim team when at Chicago and had worked as an astronomer his entire professional career. So had Kate, on both counts. He had married his college sweetheart, and after nearly 40 years, they were still the happiest couple she knew. Kate…well, maybe she wasn't exactly like her father.

Back in the bathroom, Kate fished her toothbrush out of the sink drain. The stopper had gone missing the week before, leaving an open hole in the bottom of the sink. She had lost an earring down it two days earlier or was it three days now? It's been a long week, she thought, as she inspected the toothbrush.

Kate had problems with men, not all men, just most men. A girlfriend had once told her to stop looking for her father in every man she dated. She didn't think that was the problem. The problem was she just hadn't found the perfect person, someone like her father. Besides, she had been so busy with the promotion and new job that she really hadn't had time to date.

Kate had worked at the U.S. Naval Observatory for seven years when this position came along. Her then manager and good friend had urged her to take it.

"A great career move," she had said. "You need to do this."

The job did look interesting, and it came with a big title, Site Technical Manager––not that that made any difference to Kate. The important thing was that the project looked very interesting and the job was in Hawaii, a place she had always wanted to work. Her small research organization was preparing the military's Advanced Electro-Optical System (AEOS) telescope, so that it could be used as part of a joint NOAA/Military program. The program was called the Hubble Project, named after the early 20th century astronomer. The AEOS telescope has extremely high resolution. It was the largest electro-optical telescope within the Department of Defense.

Although still technically a Naval Observatory employee, Kate reported to Captain Richard Bennett. Captain Bennett worked at the United States Pacific Command, or PACOM for short, and oversaw all Pacific region technical programs. Hubble was just one of many.

All Kate's big title really meant was that she was responsible for dealing with people problems, as well as the technical issues that were encountered. It was Kate's first leadership job, and she was having trouble being a manager.

"You're not managing *down* very well," Bennett had told her during his last visit. "You have got to get your people to do their own work. Hold them responsible. You can't do everything yourself. Your first job is to manage, not to do the analysis."

Kate had bristled at the admonishment, and at first, she wanted to blame her people. Why didn't they just do their work? They were all more than qualified, but they just didn't seem to get around to getting done with their assignments. One more thing to research, one more analysis, one more test. It was easier for her to just do it than coax them into completing their tasks. But Kate knew better, and she knew Bennett was right. She wasn't managing her people.

Her other big problem was the Air Force, specifically one Air Force colonel. As at most other observatories, vying for telescope time was a dog-eat-dog endeavor. Everyone felt their project had top priority. Unfortunately, Frank Elder, the Air Force colonel in charge of the observatory, thought that everyone (everyone else that is) was right. Colonel Elder was not particularly happy about being forced to support a navy project with his high value telescope. AEOS was in near constant use, tracking foreign satellites and near-earth objects. Elder thought "philosophical experiments," as he called them, were not the best use for tactical assets. The colonel had put the Hubble project at the bottom of his priority list. As a consequence, Kate had been allocated fewer and fewer telescope hours at increasingly less optimal time frames over the last two months. It was becoming increasingly difficult for her team to meet schedule. When she talked to Bennett about this problem, he had suggested that working it out locally would be better than running it up the chain of command. This only made Kate feel like she was not being supported by her boss, even though she knew he was also right about this issue. Apparently, she wasn't managing *up* all that well either. At least that was the impression she had when they finished discussing the problem. And so lately, Kate had been asking herself whether she really wanted to be a manager.

———•———

Negotiating the now familiar winding road to the observatory, Kate thought about this new telescope problem and the effect such an error would have had they been taking real sightings rather than just test measurements. The AEOS telescope was one element in a large array of linked telescopes that would, when fully integrated, take the appropriate astronomical and time measurements. AEOS and 43 other electro-optical instruments around the globe were being linked by a sophisticated network. The timing measurements taken by these instruments would then be compared with various atomic time and frequency standards, including the Naval

Observatory's own Hydrogen Maser Master Clock. The hope was to synchronize all global time, improving the accuracy of astronomic, navigational and other scientific research.

To Kate, the jury was still out on whether the required accuracy could be achieved. The technical problems encountered on the project were numerous. At AEOS there were major technical areas of concern that would invalidate their data. And as would be expected, most of the group's time was spent ferreting out the bugs. Like most experimental scientists, Kate found herself always dealing with the engineering issues. "Ah Kate, you have become an excellent engineer," she said to herself, mimicking her father's tone of voice, "if only a mediocre manager." She smiled to herself. OK, she would work on the management thing a little harder.

The project had been back on schedule for a trial run on Friday, until timing problems started showing up over the last weekend. Working with the Air Force facility personnel they had managed to get back on schedule by working double shifts for the last several days. Kate hoped this new problem could be solved quickly. Phil Beckman was right. Another schedule slip would not go over well with the project office.

As Kate entered the facility parking area, she started going over this new problem. The telescope's sightings were being taken to the south. Phil was right about one thing. Clock errors would show up as azimuth, not elevation. As much as Kate wanted the fix for this new issue to be minor adjustments to the instruments clock, that probably was not going to be the case.

———————•———————

By the time she arrived at the facility and cleared through what appeared to be an equally tired Air Force Security guard, the team had run six diagnostic routines of the atomic clock that provided the time reference for the telescope. All of the self-diagnostics had shown the clock to be stable. However, when they compared the local clock to National Standard clock in Boulder Colorado, there were small variations in the two intervals. The local clock appeared to have slowed slightly at 9:43 a.m. the previous day, losing 0. 27 microseconds over a period of 20 minutes.

"If the clock is off, why aren't we seeing the error in right ascension, rather than elevation?" Kate asked. Phil Beckman was the lead systems engineer in Kate's group. The research team was gathering in the small conference room that adjoined Kate's office.

"It's doubtful we would see a fluctuation that small in our sighting," Phil said. "But whatever it was, it's gone. The latest runs show no error. We're replaying the tapes and correlating all facility events. Probably a power surge," he added.

"Not likely. We have the most stable power on the Pacific Rim at this observatory," Jim Stevens said, sounding irritated. He was the only member of the team permanently assigned to the observatory. Jim worked directly for the base commander, Colonel Frank Elder.

"Sounds like a software problem," Tom Nelson piped in. "Software problems are going to kill this program," he added.

With the long hours in the last week and double shifts to meet the Friday deadline, everyone was showing signs of stress, particularly the handful of people that now sat in the conference room. At the far end of the table was Jim Stevens, the observatory's chief engineer. Tom Nelson was to Kate's immediate right. He was a network administrator on contract to the program from Microdata Systems, Inc. His company manufactured the network interface hardware used on the project. Mary Martin, a software engineer from Kate's old program at the Naval Observatory, sat between them. Mary was primarily liaison between the Hubble Program and the local Air Force software team. To Kate's left was Phil Beckman, systems engineer, also from the Naval Observatory, responsible for local project engineering and engineering liaison between the local site team and the program office. In his early 30s, Phil was short, prematurely balding and a bit on the heavy side. He also wore glasses, with thick black rims. He seemed to wear the same khaki pants and flannel shirt every day, Kate thought. He must have more than one of the shirts. The one he now had on didn't have the ink stain below the pocket. Actually, Kate got along very well with Phil. He was an excellent engineer, and she trusted his judgment on nearly all technical issues.

"We are running a full software regression test," said Mary. "So far, no errors. We should be done by 3:30 this afternoon. Personally, I don't think it's software. It must have something to do with the clock error."

"If it's a clock error, why aren't we seeing it in right ascension rather that elevation?" Kate repeated.

"Good question," Phil responded. "It doesn't make sense. But then, that's what I've been saying all along. I'll see if I can get John Martin's group involved with this. Maybe there is some physics here we just don't understand."

John Martin was the lead scientist of the R&D group at the Naval Observatory in Washington DC.

"OK. We'll leave the theory to the theorists," Kate said. "We need to get back to work and find the problem."

The meeting adjourned with Phil taking the lead on the anomaly investigation. Kate returned to her office and started revising her briefing charts for the upcoming meeting with Captain Bennett.

———•———

Captain Richard Bennett arrived 15 minutes early for the weekly briefing. Bennett was a Naval Academy graduate, an MIT graduate with an advanced degree in physics and to date, had a distinguished career with the navy. He was a bright and capable scientist, but as with many others in his profession, his advancement within the navy took him farther away from science and closer to the politics of the military and the responsibilities of his rank. At 49 and a senior captain, he had done well. He looked forward to retiring within the next year and maybe do a little teaching. He enjoyed teaching but hadn't had a chance to do any since his assignment to the Naval Post Graduate School years earlier.

Steven C. Golly

Bennett had been instrumental in getting the Air Force to allocate AEOS telescope time to the Hubble Project. He used the weight of his position to do so, and in the process alienated the Air Force Commander, Colonel Elder. Bennett, on more than one occasion, had tried to call a truce with Colonel Elder without success. Elder was a politician, not a scientist. Bennett wondered how the man had ended up in charge of the observatory in the first place. He didn't understand the science of the facility, and he wasn't even a particularly good military officer from Bennett's point of view. In fact, the Colonel was the only downside to these once-a-week excursions away from the military formalities of PACOM headquarters.

Bennett liked this little science project. The field of general relativity, however impractical, was a subject that had always interested him, and the research conducted in support of the Hubble Project relied heavily on Einstein's original work. He liked the people working the project, Kate in particular. She was a good scientist, if a little out of her depth in dealing with Elder. She reminded him of his baby sister, always trying to do what's right and not always sure how to make it happen. He could tell the job was starting to get to her. She had been looking frazzled these last few weeks. Too much work, not enough play. She needed to get out more.

————•————

The weekly briefing had started out somewhat unusual. Colonel Elder had arrived early and commandeered Kate's office for a private meeting with Bennett. Later, when the two military officers joined the team in the small conference room, the tone was serious; it was not the false joviality they usually showed.

"...but I don't understand how a time interval fluctuation can cause a declination error. Shouldn't you see it in right ascension?" Bennett was saying, as Phil Beckman entered the room.

"Sorry, I'm late," Phil said. "I spoke to John Martin at our R&D lab this morning. His research group is going to look into it. Stranger things have been known to happen, Sir."

"So, in summary, at this time we haven't found root cause, it hasn't re-occurred and we haven't been able to re-create it." Bennett summarized the anomaly findings in one sentence.

"We've offloaded the investigation to the research folks, and we're still on schedule for system test on Friday," said Kate, trying to make the best of the situation.

"And the anomaly does not appear to involve facility assets," Colonel Elder added. He wanted to make sure his bosses at PACOM knew the problem was not in his equipment.

"OK, thanks folks. Good job jumping on this thing this morning. We are almost there," Bennett said, signaling an end to the meeting. "Kate, I have another issue I need to speak with you about," he added, as Colonel Elder and the others were leaving the conference room.

Although his usual alert self, Captain Bennett had more than the Hubble Project on his mind that morning, and Kate sensed it. The scientist in him usually spent a lot more time mining for information. She got the feeling that these weekly excursions away from navy work were Bennett's only opportunity to be a scientist rather than a politician. In fact, it was his eagerness to be involved that put off many in the team. They thought he was micro-managing.

Colonel Elder must have aired some gripe he had with Kate's group at his private meeting with Bennett. Whatever it was, it seemed to have put the captain off. Bennett closed the conference room door after the others had left.

"We have bigger issues," he said, sitting back down at the conference table. He reached for his attaché case.

"SVN-28, 31 and 35 lost clock sync last night at the same time as your anomaly. No error signals from the satellites but estimated navigation errors in the Eastern Pacific were large.

Kate recognized the designation for the three satellites. They were part of the Global Positioning System, or GPS. Loss of three satellites out of the 28 wouldn't normally be an issue, unless they were over the same region when they failed. And they were.

Bennett continued, "NAVCAMS Honolulu lost sync with their Comsat bird as well as with the DSCS satellite last night. There were other assets affected also," he continued. "We have reports of hardware anomalies all over the Eastern Pacific Forces. Hell, my kids say they lost the satellite TV signal last night."

"I have a 10 o'clock flight back to Oahu this morning, and a 12:30 p.m. meeting with Admiral Wells," he said. "Your team has as much information about what is going on with this issue as anyone. I'd like you to be there."

———•———

Captain Bennett was on the plane and talking via cell phone with the technical advisor to the Navy's Pacific Fleet Commander, when Kate boarded. She had just enough time to get home, feed the cat, throw a couple of things in a bag and get to the airport in time to catch the flight. She brought copies of several error plots from the anomaly, and asked Phil to e-mail her any new info they found that morning before she left the observatory. Now, sitting in the cramped airline seat with her laptop balanced on her knees, Kate tried to organize her thoughts. Astronomical observation errors, navigational satellite timing errors, communications satellite outages—most of these things had nothing in common. In trying to make sense of it all, her long hours at work caught up with her. Kate was asleep before the plane took off.

3. Aground

1645 27 March 2007 11° North, 109° West

Alan awoke to the sound of the radar's contact alarm. He sat up, looked at his watch, then scanned the horizon. He had been cat-napping for the last two hours. The sun was still high over the western sky. The ocean looked like a pond. There was no wind, except that being generated by the boat's engine moving her through the otherwise stale air. He scanned the horizon again, seeing nothing but the blue of the ocean melting into the blue of the clear sky. He stuck his head down the companionway and looked at the radar screen, at the same time noticing with relief that the cabin floor was dry. The bilge pump was doing its job.

As the circular scan of the radar came around to the top of the display, he saw the bright line of a radar contact form on its upper left edge. It corresponded to what was probably a land mass ahead and near the outer limit of the radar's range. The audible alarm sounded, as the contact illuminated on the screen. Stepping into the companionway hatch and resting his elbows on the hatch cover to steady the binoculars, he studied the hazy line of the forward horizon again. There was now a dark spot in the haze.

Wind Gypsy had run under nearly full power for the better part of four hours. Alan estimated the boat's speed to be seven to eight knots. That would make the distance traveled, since he started the engine, nearly 30 miles. If his noon fix was right, the island should be 15 or so miles ahead. He went below to the navigation station.

Even with a water-cooled exhaust, the heat from the engine made the boat uncomfortably warm below deck. Adjusting the radar controls, he determined that the land mass was 14.7 nautical miles from the boat. The island was two hours away.

He lifted the bilge access panel. Water was still flowing along the trough of the keel and into the bilge. The pump was submerged and running. There were ripples on the water surface from the engine vibration, and as he watched, the water didn't seem to be receding. The pump was just keeping up with the leak, or, perhaps, just beginning to lose the battle.

At the galley basin, Alan splashed some fresh water on his face, grabbed a can of beef stew from the cabinet and a spoon from the drawer. With the chart and sailing directions under his arm, he escaped from the heat in the cabin to the cockpit.

Land was now clearly visible. Alan wolfed down the beef stew straight from the can. He took a few minutes to study his chart and reread the sailing directions, glancing below every few minutes to check for water.

———————•———————

The sun now hung low over the vast open waters of the Pacific Ocean to the west. A white coral reef capped with an occasional palm tree occupied the southern horizon dead ahead. Alan turned on *Wind Gypsy*'s depth sounder. Bars appeared across the digital display, indicating the water was too deep for a sounding. The instrument could only read to a depth of 300 feet. The ocean depth in this region of the Pacific was in the neighborhood of a mile. He didn't expect to see anything on the display until the boat was much closer to the island.

During the last 45 minutes, Alan's view of the island had morphed from a hazy dark blotch just above the horizon into white beaches and palm trees. Clipperton Rock was visible above the treetops on the far side of the island. His last check of the radar showed the range to the shoreline to be 3 nautical miles. Alan adjusted the autopilot to steer along the western coastline and went forward to drop the two headsails. A very slight breeze was now blowing. He would wait until the boat was aground before dropping the main. That way, if the engine failed for some reason, he could still maneuver under sail.

From the bow, he had an uncluttered view of the island. Clipperton was his first open ocean landfall on a journey that he hoped might take him around the globe, or at least across the Pacific Ocean. Although unanticipated and brought on by less than pleasant circumstances, he was enjoying the approach to the island and for the first time in a long time, he felt satisfied with himself.

In the three miles of open water between *Wind Gypsy* and the coral reef that formed the land mass of the atoll, the color of the ocean water changed from the deep blue to lighter and lighter shades of turquoise, terminating in the white sands of the beach. An occasional dark spot in the lighter water indicated a coral head, pinnacle of live coral growing just below the surface. Grounding on one of these coral outcroppings during an approach to the beach would be a disaster.

Alan's attention moved from the shallow water to the sandy reef of the island. He could see remnants of the structure mentioned in his sailing directions, just visible through the palm trees on the northern side of the island. The tall pole was missing. A large palm thicket stretched to the west of the structure, covering the northwest shoreline. The trees thinned to just the occasional lone tree with stretches of bare coral sand as his eyes followed the west side of the island southward. A thick stand of palms was visible on the southern end of the atoll. This thicket covered the south reef all the way to the base of Clipperton Rock. Clipperton Atoll was a beautiful island he thought, and as far as he could tell, he had it to himself.

Returning to the cockpit, Alan glanced down the companionway. The cabin floor was awash. *Wind Gypsy* was again taking on water faster than the pump could keep up.

He clamored down the companionway ladder and sloshed forward through six inches of water to the forward compartment.

A gushing sound from the leak was audible over the engine noise. Lifting the access panel off the berth, he could see that the hole had gotten noticeably larger and that the temporary patch was failing. The towels he had used earlier were inadequate for the increasing size of the damaged area.

Alan stripped the bedding from the forward bunk and wedged it between the framing and the damaged section of hull, pulling some of the earlier shoring out of the way. To hold the bedding in place, he used anchor chain he had stored in the forward locker. He piled chain onto the patch until he could lift his left hand off the sheet without the flow of water washing the towels and bedding from the hole. He glanced back into the main cabin. There was nearly a foot of water over the cabin floor. He piled 20 or 30 additional feet of chain on top of the blanket and then sloshed aft through what seemed to be still rising water to the main cabin. He retrieved the manual bilge pump handle from its mounting bracket and climbed the companionway ladder to the cockpit.

To the east, land was close, a bare section of coral reef perhaps 400 yards away. The large thicket of palm trees he had seen on the southern end of the island earlier was now visible. The closest point of land was the sandy beach on the southwest side of the island. This section of the reef was wooded, but the trees were not nearly as dense as the southern shoreline.

Alan disengaged the autopilot and turned Wind Gypsy toward the beach. He pushed the throttle lever to wide open. Moments later live coral was visible in the clear water off either side of the boat. The depth sounder showed 43 feet under the keel. With little wind, the surface of the water was nearly glass. Alan glanced down the companionway. The water in the main cabin was still rising. He removed the cover from the manual bilge pump access port, inserted the handle and began pumping with his left hand, while steering with his right. If water reached the air intake for the engine, he would lose the engine and the boat would drift in the shallow water of the reef until it sank. It would be too slow under the main sail alone to reach the shore. Judging by the rate at which the water level was rising in the cabin, that process wouldn't take all that long.

On the other hand, it seemed to take forever to traverse the 400 to 500 hundred yards to the beach. At 150 yards out, Alan scanned the shoreline. There was a steep coral sand beach dead ahead gave way to a rocky shoal lined with a dense coconut palm thicket to the south. Clipperton Rock was just visible above the treetops. Alan's eyes flashed between the rapidly approaching beach and the depth sounder. He grimaced, as the hull screeched over a coral outcropping 20 yards out from the beach. The sound reminded him of fingernails on a blackboard.

A few moments later *Wind Gypsy* came to a crunching stop, as the keel sliced into the coral sand, and the bow lifted onto the steep bank. Alan noticed that the boat was listing slightly to port but seemed stable. He exhaled audibly, realizing that he had been holding his breath.

Ten days out of Acapulco headed for the Marquesas Islands, Alan Peterson was aground on a small uninhabited island in the middle of nowhere.

4. United States Pacific Command (PACOM)

1230 27 March USPACOM, Camp Smith, Oahu

It was hot in the commander's conference room, the small auditorium adjoining the flag offices. Although Kate didn't recognize most of the people in attendance, she did recognize General Morris, the Deputy Commander, and Commander Jenkins, the senior Technical Advisor. Captain Bennett was chairing the meeting. There were technical representatives from various service components and commands within PACOM in the room, at least the ones that could make it to Pearl on short notice. The senior officers and government representatives sat at a table to the front of the large room, while Kate and other attendees sat in chairs facing the table.

Commander Jenkins was summarizing the Navy's Third Fleet operational reports concerning anomalies within the Eastern Pacific, when Admiral Wells and two other men entered the conference room. Everyone stood.

"Sit, sit," Admiral Wells said, as he settled into the chair next to General Morris. His voice was as usual, relaxed. "What do you tech folks know?" he said, smiling at Bennett.

"Well, Sir, we have seen significant communications disruption in the Eastern Pacific region over the last 24 hours, starting with a possible atmospheric anomaly that occurred at approximately 0945 Zulu last night. We have also seen timing errors in the GPS constellation over the Eastern Pacific, occurring in the same time frame. Cause is unknown. There may be ionospheric disruptions associated with the phenomena," Bennett said. "We are dealing with elevated solar activity and…"

Kate watched the men at the table, as Bennett summarized the information that had been covered at the meeting before the Admiral arrived. She now recognized one of the two men that had joined the meeting with the admiral. The short heavyset officer was Admiral Palmer, the PACOM Operations boss. She didn't recognize the other man in civilian clothes.

Bennett finished his summary and was about to turn the podium over to an INTELSAT representative, who would address anomalies seen in their global communication satellite constellation during the event.

"I'd like to discuss what Mr. Evans here has to say first, if you don't mind," said Admiral Wells, as he leaned over and whispered something in General Morris' ear.

Evans was the civilian that had entered the room with the admiral. He looked to Kate to be in his mid-50s. He wore an expensive suit and was definitely better dressed than the rest of the civilians at the table. Evans was of average height and weight and looked fit. He must be a senior advisor to the admiral, Kate thought.

General Morris reached across the table and flipped a switch next to the podium. On a small cluster of darkened signs at either end of the room the red TOP SECRET sign lit. The general asked that anyone without TSSI clearance leave the conference room.

Most of the staff left the room. Kate had obtained a clearance, while working on her previous program at the Naval Observatory. Bennett nodded at her to remain. As people filed out of the auditorium, Kate moved down to the front row along with three other people, who had been invited to stay. Admiral Wells waved Kate and the others up to the conference table, as there were now enough seats for all that remained.

After the room had settled, Mr. Mark Evans removed a stack of 24"x24" images from a large folder he had been carrying.

"We've pretty much ruled out solar activity or any ionosphere disturbance as the cause of these anomalies," Evans began. "This is a TYCO satellite image of the equatorial region, Eastern Pacific, taken at the time of the event."

Kate concluded that Mark Evans was CIA. And although she was not familiar with the code name TYCO, she concluded that it must be a satellite imaging system.

"This image is time lapsed, over roughly a 14-minute interval starting at 0941.89 Zulu last night. The lines that you are seeing are two tracks, both emanating from position 10 degrees 17.53 minutes north, 109 degrees, 13.46 minutes west."

"The image angle is bad," Evans continued. "We lost the bird that was over the area when the event started." He paused, lifting the second image over the first. "This is a RYNO satellite image of the same location taken at 1023 Zulu. The lines you see here and here are projections of the tracks from the TYCO bird taken back to the point of origin. The rest of these images are higher resolution views of the source location. They are also taken by a RYNO bird, and as you can see, they are all time-stamped. We believe this is the point of origin for the objects."

The images had all been electronically oriented, so that north was at the top of the sheet. Unlike other satellite images that Kate had seen on the previous program, these were in color.

The senior people at the table seemed to understand exactly what they were looking at, Kate thought. But from what she could see from where she was sitting, the images made no sense. The first one looked like red lines on a black background with red blotches. The second and subsequent images were obviously taken with a visible spectrum camera. They were pictures of what looked like a nearly circular island with what appeared to be a large lake in the middle and a small mountain on the southeast side. Two lines were emanating from the southeast base of the mountain, just off the southeast coastline of the island.

Bennett was the first to speak, after the images were spread out on the table.

"That's Clipperton Island," he said. "We were looking at it for a training operation a few years back."

"Ile Clipperton," Evans corrected. "It's French, although Mexico may still want to dispute France's claim of sovereignty. There hasn't been anything of military significance on the island since we left in 1944. People rarely land on the island. Jacques Cousteau, National Geographic, some ham radio guys and Mexican fishermen mainly. That's about it. It's abandoned. No permanent residents. The French wanted to do a nuke test on it in the 1980s, but we talked them out of it. They stand off the island with their navy once or twice a year now, just to let the Mexicans know they still own it."

Kate got a glance at the last image. She could just make out a green and yellow crab in the lower left-hand corner. The remainder of the photo looked like coral and water.

"If this is a launch site, where is the launcher?" General Morris broke the silence that had filled the room, while everyone studied the images. "Are you sure your track projections are accurate?"

"Yes, Sir," said Evans. "The infrared signature suggests that the projectiles we were tracking with the TYCO bird were moving under water. Speed was roughly 120 mph."

"So, do we know what they are? Where did they come from? Where did they go? Who made them? I don't see a launch point in these images either." The staccato of questions came from Admiral Palmer. "How do we know these objects are the cause of our hardware anomalies?" he continued. The PACOM Operations boss was a small man with an abrasive personality, strictly business.

"We don't," said Evans. "Our people haven't classified these objects, yet. They, in fact, may not have anything to do with the other anomalies; although the timing suggests that if they are not the cause, then they are probably another effect. Truth is, we don't know what they are. They do not appear to be natural or biological. We have never seen them before." Evans paused while everyone got a look at the images. After a few moments he continued; "We have other information on the island that I can discuss with the Admiral and his staff. It may or may not be significant. Oh, and Admiral, I also have the latest on the other issue, if you would like to address it later."

"OK, thanks Mark. Does anyone here have any idea what we are looking at in these images?" Admiral Wells asked the assembled group.

No one at the table could add anything to what had already been said.

"Well, I guess we had better hear what else you have to say then, Mark," said the Admiral. "Looks like we have most everyone we need here. Bob, could you chase down Ben and Paul (referring to the PACOM intelligence and communications officers). Ask Ben to bring everything we have on Clipperton. How about back in 20 minutes."

The Admiral stood. The other senior officers remained seated, still studying the images. It was a cue for everyone not on the PACOM senior staff to leave. Several people got up from the table and made for the door. The three flag officers and Mr. Evans remained, studying the information before them. As Kate left the room, a young lieutenant, who had, apparently, been waiting outside the door, passed a note to her. It was from Phil Beckman. "We've got something," is all it said, followed by Phil's phone number at the observatory.

———————•———————

Kate listened intently to what Phil was saying. She had borrowed the phone of a secretary outside the flag offices.

"We did an analysis of a wide field image taken by our telescope during the anomaly. It was accidentally snapped, while we were training the telescope between two of the target settings. We have Spica, Arcturus, Denebola and Zubenelgenubi in the image."

Kate formed a picture in her head of the stars that Phil had listed. They were all in or near the Constellation Virgo, which would have been in the southern sky at the time of the anomaly.

Phil continued, "John Martin's group did the translations. You remember these stars all showed declination errors, but they were not all the same."

"Yes, I remember that," Kate said.

"Well, in this case, they should be, since they are all in the same image. I mean, if it's calibration," Phil paused to give Kate a chance to think it over. "Well, they're not," he continued. "The positional errors are different for each star on the single, large-scale image. Each star has the same error, as in the individual images at higher resolution."

Kate was thinking as fast as she could about what Phil was saying.

"It can't be an offset error," she said almost absentmindedly. "How could that happen?"

"I don't know, but it has," he replied. "John says there is some kind of lensing, a near spherical dispersion going on in the image. But it can't be atmospheric, we've checked the DMSP satellite weather data. It was very clear last night, and the telescope calibration is dead on."

"So, what does John think it is?"

"He doesn't know. They want more data."

"Give them everything we've got."

"Done," Phil said. "Oh, John had something else interesting. He said something happened with the South Atlantic Anomaly, at the same time we saw these errors. He really didn't mention any specifics, but he thought you might be interested. So, what's going on down in Pearl? When are you coming back to work? It's starting to get interesting here."

Kate told him what she could about the meeting. As she was finishing, Bennett passed by on his way back into the conference room with a stack of red folders.

"Got to run," she said. Thanking Phil, she hung up and caught up with Bennett. "We've got more information on the telescope errors back from John Martin's group."

"OK, let's go over it when I get out of this meeting." Bennett looked at his watch. "In about an hour."

Without looking back, he entered the conference room, leaving her standing in the hallway.

Kate had been on the phone with Phil Beckman for the better part of an hour. She also retrieved copies of the most recent data by accessing the observatory's server. She was using the computer in the small office that Bennett had provided for her use when she was at PACOM Headquarters. Her "office" was a little room across the hallway from Bennett's office. It contained an old, gray, metal desk, an older, gray, metal filing cabinet, and a picture of the Naval Observatory, circa 1870 on the wall. The old, gray, metal wastebasket was missing. The old, gray, metal chair wobbled. Everything was dusty. It was standard military furnishings, from the late 1950s.

The R&D group still hadn't come up with a plausible explanation for the offset errors they had seen, and Kate's conversation with Phil was starting to lose steam.

"Maybe this is a gravitational effect," Kate offered.

She had proposed the idea earlier in the conversation, and it was met with laughter on the other end of the phone. Phil didn't laugh often, so the suggestion really must have struck him as funny. Or, maybe he was just getting punchy from lack of sleep.

"Let's see, you think there's a black hole over the South Pacific," he said. The comment was then followed by a litany of geological calamities that would precipitate from such an event. Kate listened to Phil's arguments for why her conjecture was in error. At the same time, she reminded herself that Phil didn't know about the equally implausible events that were occurring on the little island in the Eastern Pacific. Nor did he know about the problems that had occurred with communications and navigation satellites or any of the other affected assets in the region. What she could tell from the conversation was that neither Phil nor John Martin and his R&D

group were offering another explanation for the phenomena. A gravitational anomaly, however implausible, could cause just such an effect as they had seen at the observatory and possibly even the satellite and other anomalies she had heard about at the earlier meeting. At least she thought it could.

"Ask John what he thinks about gravitational lensing. If he thinks it's not possible, I'll let it go."

"OK, Kate. I'll see what he has to say. It may be a short conversation, but I'll let you know. Are you coming back tonight?"

"I may stay on Oahu tonight. If I don't talk to you before, I'll see you in the morning."

Kate hung up the phone and glanced up from her computer screen to see Bennett enter his office. She put her most recent data in a folder and crossed the hall.

"The research group found something important in our data," she said as she entered Bennett's office. "I think it's relevant to what's going on here," she added.

"What have you got?" Captain Bennett appeared to be deep in thought, distracted by something other than what Kate was mentioning.

"What we were seeing wasn't an offset error per say. They say it looked more like lensing. And it's not atmospheric. And it's not the equipment."

Bennett now had a puzzled look on his face. She had gotten his attention.

"What do they think it is?"

"They don't know. But I think it's gravitational," she said. "And I haven't heard a better explanation."

Bennett sat back in his chair staring at her for what seemed like several minutes. She was becoming uncomfortable. He was obviously thinking through something. Finally, a smile came to his face.

"Tired?" He finally spoke.

"Dead," she answered. "I'm thinking, maybe, I'll stay over in Honolulu tonight and get some rest."

"What you need is a sea cruise. Sail the South Pacific aboard the pride of the Third Fleet. Soak up rays on the beautiful beaches of Clipperton Atoll."

Kate's blank stare told him she was indeed tired.

"We're sending a ship down to Clipperton. There'll be a technical team aboard. I'd like you to be part of that team. I don't know how long you'll be there, but I think you're on to something. Your input may be important to the team. Are you up for it?"

Without even thinking Kate responded,

"Sure, I'll need to..."

"Great," he interrupted her. "You'll need to be at Hickam Air Force Base by 2000. That's in about an hour," he added matter-of-factly. "You'll be catching up with the *Fort McHenry*, LSD-43. She is enroute now." He looked at his watch. "Or, she will be in less than an hour. Lieutenant Park will get you directions and a map," he continued. "I'll talk to you on the ship. Thanks," he said as he stood up. Kate stopped at the door.

"I'll need to find someone to take care of my cat." This was happening way too fast for Kate to keep up.

"I'll find someone," Bennett said. He still had the smile on his face.

"...but where is Hickam Air Force Base?"

Lt. Park was waiting outside Bennett's office as she left. He knew the way.

5. The Atoll

0615 28 March 2007 Aground, Clipperton Atoll

Someone was knocking on his door. He answered. It was Ketut.

"You must come quickly, Sir," the young man said. Alan glanced over Ketut's head just in time to see an enormous explosion at the base of the mine. "Fifth level," he thought. ...Interesting. That could do some serious damage. I wonder what would have caused...

And then the blast hit.

Alan opened his eyes to see a blue-footed booby perched on the stern rail, one of its big, webbed feet resting on the boat's GPS antenna. The big bird was pecking at the stern running light with its heavy, hammer-like beak. It made the same sound as Ketut's knocking.

He had been dreaming about the accident again. Alan's last job was managing a remediation effort at the site of an old mine located at a remote island in Indonesia. The site was an exhausted open-pit, gold-and-silver mine from the 1980s. It was situated along the Kelian River. Remnants of the old mine included a huge open pit, covering thousands of acres. Tailings from the mining effort had produced a sediment-filled delta at the mouth of the river. Alan's job involved reforestation and wetland recovery, as well as the recovery of any remaining gold and silver in the waste material and sediment around the mine site. Alan knew that the two efforts, environmental remediation and the recovery of gold and silver, were competing activities. But he thought he could manage the conflict. He soon realized he was wrong.

As an outsider he simply could not influence the social and political forces that were involved in the region. The mine owners and the Indonesian government wanted to continue mining. At the same time, several activist environmental organizations, most notably the DDE (Don't Destroy Earth), were actively trying to disrupt their effort.

Then there was the local population. There were about 2,000 people, most of whom were not native. They had come to the remote river area in order to get rich, panning for gold. It reminded Alan of what it must have been like in California during the gold rush, notwithstanding the dense jungle and oppressive heat. These islander-miners were up in arms because the government had passed a law making it illegal to pan in the Kelian River.

After two years of work, the project was hopelessly behind schedule. Most behind was the reforestation effort, primarily due to vandalism and personnel turnover. The area was becoming volatile. Good workers were leaving for friendlier territory. Meanwhile, rampant vandalism was seriously affecting the work. Half of the equipment was inoperable at any given time due to vandals.

He had asked for security, but the company and the government were slow to respond. Most of the vandalism, it seemed, was occurring to equipment being used for remediation. The mining effort was proceeding on schedule.

In his last week, he had brought his concerns to the attention of the government and owner representatives for the final time. He informed them that they would have to cease their mining effort and focus attention on wetland recovery and reforestation, in order to have any chance of meeting the current schedule goals. The schedule had been continually revised and slipped for the last year. He saw a budget crisis looming, due to the overruns caused by the slips. The company and government officials took his comments under advisement. Two days later the explosion occurred. It was a huge blast, destroying most of the equipment being used for mining at the site. It killed 23 people, including his assistant manager and good friend, Ketut. The company representatives at the site blamed Alan for the blast, going so far as to insinuate he may have facilitated the sabotage. Truth be told, it was probably the work of the environmental extremists from DDE or possibly the locals. Either way, he was lucky to have gotten off the island and out of the country alive.

Alan spent several months back at the corporate offices in San Francisco going over the "couldas and shouldas" with his bosses. He was offered a new project. He questioned the amount of oversight the company wanted over his work. In the end, Alan found that his patience with corporate management, actually any *authority*, had waned. He needed to get away from excuses and rules and greed and apathy, and, well,…people.

His mind came back to the present. The bird was still pecking at his stern light.

"Wonderful. Boobies. The island has boobies," he grumbled.

Alan had dealt with these creatures along the Mexican mainland. They were extremely curious, and their antics were often funny and very entertaining to watch. However, after paying an exorbitant price for the purchase and shipment of a replacement mast top wind gauge, when one of the birds destroyed it, Alan lost his sense of humor with their shenanigans. The more he was around them, the less fond of them he became. In fact, they were now on his list of obnoxious, messy and destructive creatures––right next to corrupt government agencies and other such *authorities*.

He waved his arms. The bird looked at him disinterestedly for a moment then continued pecking. Expecting as much, Alan reached below and retrieved the boat hook from its mount. The device's retractable handle could be extended to over 10 feet if needed. The hooked end-piece gave the device its name. It was used to retrieve lines or buoys and to fend off while docking. He extended the handle and waved the hooked end around the bird's head. No effect, other than it seemed to Alan that the pecking became more vigorous. A moment later, the plastic lens cover cracked under the pounding the bird was now giving it. Alan stifled an expletive. He lowered the boat hook, smacking the fowl on the top of the head. The big bird squawked and took off screeching. It landed a few hundred feet north of the boat amid a flock of maybe 10 birds that looked like they had taken up residence on the sandy beach.

Alan put the boat hook away and went aft, leaning over the pile of sail bags and other equipment he had lashed on deck. He examined the stern light. The lens was indeed cracked, but still in place. He'd fix it later.

<hr>

It was now fully daylight. Alan stood up and took a good look at *Wind Gypsy*. The boat was a mess. There were lines and sails cluttering the deck. The remnants of the previous night's meal, a half full can of chili and an open container of crackers were sitting on the small cockpit table. There was a Mexican soda bottle (not a particularly good flavor as he recalled) in the drink holder. The cracker box had spilled over and there were cracker bits all over the cockpit. "That's what must have brought the birds," Alan thought.

Through the trees, low, puffy clouds hung over the eastern horizon. The sky was a watercolor of magenta, gold and blue. He was fortunate that he had dropped the mainsail the previous night, as a stiff breeze now blew from the northeast.

Wind Gypsy was still listing slightly to port and was hard aground. Alan glanced over the starboard rail. A foot of water surged over the coral sand some eight feet below. The tide was out and it looked like the damaged section of the hull should be well out of the water. Now was the time for inspection and, hopefully, to repair the hull damage, he thought.

The boarding ladder was still lowered over the side from the previous evening. Alan pulled on his old tennis shoes and climbed down the ladder onto the beach.

Upon initial inspection, it became immediately apparent that there was little holding the boat upright. The keel had buried itself a foot or so into the coral sand when the boat slid up on the beach. Then, as the water receded with the tide, the boat had tipped slightly to port, and the keel came to rest against the trunk of a downed palm tree. The tree was now wedged between the boat and the beach sand, just below the damaged section of hull. Alan was grateful that the tree trunk didn't block access to the damage. However, the balance of the boat was precarious. If the boat were to lean a little farther over, the keel could kick loose from the sand and the boat would topple over onto its side. It was too dangerous to stand close to the boat, particularly under the hull. But then, that was exactly where he needed to be in order to do repairs. *Wind Gypsy* weighed more than 34 thousand pounds with her current cruising load. Alan pictured her falling over. There would be considerable damage. He then erased the picture from his mind as quickly as possible. It would be a disaster.

It was clear that the boat would definitely need to be braced before he ventured under the hull. What he needed was bracing material, something to fashion a temporary cradle that would support the boat upright.

Alan scanned the beach in both directions. The landscape was low coral reef, palm trees and broad-leafed brush to the south and east. To the north, the ground foliage thinned, and there was just sandy beach with the occasional palm tree. No usable materials for bracing were visible. He remembered the ruins he had seen the previous day, as he approached the atoll in the boat. They were perhaps two miles up the narrow strand of beach to the north. He suspected, it would be the most likely source of timbers for bracing, although there may be driftwood on the reef. The prevailing currents would deposit such flotsam on the northern and eastern side of the atoll. He estimated that there should be a lot of floating debris on the eastern reef.

He made his way inland from the beach through a small grove of palms and brush. The trees were heavy with coconuts, and the base of the trees were surrounded by coconut husks. There were crabs everywhere. Small crabs scurrying along the foamy water's edge, large coconut crabs here and there at the base of the palm trees. And birds, lots of birds. The dominate species appeared to be blue- and red-footed boobies. Although, he spotted several other species, as he walked toward the interior of the island.

Weaving in and out of thick underbrush, Alan came to what looked like a trail 200 feet or so in from the beach. The trail was little more than a bare path of sand through the heavy brush. It appeared to run north and south. To the north, it disappeared as the brush thinned. To the south, it tracked parallel with the shoreline, following the reef and disappearing as it turned to the east. Alan crossed the trail and continued east through the brush and thinning palm trees. At 100 feet past the trail, he stepped out onto the dark sand shoreline of the lagoon.

Clipperton Island is an atoll. Alan remembered what he had read about the Tuamotu Islands, the string of atolls that lie along his intended sailing route. Atolls are the oldest of islands he recalled. Like all other islands, they are formed by the tops of mountains, which are high enough to protrude above the water level of the ocean. But unlike other islands, the mountain tops that formed them no longer exist, having long ago eroded away under the forces of wind, rain and ocean currents. What remains is the coral reef that grew around the mountain in the warm shallow waters of the coastline. With time, the mountain top eroded away, and the coral died and eroded into sand. But not all the coral died. New coral grew in the shallow water above the sandy skeleton of its predecessor.

As atolls go, Clipperton is not particularly remarkable. It has three characteristics of note, and Alan now stood examining all of them. As his eyes quickly followed the shoreline around the circumference of the lagoon, he verified what he had read in the sailing directions. The stagnate water of the lagoon was completely enclosed by the reef. Clipperton is not unique in this regard, but it is unusual for an atoll to not have at least one channel or pass, as they are called, between the lagoon and the ocean. Alan noticed that the water of the lagoon, particularly at its center, was very dark. Clipperton's lagoon fills the crater of an ancient volcano and is significantly deeper than that of a normal lagoon. This characteristic is also not unique but, again, unusual.

The stiff breeze that had built overnight, was kicking up a chop on the lagoon surface. The water looked murky. Alan couldn't tell whether it was naturally so or whether it was just silt agitated by the wind chop along the shoreline. He stepped out into the lagoon until the water was waist deep. It was bathtub temperature, already heated by the morning sun, or maybe, this temperature was cool for the lagoon. He scooped some water in his cupped hand and tasted it--slightly salty and stale. It had an unpleasant sulfur smell.

Standing in the lagoon 50 feet from shore, Alan turned around and, again, traced the shoreline, this time clockwise starting along the west side of the island. The sandy band of land on the western side of the island narrowed before turning east. The northwest side widened again, and there was a thick stand of palms. Just to the east of this thicket, the remains of the old building were visible on the northern reef. East along the reef, the trees thinned again, and Alan could make out the spray of what must be significant surf rising above the reef on the northeastern side of the island. As his eyes followed the sparse tree line south, he noticed the reddish colored remains of an old ship to seaward of the reef and on the opposite side of the lagoon. He couldn't make out what type of ship it was from this distance and angle. Although, it may have been painted red, he suspected it was more likely rust.

Alan continued scanning the shoreline. His eyes followed the reef south from the wreck to his first unobstructed view of the third notable characteristic of Clipperton Island--The Rock. It was as described in the sailing directions. It was steep on all the faces he could see with a ragged peak. It was dark in color. Although, all of its horizontal or near horizontal surfaces were gray-white from bird droppings. Staring at The Rock, Alan became aware of the odor that had been in the air since he landed on the island. It's not that he hadn't noticed it before. It was just that he had been preoccupied with other more pressing events––such as avoiding sinking and crashing onto the beach.

The island smelled like a bird cage, with just a hint of burning sulfur for good measure.

He wrinkled his nose, wishing he hadn't noticed.

———•———

Back at the boat, Alan decided that his best course of action was to inflate the rubber dinghy, install the outboard motor and use the small craft as transportation to and from the site of the old building. It would be just a matter of moving any materials he could find to the waterline, tying them to the dinghy and towing them back to *Wind Gypsy*'s location. Although it may have been best to put the dinghy in the lagoon, as the water there was quite a bit smoother than in the ocean, he decided against it. An anchor needed to be set off *Wind Gypsy*'s stern as soon as possible, while he still had the weather in his favor. The wind had stiffened all morning and was shifting from the west around to the east. Although Alan had been too busy to wait for a weather report on the side-band radio, he knew a storm was coming. The Coast Guard broadcast cycles through a complete synopsis of the Pacific Ocean weather about once every two hours. He didn't have the time now to wait for a local report. He told himself he needed to do so before the end of the day. Right now, however, he needed to put the dinghy on the ocean side of the reef and set an anchor. Ultimately, that same anchor would be used to pull the boat off the beach, after the repairs were complete. Now, it was needed to keep the boat from being pushed farther onto the beach in the coming high surf and stiffening wind. The anchor was now his top priority.

———•———

Alan spent the remainder of the morning getting the dinghy inflated and rigged and getting the stern anchor set. He used his *storm anchor*. The massive hunk of steel was a standing joke between Alan and his sailing friends back in California. It weighed well over 100 pounds and was "the most massive Danforth anchor ah has ever seen, mate," his friend, Brian, had taken to saying. "Is that an anchor, or are you goin' fishin' for whales?" "Guess with that, you can save on ballast." "At least, if you run across a battleship in distress, you will be able to help." Alan ignored the kidding. He had purchased the anchor at a marine equipment sale. It had been salvaged off a 100-foot fishing boat. His friends were right. It was too big for *Wind Gypsy*. It was heavy and awkward to store and handle. It was particularly awkward to handle in the dinghy. But then, it was a bargain (he had also endured a lot of bargain jokes). On the other hand, the large anchor had one massively redeeming quality––once it was set, it held. And, he thought to himself, it will take all its holding power to get the boat off the beach once the repairs were complete.

———•———

By the time Alan completed setting the big anchor, the tide was high, and the damaged section of the hull was underwater again. It would be the following day before the repairs could be completed, assuming he could rig a cradle for the boat by then. He checked the weather channel again but just missed the local report. He decided to go after bracing material.

Alan set out in the dinghy and headed north along the western side of the atoll. He motored the small inflatable along the narrow section of reef to the north of *Wind Gypsy*'s location. The water was shallow. It was less than 100 feet in depth, several hundred yards to the west of the island. He maneuvered the dinghy to stay in the shallow water where the ride wasn't so rough.

As he approached the north side of the island, Alan could see that the area of shallow water over the submerged reef narrowed to less than 100 feet. There were frequent coral heads extending up from the bottom to within a few feet of the surface. The dinghy passed easily over them in the water of the high tide, but they could very well present a hazard as the tide receded.

Alan had put his dive bag in the dinghy. It contained a collection of face masks and snorkels. As he approached one of the coral heads, he put on a face mask and leaned over the side of the boat. The water was clear, much clearer than the North American coastline. The visibility was at least 150 feet. The bottom was covered with multi-colored coral and alive with tropical fish and other marine life. A good place for snorkeling, once the boat was repaired and re-floated, he thought. And he certainly had the place to himself. The reef looked pristine.

He was thinking about where he had stored his underwater camera, when the dinghy passed over the coral head. The depth under the boat went abruptly from 30 feet to three feet. Alan pulled his head out of the water reflexively. At the same time, the outboard motor hit a coral outcrop at the top of the coral head, bucking and jarring the boat.

"Pay attention to what you are doing," Alan chastised himself.

Bringing the dinghy's heading back on course, he threw his facemask in his dive bag and continued scanning the shoreline for bracing material. So far, he had found nothing usable on the western side of the island.

As he motored around the northeastern side of the atoll, the dinghy nosed into a stiff breeze. Unprotected by the wind break of the island, there was a significantly larger chop on the water surface here, much larger than he had encountered on the island's western side. The small boat bobbed in the swell, its bow becoming airborne at the crest of an occasional larger wave.

Toward the shore, there were several lines of coral outcropping. Surf was breaking over these shallows and forcing him to stay well out. This far to sea, he was in the deep blue water of the open ocean and getting wet from the spray that blew over the bow of the little boat. He backed off on the throttle and scanned the shoreline, looking for a break in the surf that might provide access to the beach.

Alan had searched along the northern shore of the island for over half an hour without success. He stopped the engine just offshore from the dilapidated structure and studied it using his binoculars. It looked like a good source for bracing material. Unfortunately, there was no place to land without risking damage to the dinghy. The wind was still increasing in strength, and the seas had grown. He considered going back and landing at the narrow section of reef just north of *Wind Gypsy*'s location. From there, he could drag the dinghy across and into the lagoon where the water was much smoother. It would be easy to land the dinghy on the lagoon side of the northern reef.

It was tempting, but he decided to continue eastward. He wanted to explore the rest of the island's shoreline, anyway, and he may find a good landing spot somewhere along the eastern reef.

Rounding the northeastern side of the island, Alan could see the profile of the rusting hulk midway down the eastern reef. He recognized it as an old landing craft. He estimated that it was about a mile south of his position. It was possible that the ship's hull could provide a breakwater he thought, allowing him to land on its southern side. He could then scout the flotsam on the eastern shoreline, perhaps finding the materials he needed on the reef. If he didn't find what he needed, he could still just return and beach the dinghy on the island's northwestern side. From there, he could walk the rest of the way to the shack. Alan pointed the dinghy south, reaching the rusted hulk in 15 minutes.

Alan watched as continuous rows of surf broke on both sides of the old vessel. There was no place to land. The large ocean swells now created a continuous line of surf along the eastern shore. He now recognized the wreck as an old LST with its high superstructure. A relic, he thought. The design was significantly different than the LST's in use when he was on active duty. The entire ship was rust red. Not a square inch of paint was visible. It would be something to explore after *Wind Gypsy*'s repairs were complete, he told himself as he headed the dinghy toward The Rock.

———•———

Twenty minutes later, he was 200 feet off the base of Clipperton Rock. From here, it was clear what the rock formation was. Having been trained in geology, Alan recognized the dark jagged rock formation as a volcanic plug, the last remnant of the volcano that is now Clipperton Atoll. It seemed somewhat out of place. Clipperton Rock would have to be nearly solid iron in order to show so little erosion, given the obvious age of the island. The old volcano must have lain dormant for eons, eroding away while the atoll formed and then erupted again in the not-so-distant geological past, to form this rocky mass. It spoke of an unusually long lapse between volcanic activity. Strange, Alan thought.

On top of the mound, Alan could see the remains of an old lighthouse. There were a few timbers and some other debris below the old structure in a thicket of palm trees to the northeast of The Rock.

He scanned the shoreline. Light surf was breaking on the reef 30 feet to his west. He could see a small channel through the surf, perhaps 20 feet wide. It led to a narrow beach at the base of The Rock. The water was deeper in the channel, too deep for surf to form. In the clear water of this channel, he could see the bottom all the way into the beach. It looked passable.

Alan decided to try landing on the beach. He would approach through the channel and collect the material he could see in the thicket below the lighthouse remains. As he eased the boat forward, a bright blue light flashed from the base of The Rock, followed by a large splash at the channel head. Within a second, a bright blue object passed underwater at high speed just off the bow of the dinghy. The small boat was knocked violently by the object's wake. Within seconds, another flash and another object repeated the trajectory. Alan struggled for a moment to get control of the dinghy and get it out of the way of the second object. By the time he had settled the boat down and looked, both objects were gone. He could just make out the wake of one to the south, just moments before it disappeared amid the ocean swell and wind waves.

6. The Ship

2230 27 March 2007 Enroute USS *Fort McHenry*

By the time Kate arrived at Hickam Air Force Base, the research team was already embarking aboard a large helicopter for transit to the ship. Heavily loaded and loud, the CH-53 Sea Stallion was not a comfortable ride. It did, however, have the range to reach *Fort McHenry*'s position and the capability of landing on the ship's small flight deck.

Kate recognized Commander Jenkins as she boarded. The other four passengers were civilians that Kate had not met, although one man looked familiar. He was short and pudgy wearing shorts, a Hawaiian shirt and sandals. His hair was bright red. He was at the PACOM meeting earlier in the day, she recalled, a little better dressed. He was one of the people that left when the meeting became classified.

Kate sat in a web cargo net seat next to a small window on the left side of the aircraft. The red-haired man sat next to her.

"You're Kate Harris," the man said in a matter-of-fact manner. "Are you working on the big project? You're an astronomer, right?"

Kate looked at him with a puzzled expression.

"I'm sorry. We haven't met. My name is Sam Irvington. I work for Captain Bennett at PACOM. I've seen you around the office, and someone mentioned that you were an astronomer. So how close?"

Mr. Irvington seemed eager to strike up a conversation, but Kate was having a hard time following him. He was a very animated character. Although he spoke in a low, almost secretive voice, his hands appeared to be constantly in motion with gestures. And he spoke rapidly. Kate was having trouble hearing and digesting the barrage of questions over the helicopter's engine noise.

Mr. Irvington apparently knew about the Hubble project and was interested in it. More likely, he just wanted to make small talk.

"Well, it looks like we will be able to get the first system test done this Friday," Kate said.

Now, Irvington looked confused. "So, we'll know what we are dealing with by Friday?"

Kate realized his question didn't make sense. "Are you talking about the Hubble project?" She finally asked.

Sam Irvington's face turned as red as his hair. He became self-conscious, glancing at the other passengers before responding.

"I'm sorry, I made an assumption I shouldn't have," he said.

The big, turbojet engines of the CH-53 increased pitch, and the helicopter's blades began to turn. The noise level in the cabin became too high for conversation. Sam Irvington opened a book he had been carrying and began to read. Kate looked out the window. In what seemed like just a few minutes, the ocean was passing several thousand feet below them, and the evening sky turned to dusk...then darkness.

The harsh sounds of the helicopter engines had subsided, giving way to the rhythmic drone of the blades. It was the first time Kate had ridden in a helicopter. But after three hours of flight, her original excitement was now overcome by her fatigue. She was beginning to nod off.

———————•———————

The engine noise changed pitch as the helicopter started its descent. Kate opened her eyes and looked out the window. Outside was total darkness, except for a speck of light below and ahead of the aircraft. As she watched, the light turned into several lights of different colors: red, white and green. Minutes later they landed on the ship.

The USS *Fort McHenry* was 600 miles out of Pearl Harbor in transit from San Diego, California, to Okinawa, Japan, when orders were received diverting her south to Clipperton Island. For the ship's crew, it was the beginning of a normal six-month rotation to the Western Pacific, or WestPac as it was called. Aside from the ship's complement of officers and men, there was a small contingent of marines aboard. Many in the crew wondered whether the diversion south would extend the deployment.

It was after 2 a.m. before the big helicopter landed. The research team disembarked and were escorted to their quarters.

Fort McHenry was an amphibious assault ship. As such, she was designed to carry troops, some 700 (usually Marine) officers and men. With only its current small contingent of marines, there were ample quarters available for the research team. Kate was assigned a 12-by-15-foot room on the O-2 level, some distance aft and one deck up from the eating facility, or wardroom. Her room was designed to accommodate two junior officers. There were two twin beds, one on either side of the room with a small table and two chairs between. There was a basin, mirror, and medicine chest to the right as you entered the room. Next to those was the bathroom entrance.

She dropped the carry-on bag she had packed the previous morning for a day-trip to Honolulu on one bunk and lay down on the other. With her ears still ringing from the helicopter noise, she could just make out the sound of what must be the ship's ventilation system...maybe engines...maybe power plant. In 30 seconds, Kate was fast asleep.

———•———

Kate awoke to the low-pitched droning of the ship's ventilation system. She couldn't place the noise. She opened her eyes to see gray plumbing and wiring running across a gray open beam ceiling with black stenciled printing along the side of each beam. She was momentarily disoriented. Then she remembered that she was aboard a ship. Achy, she sat up and looked around.

The lights in the small compartment were on. She hadn't turned them off before falling asleep. Looking around the room, she remembered coming in the previous night. She spotted something new on the bed across from her. There was a pile of khaki-colored clothes, a blue jump suit, tennis shoes and socks and a small night bag lying next to her carry-on. She stood and walked around the table. Next to the clothes was a white bag made of netting material with the biggest safety pin she had ever seen holding the top of the bag shut. There was a label on the bag with her name stenciled on it in black, block letters. There was a small envelope on top of the bag. The card inside had an oval-shaped, military emblem with the engraving USS *Fort McHenry* along the top and LSD-43 on the bottom. The message read:

"Compliments of the Ship's Captain, and with
regards from Captain R. L. Bennett, PACOM"

Kate noticed, when leaving the helicopter the night before, that the other passengers had significant amounts of luggage with them. They obviously, had more time to prepare for the trip. But then, she was a last-minute addition to the team. In any case, she was thankful that Bennett had thought to take care of her.

Kate went through the clothing in the stack. It all looked like it would fit, and after she cleaned up, she changed into the jumpsuit and tennis shoes. Pleased that they did fit, she took a seat at the small desk and began going through her notes from the previous day. Ten minutes later there was a knock on the stateroom door.

"You have message traffic, Miss Harris." The steward stepped into the compartment and walked across the room to the desk. He put a folder down before her.

"Do you have laundry?" He asked.

Kate realized that's what the net bag was for.

"Yes, I do. Just a moment." She stuffed her previous day's clothes in the bag and securing the bag closed with the giant safety pin she handed it to the steward.

"Brunch is served until 1030," the young man said. "Do you remember where the wardroom is?"

The research team had been escorted from the flight deck to the wardroom, where they had briefly met the ship's captain and executive officer before being escorted to their quarters for the evening. Kate couldn't remember either officer's name, but she could remember the route between the wardroom and her stateroom. Her father always marveled at her exceptional sense of direction.

"I think so," Kate said. "It's down one floor, right?"

"Yes, Ma'am. O-1 level forward. Do you want me to show you?"

Kate glanced at the young man's white uniform. There were three black hash marks just below his left shoulder, the insignia for a rank of seaman. His name tag, pinned above his left breast pocket, said "Franks."

"Thank you, Mister Franks. I can find it." Kate extended her hand. "I'm Kate Harris."

"Seaman Franks." He said, taking her hand. "I'll be getting your clothes to the laundry Ma'am. Let me know if there's anything else you'll be needing." Seaman Franks stepped out into the passageway and closed the door.

Kate glanced at the folder the young man had left on her desk. Opening it, she found a message from Bennett, a large pile of data from Phil on the technical findings concerning the telescope anomaly and a note from Commander Jenkins. Jenkins' note advised her that there would be a team meeting in the wardroom at 1300. She looked at her watch. Three hours. She sat back down and started through the data.

———————•———————

With the small team seated in the wardroom of *Fort McHenry*, Commander Jenkins introduced the team to each other and to the ship's senior officers.

"This research group has been brought together very rapidly, Captain Arthur."

Jenkins addressed the introductions to the Commanding Officer of the *Fort McHenry*.

"I know you already met the team members last night, but let me tell you a little bit about us and what we are trying to accomplish. This can also serve as an introduction for the team as well. Some of these people, I have not met. I'm reading from my notes of yesterday, so, please pipe up if I get your backgrounds wrong.

As you have no doubt seen in the message traffic, if you did not in fact experience it directly Sir, there was significant communications and navigational satellite disruption in this region some 36 hours ago. There was also some…*activity* observed in the vicinity of Clipperton Island in the same time frame. PACOM believes the two events may be related. As a result, our little band here was put together to investigate the sightings on Clipperton. We are also going to request some help from your marine detachment during our excursion."

Kate noted that there were two officers in marine uniforms in the room. A captain and a second lieutenant if she had her Marine Corp ranks correct.

Jenkins continued. "I know that recent events have changed the priorities here, but as of now, we still plan to land the team on the island. Hopefully, with marine support." Jenkins smiled at the marine captain. "Assuming no changes, that landing should be happening in approximately (he looked at his watch), 30 hours."

Why would that change? What recent events? Kate had seen nothing in her note from Captain Bennett to suggest the investigation was to be called off. All he had said was that he hoped the trip went well and that he would try to get her access to the additional data that Evans had presented to the senior staff. He also let her know that he thought Jenkins was a good guy to work with. What's changed?

Jenkins began the introductions by seniority, that is to say military first, then government service and lastly civilians. Commander Norman Jenkins himself was now assigned as scientific liaison for the US Pacific Fleet (PACFLT) stationed in Pearl Harbor.

Jenkins was the beneficiary of a navy officer training program that allowed selected personnel to attend graduate education programs at the navy's expense, while drawing full pay. He received a PhD in chemistry from Duke University, compliments of the navy. He had used this advanced training at his previous assignment, which was at the Naval Weapons Laboratory in China Lake, California. In his early 40s, Norm Jenkins was average height and build, clean shaven, with short dark hair. Kate noticed his wedding band.

Robert Fulton, who looked to be in his late 60s, was the oldest of the group. Professor Fulton was a nuclear power expert, semi-retired from government service and currently full-time professor of engineering at the University of Hawaii. The professor was also working part time at the Naval Submarine Base in Pearl Harbor. He had published extensively in elementary particle theory and nuclear power plant design. He reminded Kate of one of her undergraduate mathematics professors. Murphy was his name. Professor Fulton was tall, well over six feet, and thin, with a gray beard and mustache. He wore thick glasses, and he had a cane. He actually looked more like a professor than did Professor Murphy, Kate thought. She smiled, at the same time wondering why a nuclear engineer was needed on the team.

Jenkins nodded toward Samuel Irvington. He looked heavier and shorter than the previous night, perhaps 250 lbs. and 5'4." Kate learned that he was a marine biologist of general background. He was currently working on a new formulation of paint that could "revolutionize the marine growth inhibitor industry," so Jenkins said. Irvington's previous experience was with the navy's marine mammal program. Although Kate suspected otherwise, maybe it would turn out that this was all just about fast swimming fish.

Jenkins introduced Kate, next. She could tell that he wasn't familiar with the Hubble Project or the Air Force Observatory on Maui, for that matter.

The last man on the team was Mr. Geoffrey Fox. He, apparently, worked for the U.S. Consulate in Honolulu. Jenkins was careful to point out that Clipperton Island was a part of French Polynesia and a French held island. As such, some diplomatic expertise may be needed. Jenkins also mentioned that Fox was an associate of Mr. Evans, the man with the satellite photos from the previous day. Kate concluded that Geoffrey Fox, or whatever his name was, was CIA. She began to feel out of place. Although it had originally sounded exciting when Bennett mentioned her joining this team, Kate now wondered what she could add. She had never been involved in field operations before. All her previous assignments had been at an observatory or in a lab. Last night had been her first time on a helicopter and this was her first time on a ship. Spies and nuclear engineers...what could an astronomer add to the mix?

Jenkins finished the introductions.

"This is our team, Skipper. We will be going over the data we have on the anomaly to date. I would request that your navigation and communications officers become familiar with the data. We would also request the use of a section of the wardroom for a conference and analysis area. I'll also need to brief the marine captain at his convenience," Jenkins glanced at the marines who were standing at the back of the wardroom. "For now, that's all I have."

The meeting was breaking up. Kate saw Sam Irvington headed her way from across the small wardroom and groaned. She found a tray of vegetables with ranch dressing, scooped up a hand full of carrots in a napkin and put them in her pocket.

"Ah, Miss Harris. How is your room? I don't do well on ships and they've put me in a room without a window. And the air conditioning is so loud. I hope you at least got some sleep."

Irvington was apparently not enjoying the ship portion of the trip. Kate thought he looked a little peaked.

———————•———————

Kate had taken copies of all the background information on Clipperton Island, as well as timing data from the GPS satellites affected by the anomaly. She sent a message to Phil Beckman, via the observatory's communications office. She requested that he send her what he could find on the geology of Clipperton Island and any new data on the telescope anomaly. She also sent a message to her old boss asking for information on what had happened with the South Atlantic Anomaly at the time of the incident. Phil had mentioned that something *odd* had happened there at the same time as the incidents in the Pacific.

The South Atlantic Anomaly, or SAA, is most easily described as a region over Brazil and the southern Atlantic Ocean, where the earth's magnetic field is weaker than other regions. This dip in the earth's magnetic field strength causes a significant increase in radiation in the region, much like what occurs in the Van Alan Belts. This high radiation has caused catastrophic loss of many satellites and remains a major design and operational constraint for most low-earth- orbiting satellite systems.

Although the SAA phenomena would nominally fall within the purview of elementary particle physicists, Kate's previous research program relied on astronomical measurements as well as particle physics. After the six months wait for her security clearance to be finalized, Kate had worked for two years on the program. She had learned a great deal about satellites, particle physics, and the environment of space. She hoped to use that knowledge to understand what had caused the GPS and other satellite outages that occurred at the same time as the anomalous measurements at the observatory and the sightings at Clipperton Island.

Leaning back in her chair in the little stateroom, Kate took the bundle of carrot sticks out of her pocket and popped one in her mouth. She sat quietly for a moment, noticing the ever so slight motion of the ship and the sound of machinery. She wondered what the recent events were that Commander Jenkins had mentioned during the meeting.

7. The Cave

1700 28 March 2007 Clipperton Atoll

Alan had almost convinced himself that the objects he saw near the base of Clipperton Rock were part of some type of oceanographic instrument or experiment. He was also fairly sure that had he ventured into the channel a few seconds earlier, he would now be the victim of an experiment gone awry. In fact, he thought he may already be a victim of whatever this device was. It seemed possible that what hit *Wind Gypsy* may have been an earlier projectile of the same type as the ones he saw leave The Rock. He decided he would approach the spot where the objects appeared by land, after he had refloated the boat. He wanted to take a closer look.

A big thunderhead had formed over the island that afternoon. It was raining hard as Alan beached the dinghy near the palm thicket at the northwest side of the island. He took the dinghy as close to the old ruins as he could. It was still a hike. The path, that he had found just inland from where *Wind Gypsy* was beached, reappeared at the beginning of the palm thicket. Alan considered taking this path but decided to stay close to the lagoon shore, instead. The darker, silt-laden sand along the lagoon was hard-packed and easier to walk through than the soft, coral sand of the path. Still, it was a workout, trudging through the sand and torrential rain to the shack.

The old building was a small structure, perhaps 15 feet on either side finished in some rough sawn and some hand-hued lumber. The material looked to Alan like pine, but he guessed it could be indigenous palm. The floor was finished in rough lumber, somewhat over an inch thick. There were pole rafters on the roof and the remains of thatching on the northwest corner. Otherwise, the rafters were bare of roofing material. Alan stood under the thatching and studied his surroundings. The corner posts and plates were palm poles, their surfaces hued with a bladed tool, probably an adze. They would work fine for what he needed, but he would have to demolish the structure to get at them. Through a window opening, on the west side of the building, he could see where someone had fashioned a newer structure, a lean-to on the side of the old building. It appeared to be haphazardly built out of more modern materials, dimension lumber. The remains of a corrugated metal roof, that was red with rust, covered the structure. It looked much more promising as a source of material.

Alan waited a few minutes under the thatched section of roof, hoping the rain would let up. It didn't. Resigned to remaining drenched for the rest of the day, he went back out the entrance and around to its west side. There he had a good view inside the lean-to. It was full of lumber! Near the entrance was a stack of the same 2x4 and 4x4 material that was used to construct the newer addition. He stood under the metal roof for a few moments, again hoping the rain would let up. And as before, it didn't. So, with only a small amount of grumbling, Alan commenced packing 4x4s––one at a time––back to the dinghy.

It turned out to be what he had expected––a tiring task. The equatorial heat combined with the rain made the job seem like working in a steam bath. He spent the remainder of the afternoon moving lumber from the shed to the dinghy. As the wind built, the rain increased making the job even less pleasant.

———————•———————

Alan had a good start installing bracing under the hull the previous evening. He had worked all day finishing the construction of the cradle, making two more trips to the old shack for material. He had taken only one break late that morning, after a fit of nausea overcame him while he was packing 2x4s between the old building and the dinghy. It seemed like the heat was getting to him. So, he added a little salt to the can of chili he had for lunch. It seemed to do the trick.

The result of his work was a makeshift––but strong––cradle that he completed before nightfall. At dusk, the rain and wind subsided, and the skies cleared over the island. At the same time, a line of dark clouds had formed to the east, suggesting a larger weather system was approaching. The weather change didn't concern Alan. *Wind Gypsy* was well braced and tied off, and he felt more secure aboard the boat than he had at any time since the collision. He slept below deck that night, for the first time since leaving the mainland. His sleep was sound and dreamless.

———•———

Alan awoke to an intermittent thumping from the cockpit. Making his way back to the companionway hatch, he could see several booby birds perched on the railing. There was also one standing on the compass pecking at the engine start switch. Alan groaned.

"Get away from that," he yelled.

The bird switched to pecking at the engine's oil-pressure gauge, while the others watched uninterestedly. Alan retrieved the boat hook and brought it up into the cockpit in view of the birds. The one that was pecking the oil gauge squawked and flew off.

"Ah, we've met," he said watching the bird fly down the beach, "and, apparently, we haven't," to the other three. They still sat on the cockpit rail now looking at him with that same disinterest.

He waved the pole over them. They got the hint and flew off in the same direction as their friend.

Alan looked around. The eastern sky was multiple shades of red, yellow and blue, studded with beams of sunlight through dark clouds. Overhead, high cirrus clouds moved rapidly to the west. There was a stiff breeze blowing, and it was cooler than it had been the previous day. The weather was changing for the worse. Alan realized he had not listened to a weather report since arriving on the island. He made a mental note to turn the radio to the weather channel when he went back below.

Glancing over *Wind Gypsy*'s rail, Alan noted that the tide was again out. Just as on the previous morning, a foot of water sloshed over the coral sand eight feet below the cockpit. The weather could wait he thought.

———•———

It took nearly two hours to complete the hull patch, which consisted of epoxy resin and multiple layers of fiberglass cloth. Alan stepped back and inspected his work. It was not pretty, but it would be strong once the resin cured. He climbed back aboard the boat and stowed his tools and patching materials back in their locker. He then opened a can of tuna fish and a package of crackers for lunch. It was far too hot below deck to use the cookstove. Taking a cold bottle of soda from the icebox, he escaped to the cool breeze now blowing through the cockpit.

He had installed a small battery-powered refrigeration unit in the icebox before departing the San Francisco Bay Area. Although it was a big draw on the batteries, it was a wise decision. He really didn't like warm soda. Besides, between the small generator that he stored in the cockpit storage locker and the big generator installed on the auxiliary engine, he was able to easily keep up with the electrical loads of the boat, including keeping the batteries charged. The small gas generator had also come in handy several times during his trip. It enabled him to run the few power tools that he carried. He would use it again to power his small grinder, once the epoxy resin in his hull patch had cured, to smooth the surface of the patch.

Alan pressed the ice-cold soda bottle to his forehead and took in his surroundings. The breeze that had increased in strength over the night had stiffened even more, and dark clouds hovered over the small island. He knew that the fast-curing epoxy resin he had used for the patch was already set up and would be impervious to the weather or tide. By the time the tide was high enough to refloat *Wind Gypsy*, the patch would be at full strength. He had several hours, yet, to do the grinding and wait for the tide. It was plenty of time to explore The Rock.

———•———

With a small pack containing a can of chili, a bottle of water, his flashlight and a sheath knife, Alan made his way through the palm thicket off the bow of the boat. He followed the same route he had used the previous morning to the shore of the lagoon, crossing the trail he had found that previous day. He decided to walk along the lagoon shoreline to The Rock, rather than use the trail. As with the northern end of the island, the volcanic sand along the lagoon was much easier to walk through than the soft, coral sand of the trail. Reaching the lagoon, he stood and studied the features of The Rock. The top was very jagged, typical of a volcanic plug.

"It looks like a recent formation," he told himself again.

From this distance and sun angle, it looked almost as though it were snow-covered.

"Guano," he said, remembering the smell. He realized the stench was still there, even in the stiff breeze.

As he started to step off through the dark sand, he felt something at his feet. He looked down. There was a red-footed booby pulling on his shoelace. There were 10 or 15 others watching from the tree line a few feet away.

"Stand still long enough, they will make a nest out of you." Alan wiggled his foot, and the bird ran off.

———•———

The sandy beach of the lagoon had given way to a rough, rocky shoreline at the base of Clipperton Rock. The smell of sulfur had grown stronger. The water itself looked yellow and stagnant. Green algae grew over the surface in the shallows near The Rock's bluff-like face. The rocky bottom in this area was slippery, and progress was difficult. Alan waded out farther into the lagoon to skirt around the rocky area, wishing he had taken the trail.

Aside from a small piece of old fish netting and a weathered Styrofoam float, he found no signs of civilization. There was certainly no sophisticated technology or complex instrumentation on the lagoon shoreline near The Rock. Reaching the northeast side of the outcropping. Alan made his way through a palm thicket and onto the coral sand beach of the southeastern end of the island. The sandy beach ran southwest to the base of The Rock. He realized the dinghy was just seaward of this point, when he saw the blue objects appear the previous day.

The sun had broken through the cloud cover and was now high in the sky. Sunlight reflected off the white coral sand of the beach and the surface of the water. With the trees and undergrowth blocking the east wind, it was hot. Alan sat down in the shade of a palm tree and unpacked his water bottle. The channel through the reef, that he saw the previous day, was clearly visible. He could also make out another channel running to the south. The sheer face of Clipperton Rock was directly in front of him. It extended from the tree line on his right to the water of the Pacific Ocean on his left.

He took a drink from the bottle. As he did so, a blue sphere appeared and shot past him into the narrow channel. The object made no noise as it passed about 40 feet away from where Alan sat. There was, however, a tremendous splash when it hit the water. The object moved down the channel under water at high speed, turning north once it cleared the reef. Within seconds, it was gone. Alan lowered his water bottle. Although he was within feet of what must be the source of the object, all he could see was a solid rock wall. He scanned the rock surface looking for something that might be a source. As he did so, another sphere appeared before his eyes. It took a similar trajectory through the coral reef. Once clearing the reef, this object turned southeast rather than north. In a few seconds, it was gone.

Alan stood up and looked back at The Rock. For an instant, he had a sense of vertigo, followed by a rather strong feeling of nausea. In the palm thicket to his right, he heard the crash of a falling tree. He sat back down, fighting back the nausea and still staring at The Rock. Just as quickly as it had come on, the nausea subsided.

Alan sat for several minutes with his eyes fixed on that location at the base of The Rock where the object had appeared. He collected his thoughts and his wits. From this close, the objects were frightening. Large, maybe five feet in diameter. Their surface was shiny blue and appeared smooth, almost metallic. Although there was no visible source of propulsion, their motion was accelerated. He had no idea what they could be, but whatever they were, he did not want to be in their path. Several minutes had passed without the appearance of any more objects. The same thing had happened the previous day. Apparently, just two of these things were emitted per, what would you call it...per *event*.

He stood slowly, checking his balance. The vertigo was gone. Cautiously, he walked toward the base of The Rock. He kept well to the right of where the objects had appeared, avoiding any chance of placing himself in the path the objects had taken earlier. Along this section of The Rock, its face was nearly vertical, rising straight up out of the coral sand to a height of approximately 12 feet. There, the sheer face broke onto a narrow ledge that ran horizontally and out of sight in both directions. Above this ledge, the rock face continued nearly vertically up to the jagged peak.

Reaching The Rock, he edged his way along its face, running his hand over the surface. It was slippery, covered with algae and wet bird guano. The birdcage smell was particularly strong. "Is this what it's like being in a birdcage?" he thought, trying to take his mind off his nervousness. It didn't work. He was still nervous.

Closer to the location where the spheres had appeared, the rock face seemed to give way under his hand. He glanced down and was shocked to see that his hand had disappeared into the rock. He yanked it back instinctively. His hand reappeared. He

Steven C. Golly

inspected the spot in the rock surface where this odd illusion had occurred, moving his head from side to side. It looked like solid rock from all angles.

Tentatively, he reached out to touch the rock again. He felt nothing. His hand simply passed through what appeared to be solid rock.

"The best camouflage I've ever seen," he said out loud, moving his hand in and out of the rock several times. He concluded that he was looking at a hologram. It was certainly an elaborate disguise for a scientific instrument he thought. What was it being hidden from? The boobies? This may be a weapons system of some type. Maybe he's shipwrecked in the middle of a weapons test! "Wouldn't that be just grand," he said.

Stepping back away from The Rock, he estimated that he was still several feet from where the spheres had appeared. He thought about it for a few minutes.

"So, I'm about to prove that curiosity killed the cat...and the sailor" he said, trying to talk himself out of continuing. He stepped back to The Rock and found the camouflaged opening again. He felt around the edge, then passed his head through. There was no sensation at all. There just wasn't anything there to feel. He looked around. What he could see appeared to be a cave opening, perhaps 20 feet at the mouth and extending 20 to 30 feet back into The Rock. He stepped in and looked behind him. The channel through the reef and the open ocean were visible to the east. The camouflage that looked like a solid rock face from the outside was not visible from the inside. As he watched, surf broke on either side of the channel. He realized he couldn't hear it break. In fact, he couldn't hear anything--not the wind, not the birds. Nothing. Nothing except his heart pounding. Apparently, the camouflage blocked sound from the outside. Do holograms do that he wondered? He didn't know.

Alan stood for a moment looking around the cavern. There were no birds, no crabs and no foliage of any type visible. There didn't even appear to be any algae on the rock surfaces. Nothing living. There was, however, a shaft at the back of the opening.

From where he stood, the shaft looked like it was in line with the channel through the reef and the path of the blue spheres. There didn't appear to be any equipment in the cave, nothing that could have generated the spheres. The source of the objects must be at the other end of the shaft.

Alan's palms began to sweat. He was becoming less interested in the source of the objects. At the same time, he was intrigued by this cave. He hadn't seen anything like it before. With some reluctance, he made his way to the back of the cave and peered down the shaft. It was pitch black.

He dug the flashlight out of his pack. Staying at the edge of the shaft and out of what he thought must be the path of the blue objects, he shined the flashlight down. The shaft opening was nearly round and about 10 feet in diameter. It had a gentle, downward slope and disappeared into blackness. Its walls had a slight texture, a wavy surface but were otherwise smooth solid rock. There were no fissures in the surface of the rock walls that he could see, and there was no rubble in the shaft. None.

"Not a natural formation," he said to himself, taking a closer look at the rock surface. What type of boring machine made this? He didn't know. The walls were much smoother than those produced by any tunneling equipment he was familiar with. And any waste material from the shaft had been cleaned up. There was no rubble in sight anywhere—not in the cave, not in the shaft and not outside the cave for that matter. This couldn't be a natural feature. Yet, there was no indication that it had been made by any mining method he was familiar with.

"An unnatural cavern with supernatural objects emanating from it, invisible from the outside." He was dictating the entry that he would be making in his logbook.

Alan Peterson had been a mining engineer for more than 15 years. He hated being inside mines. Technical challenges were his forte, and he was considered an expert in many mining techniques. That was quite an achievement, given that for most of those 15 years he seldom ventured into a mine. He was not claustrophobic, he told himself. He just didn't like being in tight spaces in the ground.

Alan glanced back at the cave opening. He could see coral sand and open ocean beckoning him. The sunlight was fading, and darkening clouds were forming to the east. Surf was breaking on the beach and on the reef. A frigate bird flew by the cave opening. Inside, there was total *silence*.

He stood for a moment, again, trying to figure out how it could be that sound wasn't getting into the cave. The camouflage curtain, hologram, whatever it was certainly did the job. The curtain at the opening to the cave was either totally reflecting or totally absorbing the sound from the outside. He had no idea how that could happen. Turning back to the shaft, he wiped the sweat from his palms onto his T-shirt and began easing his way down.

8. General Quarters

Kate was onto something. Using the stellar position data that Phil had sent her, she plotted the Geographic Position (GP) of all the stars they found with positional errors. GP is the location on the earth's surface directly under the star at the time of the event. Further, as she went through the data Commander Jenkins had accumulated in the wardroom, she was able to glean the GP of all the affected satellites during the anomaly. She then plotted all these points on a navigational chart that Seaman Franks got for her. The plot showed that all of the anomalies happened in a roughly triangular region over the Eastern Pacific Ocean. A triangle where one corner was located at Clipperton Island.

Kate stood up and stretched while looking at her watch. It was a little before 11 o'clock. She realized that she didn't know whether it was AM or PM. Nearly her entire time aboard had been spent in her stateroom. She tried to remember back over the last couple of days. There were what, three team meetings and probably an equal number of formal dinners she had avoided. Seaman Franks had brought all her meals to her stateroom. On a couple of occasions, he had admonished her for not joining the others. She was unaware of the gross breach of wardroom etiquette she had committed by not accepting the captain's invitations to dinner. Thinking about it, she realized the only person from the ship she had met was Seaman Franks.

There was nothing in her room to indicate whether it was day or night outside. As it was located close to the centerline of the ship, her stateroom had no windows or portholes to the outside. There were five decks above her, 12 below and numerous steel bulkheads in all directions. Realizing this for the first time gave her a feeling of claustrophobia––something she rarely felt.

"I need some air," she said to herself.

Kate pulled on the jacket she found in the room's small closet; surprised that it fit. She stepped out into the passageway and made her way to the wardroom. It occurred to her that her stateroom, the wardroom and the path between were the only parts of the ship she had seen, except when they had arrived that first night.

The lights were dim in the passageway and also in the wardroom itself. It must be night, Kate thought. Piles of documents and data on the anomaly lay on serving tables, just to her right as she entered. She caught herself starting to walk over to the data. "Enough research," she said to herself. "You're taking a break, remember."

Two men in khaki uniforms were seated at a table in the back of the room. One of the men stood as she turned in their direction. He looked young, maybe mid-20s. His collar devices indicated that he was a navy lieutenant.

"Would you like some coffee Ma'am?"

"Is there any on?"

"Always," he said. "I'll get it. Please, come join us." The lieutenant motioned to a chair at the table where the two men were seated. While he went through a swinging doorway into what Kate thought must be the kitchen, the other man, a lieutenant junior grade, pulled the chair out for Kate to sit. This fellow looked even younger than the lieutenant, who returned from the kitchen carrying a platter with coffee, sugar and cream.

The men introduced themselves. Kate asked what kept them up so late.

"Just getting ready for watch, OOD," the lieutenant said pointing to himself, "and CIC," pointing to the other man.

Kate frowned.

"Officer of the Deck and Combat Information Center Watch Officer," the man clarified. "The watch changes at midnight, but we need to be up there early. We're pulling the mid tonight."

Kate was still frowning.

"You didn't take the tour," the lieutenant said.

"No. Missed it."

Kate remembered the captain had offered a tour of the ship to anyone on the research team who was interested. She hadn't gone.

Kate was beginning to realize just how little she knew about the navy. She had worked for the Naval Observatory for seven years and in her experience, naval personnel were all astronomers or engineers. Their primary job was to keep correct time and take star sights with a sextant, not to be OODs and CICs, whatever these jobs were.

"Franks says you spend all your time in your stateroom. He says you're a bookworm." said the younger officer.

"You're developing a reputation with the crew," the lieutenant added smiling. "Don't you like our beautiful ship?"

Kate blushed, taking the teasing with a smile, although, maybe it did sting just a bit. She had been shy as a small child, and she still was, maybe a little anyway.

Kate Harris spent her early teens as the tomboy of a family of three sisters, never quite fitting in when it came to the social events of the household. And it seemed there were always social events going on at their house. Her father's professorship was at the University of Ohio in Columbus where Kate grew up. It seemed he was always in his office or at the observatory. On the other hand, her mother, Betty Harris, was seemingly always involved in some sort of social club or society function. From the Quilting Club, the Bridge Club, the Faculty Wives Club, to the local Opera Society, there was always a social function of some sort occurring at the house. Kate's sisters involved themselves in all their mother's activities. They did everything with their mother while Kate found herself preferring the relative solitude of her father's observatory. As a teenager, she had developed a keen interest in his work. Delighted that one of his daughters took up such an interest, Peter Harris encouraged her. By the age of 15, Kate had the run of the small observatory near the university campus. She spent most of her free time there, missing all her high school dances, ball games and most other high school social events. She did enter her home-made telescope in the school science fair during her junior year, primarily at the coaxing of her father. It won third place. First and second went to the boys with rockets and solar powered scooters.

The older of the two officers interrupted Kate's thoughts.

"What's your specialty?" He asked.

"Astronomy," Kate answered. "I work for the Naval Observatory, but I'm on loan to PACOM for a project on Maui. How about you? What is it, OOD? Is that your specialty?" Kate didn't want to talk about herself.

The young man smiled again.

"No, I'm the first lieutenant, deck operations and ship's maintenance. I just stand watch as OOD." He could see that Kate was confused. "Everyone on the ship stands watch, as well as doing their regular, nine-to-five job. I stand watch as OOD. I am one of the five people qualified for that watch aboard the ship. When not on watch, I run the day-to-day operation of the Deck Division. He could see that none of what he was saying was making sense to Kate.

"I stand watch in CIC, but my full-time job is Communications Officer," the younger man said. "I'm the guy that authorized the Internet connection in your quarters, so that you could get online with Pearl," he added.

Kate remembered filling out a form that required the communications officer's signature in order to get the Internet line. But she was still confused. What was a watch? Stand watch? The lieutenant continued.

"There are two kinds of jobs on a ship. The administrative and support job such as maintenance, like painting, maintaining the rigging, telephones, water, trash disposal, cooking, cleaning, ordering paper clips, you know, checking the tires and changing the oil type stuff. In my case, first lieutenant stuff. Then there's ship operations: jobs that go on all the time, at least when the ship is underway. Jobs, like driving the ship, running the engines, operating the communications and navigation equipment and things done by watch standers 24/7."

"So, you drive the ship when you're watch standing…standing watch?"

"Well, kind of, but not really. The ship is *driven* by a number of people. If you would like to see how that works, I'd be happy to show you the bridge," he added, looking at his watch.

"Oh, no, thank you. I just wanted to go outside and get a little air," Kate said. "I don't want to trouble you."

"No trouble. And the bridge wing is one of the best topside views on the ship." The lieutenant stood.

"We need to get to work anyway," he said, downing the remainder of his coffee.

Kate followed the two men up five floors of stairs, which the lieutenant took two steps at a time. Then they went down a short passageway and into a dimly lit room that was full of computer screens and electronics equipment racks. Several men with headsets and microphones were seated before large consoles. Kate's guide nodded at another man in khakis and pointed toward a door at the forward end of the room. The other officer nodded back, while talking into a microphone at the same time.

"Nice to meet you," the younger officer said to Kate, as they were about to go through a door. "This is my stop."

Kate followed the lieutenant through the door and onto the bridge of the ship.

"Permission to enter the bridge," he requested, as Kate stepped through the doorway.

The room was in near complete darkness with only a few dim red lights. They gave Kate the faintest sense of the room's layout. It seemed large. As her eyes adjusted to the darkness, she could see that the entire front wall of the room was windows from waist high to the ceiling. To her right was an open door to an outside patio, the starboard bridge wing as she would learn. There was a big swivel chair mounted on a pedestal just in front of her and a similar one across the room. They looked like barbers' chairs, although they sat up higher. As her eyes adjusted to the darkness, Kate could see a man standing near the center of the room holding on to what must be the ship's steering wheel. It was nearly as big around as the sailor was tall. In front of the wheel, Kate recognized a magnetic compass, similar to the one on display at the Naval Observatory. There were two officers in khaki uniforms on the bridge. As well, there were several other men including the one at the wheel. One of the officers, that had been looking out through the windows with binoculars, turned and responded to Kate's guide.

"Permission granted," he said, studying Kate for a few seconds. He then turned back and resumed scanning the horizon with his binoculars. He was apparently the current OOD.

Kate's guide took a couple of steps forward, turning to inspect a large plexiglass board that appeared to be part of the wall between the bridge and the room that they had passed through. The plexiglass was divided by yellow lines into a table with headings that were acronyms Kate didn't recognize. There were two entries in the table. A man was changing one of them as they watched.

"Sonar has contact Tango bearing unchanged––two two zero and closing. Still probable biologicals, Sir. CIC recommends we go active."

"Very well," said the OOD, still looking through his binoculars. "Commence active sonar."

Kate was guided out onto the starboard bridge wing. There was a stiff breeze blowing, but it was warm, nearly too warm for her jacket. The sky was overcast with a patch of clearing to the rear of the ship. Looking back, she picked out Polaris between the low clouds regaining her sense of direction. The ship was headed nearly due south, she estimated. Her guide remained close to the doorway, listening to what was happening on the bridge.

"What are biologicals," Kate asked?

"Probably a whale," the lieutenant answered, pointing just to the right of the bow. "It's a long way off," he added.

Kate looked forward. The night sky was moonless. She could just make out the horizon to the south. To her right, the dim glow of a green light was just visible from behind the railing of the bridge wing. Above and to the rear, a white light was visible near the top of a tall tower just behind the bridge. She could also see a large radar antenna rotating just below the light. Kate heard talking from the bridge. She stepped closer to the door.

"...all ahead flank," the OOD was saying. The man picked up what looked to Kate to be a telephone receiver.

"Morning, Captain. This is the bridge. We have an unknown sonar contact bearing zero two zero degrees, range twelve thousand yards, speed 120 knots. It will be close. CPA close astern. I've come left. New course zero eight five. I've increased speed to flank, Sir." He paused then, "Aye, aye, Sir." He hung up the phone and glanced toward Kate and her escort. "Please clear the bridge, Mister Philips," he said.

Kate's guide directed her back through the door they had used earlier and out into the passageway. He continued down the passageway, past the stairs they had come up earlier and through a door leading to the outside. They both walked across the deck to the railing. Kate noticed that the ship was vibrating, almost like it was jumping up and down. Something metallic was rattling below her feet, somewhere on a lower deck. The young officer glanced at his watch.

"Two minutes," he said. "If it maintains its course and speed, it should pass to our stern in about two minutes."

The man was watching the horizon directly in front of them. Kate followed his gaze. This has to be an object like those that were in the satellite images, Kate thought. It's moving at the same speed and, she estimated, in about the same direction as the northbound object she had seen in the images at PACOM headquarters.

Standing at the railing seven stories above the water, they watched as a blue-glowing object appeared just below the horizon. It was, indeed, moving fast, passing astern and out of sight within a few seconds.

"Holy Jesus, what the hell was that?" the young officer said. "Pardon me, Ma'am," he added self-consciously.

From a megaphone shaped speaker mounted on the wall about 10 feet from Kate came the deafening sound of an alarm, then…

"Now hear this. General quarters, general quarters. All hands to stations. This is not a drill."

The alert was repeated several times. Kate's ears were ringing. The lieutenant escorted her back down to the wardroom at almost a run. Commander Jenkins and the rest of the research group were already there when Kate and the lieutenant arrived. The young officer dropped her off and was gone, before she had a chance to thank him for the tour.

With her arrival, all the members of the research team were now in the wardroom, and several conversations were going on simultaneously. Kate interrupted Commander Jenkins in the middle of a sentence and maneuvered him toward the kitchen entrance, away from the others.

"I was on the bridge when they spotted it. I saw it," she said. "It must have been one of the objects like those that were picked up on Evans' satellite images. It was moving fast, 120 knots according to sonar. It had a blue glow, and it was close but missed us. I don't know why the ship went to general quarters?

"If it acts like a torpedo, it could turn around and make another run at us," Jenkins said. "Putting the ship at general quarters is the prudent thing to do. We'll just have to wait it out here or in our quarters 'til the ship stands down. I'll get the tracking data on the contact for analysis as soon as I can. We can compare it to the satellite images."

"Haven't seen you in a while." Jenkins changed the subject. "Seasick? Irvington's been seasick, since we arrived aboard."

Kate glanced across the room and saw Sam Irvington sitting alone at a table, his chin propped up by his hands. He was wearing a bathrobe and the same sandals he had on when they met. He looked pale, not his normal ruddy complexion.

"No, I'm OK. I've been correlating the satellite anomaly data with stellar data we collected at the observatory during the anomalies. I have some results I'd like to go over with the group, when we get a chance."

"OK, I'll set it up." Jenkins paused. "New subject," he said. "You've been cleared for the other data, the program we covered at PACOM after you left the meeting. You'll need to in-brief when we get a chance. We can do it now if you want. I have the data in my quarters."

Kate remembered Bennett mentioning something in his note about getting her cleared.

"All right," she said, as she followed Commander Jenkins out of the wardroom. She was about to be introduced to the Hellfire Program.

9. The Machine

1430 30 March, 2007 Beached, Clipperton Atoll

Alan eased his way down the shaft. Although the surface was polished and slippery, the slope was gentle enough, and the wavy texture of the surface gave him enough traction to make the going easy. It appeared that the shaft was large enough, so that if he stayed to one side and close to the wall, he could avoid being hit by one of the spheres, should he happen upon one. That is, if he lay down flat against the side and if the spheres traveled down the middle. He knew this was a bad idea, but his curiosity had won out over caution and besides…what would he put in his logbook, if he didn't find the source of the blue objects. "Saw mysterious objects coming from mysterious cave with mysterious camouflage entrance. Passed through mysterious camouflage curtain and found mysterious shaft. Chickened out and went home." No, he would check out the shaft and see what he could find. He was OK, as long as he stayed near the side of the shaft, he told himself.

As he eased his way down, Alan steadied himself with his hand, sliding it along the surface of the shaft wall. From what he could make out with his flashlight, the shaft seemed to maintain a near circular cross section of about 10 feet in diameter for its entire length. He neither saw, nor felt, any sharp edges in the rock face. It must have been dug by some type of tunneling machine. But what machine leaves the walls of the tunnel so smooth? He didn't know of any.

Having traveled what he estimated to be 100 feet down the shaft, he could see that it opened up into a chamber. He reached the opening 20 feet farther and shined his flashlight over the walls and floor. He was in what appeared to be a long narrow cavern, perhaps 20 feet wide and running in line with the shaft he had just come through. It was partially filled with rubble. It had irregular walls. Alan studied the ceiling, pausing at features that might suggest structural weakness. It looked sound. In fact, the cavern looked more like a natural formation, he thought. The overhead, walls and floor were ragged rock. It had loose rock and rubble along its length.

On the floor in front of him, his flashlight beam fell on human remains. The skeleton was surrounded by shredded bits of an old navy uniform––a white jumper with petty officer stripes on the sleeve. The fact that his rating was on the right sleeve, a *right-arm-rate,* as it used to be called, suggested the sailor's death had not been recent. Farther back in the cavern lay the rusted frame of a machine gun. The barrel and bipod were mangled, but Alan recognized it as a .30 caliber. He remembered the old weapon from his navy training. They were no longer used by the military as he recalled. It fit with the older uniform. He shined the light farther back into the cavern. There was another decayed body. A chill went through him. Whatever the glowing objects were, they were not part of an oceanographic experiment or for that matter a weapons test. This was something older. Something that had been around at least the 50 years since the old machine gun was in use by the military, and the navy had right-arm-ratings. Whatever this thing was, it was old, and it was lethal. But he could see nothing in the cavern that looked like it might be a source of the blue objects.

The shaft he came down entered the cavern at its east end. The cavern itself ran to the west, perhaps 80 feet, then seemed to end in a pile of rubble. To his right another shaft left the cavern close to where the first one entered it. It was at what appeared to be a right angle to the one he had come down. It had a much steeper slope, dropping down and to the north. The blue spheres must have come

Steven C. Golly

from the other end of this lower shaft.

Alan switched off his flashlight and let his eyes adjust to the darkness. Save for a very dim light coming from the cave entrance 120 feet above, it was pitch black. He switched the light back on and walked farther into the cavern. There were more human remains. Alan noticed they were not wearing navy uniforms. Some had been in what looked like the remnants of business suits. Obviously, this was not a safe place to be.

He walked back to where the two shafts converged and stopped. He then peered down the lower shaft and caught something in the corner of his eye. There was something down there. He switched off the flashlight again. In the darkness, he could see a dim blue light at the bottom of the shaft. Another blue sphere, he thought, with a chill, easing his way toward the north wall next to the lower shaft entrance. He stood motionless for several minutes, his eyes adjusting further to the near total darkness. The light from the lower shaft was coming from about 100 feet below where he stood. And there was something else. He could now hear something…a faint humming sound also coming from the lower shaft.

Alan stood in the darkness, staring down the shaft at the steady blue light. He couldn't make any sense out of what he was seeing. The camouflage at the cave opening above him was what, a hologram? The blue spheres were what, projections? If they were just projections, what made the splash when they entered the water and the wake as they passed through it? And what killed the men in the cavern? Was it the blue objects?

"Projections don't kill people," he said out loud, his voice echoing through the cavern.

And these shafts, what made these shafts? Were they made with a boring or tunneling machine and then the walls polished? Were the shafts cleared of rubble? Why would anyone do that? It didn't make sense.

He stood and watched the light coming up from the lower shaft for several minutes. It hadn't changed. Whatever the source was, it wasn't moving. He switched the flashlight back on and shined it on the wall of the lower shaft. Reaching out, he rubbed his hand over the surface. It was the same smooth finish with the same uneven wavy texture as the upper shaft. It appeared to be the same diameter. It was definitely not dug by any method he was familiar with.

On the other hand, the cavern walls were irregular with rough edges of rock exposed on all the surfaces he could see. This opening could very well be a natural fissure of the volcanic plug, he thought. The cavern could have been here for a long time. The shafts looked like they were made much more recently.

Did the men whose bodies were in the cavern kill each other in some kind of shootout? Perhaps it was a chase down and shootout that ended in this cavern. Could it be that at some time more recently these shafts were dug, exposing the cavern and the remains of these old-time adversaries? Why would the people that put these shafts in the cavern leave the human remains undisturbed?

Or were these men victims of an encounter with one of the blue objects? If it were this latter case, then the source of the spheres would have to have been around much longer than the technology of holograms and projections. That didn't make sense. But even if it were the former case, he still couldn't explain how the shafts were dug, or why they were cleaned out and polished, or what the blue objects are or what their function was/is.

Clearly, his safest course of action was to go back to the surface, leave the cave and stay clear of the objects, until he could leave the island altogether. And then there was the other issue. He wasn't claustrophobic, he reminded himself. But he was down in a hole below a solid rock mountain. He didn't like that…feeling. But he hesitated. He still hadn't found the source for the blue objects, and that was what he was down in this hole to do in the first place. And that source must be at the bottom of this lower shaft.

He thought back to the appearance of the objects the day before and earlier that afternoon. As they passed in front of him on those two occasions, they appeared to act like projectiles on a set trajectory, headed for some far-off location. They didn't look like weapons aimed at a local threat. If the men whose remains now lay around his feet were killed by one of the blue objects, did they just get in the way? Then why did they have a machine gun?

Alan made a decision. "They're probably not a threat unless you get in the way," he said to himself.

As he eased his way down the lower shaft, sliding in a crab walk position along its smooth floor he added, "and I must be crazy."

———————•———————

The shaft was steep. Alan stopped a few feet past the entrance and made sure he had enough traction to get back out. Satisfied, he continued the descent. The blue light at the bottom grew brighter.

The bottom of the shaft opened into a roughly triangular chamber about 40 feet on each side and 20 feet high at its highest point. The shaft entered on what Alan estimated to be the south side of the room. Instinctively, he scanned the rock above his head with the flashlight. Above and directly in front of him a metallic looking object protruded down from the ceiling to form a point perhaps 10 or 12 feet above the floor. It looked something like a stalactite, except that its surface looked metallic rather than like a mineral deposit. It also had another distinguishing characteristic; it glowed a faint blue color. The rest of the ceiling looked like solid rock with the same polished texture as the shaft walls. Nearer the middle of each wall, the rock surface gave way gradually to a metallic looking surface with the same faint blue glow as the pointed object on the ceiling. The floor of the room was smooth and flat.

Alan switched his flashlight off and took in the strange sight. There was enough light from all the metallic surfaces to see across the room. The corners were dark, and there were eerie shadows on the floor. He turned the light back on and scanned the floor and corners of the room. There were more human remains in the far corner. To his left was a small pile of rubble where it appeared there had been a cave-in. Rubble filled a section of the west corner.

He moved along the wall to his right, reaching a point where the metallic surface seemed to disappear behind polished rock. Past that point, the metal was still partially exposed at the bottom of the indentations in the rock's surface. It looked to Alan like the metal room was *submerged* in the rock. The corners appeared to be completely covered with rock. Was this the *machine* that produced the spherical objects? Was he seeing all of it or was it bigger? How far into the rock did it extend?

Alan traced the wall in front of him with his flashlight, up to where it joined the ceiling. There wasn't really a corner at the ceiling. Rather, the walls curved seamlessly into the ceiling, and then the ceiling curved down to the protrusion at the center of the room. Actually, the room had a relatively complex curvature, rather than real corners.

And there was the humming sound.

"It must be a machine," he said to himself. There was a slight echo as he spoke.

Tentatively, he touched the exposed metallic surface. It was cold. In fact, the entire honeycomb of shafts and caverns was cold, much colder than they should be, based on his experience. He moved his hand along the metallic surface to a point where it disappeared into the rock face of the wall. He began to shake his head. This just didn't make sense. This machine…this thing…was imbedded in solid rock. He had no way of telling how big it was, and no idea what it was for. This thing, apparently, produced blue spheres that moved very fast, nearly sank boats and maybe killed people. For what purpose? As he felt his way along the wall, he realized that his hands were shaking. For the second time in as many days, he was frightened.

Steven C. Golly

10. Hellfire I

0130 30 March, 2007 USS *Fort McHenry*
Eastern Pacific

Commander Jenkins' quarters aboard the *Fort McHenry* were significantly nicer than Kate's. For one thing, they were bigger. For another, they were carpeted. There was a living room/office area at the entrance and what appeared to be a bedroom to the rear. There was artificial wood paneling on the walls. She inspected the television and remote control, as he opened the small safe that was next to his mahogany-topped desk. He removed a thick folder with a red-and-white striped cover. "TOP SECRET" in block letters was centered on the front and back. Jenkins flipped open the folder. A cover page was imprinted with the word "Secret" at the top and bottom and "HELL-FIRE" in bold letters at its center. Kate sat down across from him at the desk, and they went through the normal security procedures for clearing into a classified program. After the forms were read and signed, Jenkins started the program overview briefing.

"The Hellfire program grew out of a project first started in the mid-1940s. The project was initiated by the military after some original work had been done as part of the Manhattan Project. Manhattan, as you may recall, was the codename for the most classified development program of the Second World War; the program that ultimately produced the atomic bombs that were dropped on Hiroshima and Nagasaki." Jenkins paused. "Do you want any coffee, or anything? This will take a while."

"No thanks, I'm coffee'd out," Kate said.

Jenkins continued, "As the bombs were being developed, there were concerns expressed by some scientists that the initiation of a nuclear chain reaction in the earth's atmosphere might result in what could be referred to as a global nuclear event. That is, the chain reaction initiated in the bomb might spread into a chain reaction in the surrounding atmosphere that could propagate to encompass the entire globe…not just the fissionable material within the device itself. Although most of the Manhattan scientists considered such an event unlikely, there was enough concern that the military decided the issue warranted further looking into."

"A small research team was formed to study such a possibility. The codename for the study was Hellfire."

"Obviously, they were wrong," Kate interrupted.

"Yes, they were," said Jenkins. "But at the time, it couldn't be proven by any means other than detonating a device. And when that first bomb was detonated in the Nevada desert, there was a significant pucker factor associated with this concern."

They both smiled at Jenkins' remark.

"So, that was it?" Kate asked with a shrug.

"No, not quite." Jenkins continued. "What the Hellfire program determined was that, indeed, the likelihood of a sustained chain reaction of the atmosphere was low. But what did happen was that the concerns of the group shifted from stimulating fission in the atmosphere to something that seemed a lot more probable. That concern was the inadvertent initiation of a chain reaction in known concentrations of fissionable materials, like those at the diffusion plant at Hanford or the centrifuges in Oak Ridge. As a consequence of the original studies, a considerable amount of work was done to prevent such an occurrence at these facilities. But there were other locations of concern, as well. Locations where naturally occurring concentrations of radioactive material may be at risk of producing a secondary chain reaction. In other words, the question still remained. Was there a high enough concentration of fissionable material and sufficient moderating materials at a location, such as the uranium mines in Colorado, to result in a spontaneous chain reaction from the neutron flux of a device detonating in Japan or Nevada?

"Looks like the answer to those questions was also, no." Kate said.

"Actually, that is not entirely true." Jenkins responded.

Kate went noticeably rigid in her chair. Her eyebrows raised. Neither spoke for a few moments.

"But I've never heard of anything like this." Kate finally said.

"Exactly." Jenkins replied. "Look, there's data on the events in this folder. I'd like you to go over it this morning, although I don't think it really concerns us on this project. I'll just say that there have been naturally occurring, and not so naturally occurring, nuclear events at locations on the earth where high concentrations of fissionable material occur, be the high concentrations natural or otherwise. What does concern us is that Clipperton Rock may be just such a location."

Kate realized her mouth was open. She closed it.

Jenkins continued. "In 1944, before the first test detonation in Nevada, the military had research teams all over the world checking out known and suspected radioactive sources; they went anywhere that an inadvertent nuclear detonation might be a problem, for the Allies anyway. They were taking samples of ore and measurements with primitive Geiger counters. The data was brought back to the states for tabulation and analysis. Some of the first field radiation models were developed by these guys. Amazing what they did before the computer age," Jenkins added. "Anyway, late in 1944, a team was sent to Clipperton to chase down a reported sighting that there was blue light coming from a cave in the Clipperton Rock. They thought it might be gaseous luminescence pumped by a radioactive source. The reports of the blue light came from the caretaker of the old lighthouse that was located on Clipperton Rock back in the late 1800s and early 1900s."

"What did they find?" Kate asked.

"They didn't." Jenkins answered. "The entire team was lost when a mineshaft caved in. Shortly thereafter, the Nevada test was done. Since the island didn't blow up, the investigation of the incident was dropped. A bit later, the Hellfire project was canceled--the original one anyway. Hellfire II was initiated in the 1950s. You have not been cleared for access to the new program. Bennett didn't think you needed to be, but things have changed. I'm going to give you access to Hellfire II, now, because I think your clearance won't be here in time, and your only access to the data is here in this stateroom. It doesn't leave this room." He repeated for emphasis. "Study the data before you leave, then return it to the safe. As it is, we're really not sure whether the Clipperton incident falls into the arena of Hellfire II research or not."

Kate tried to fit what she was hearing into the context of what they were trying to find out about the current satellite and telescope anomalies. She couldn't find a link.

"Do you think what happened back in 1944 is relevant to the events that we are seeing, the objects that were picked up in the satellite images? It sounds like what happened to the original Hellfire scientists was just an unfortunate accident. Were the claims of blue lights in caves ever checked out?"

Jenkins smiled at Kate's barrage of questions. She had the skepticism of a true scientist. No wonder Captain Bennett liked her.

"When I first heard about this incident in Evans' brief at PACOM, I tended to agree with you. What does this unfortunate event have to do with the objects we are seeing now? I did some checking. The ship that carried the original Hellfire team to Clipperton, an old LST, LST-563, I think, it was referred to in the notes. Anyway, 563 went aground on the eastern reef of the island several days after the team was lost. She was abandoned shortly thereafter. Records of the investigation into the loss of the ship show conflicting reports. The OOD at the time of the grounding claimed that the ship had been torpedoed, but there was nothing to indicate that enemy forces were involved. The conclusion of the board of inquiry was that the

563 hit a submerged coral head. There are many of them around the island. Anyway, the hull was breached, and the skipper did the only thing he could do––beach her before she sank.

"But…" Kate couldn't see the relevance of Jenkins' story.

Jenkins held up his hand and continued.

"It turns out, not all of the people that were on the island were lost in the cave-in. The officer in charge of the shore party survived the incident and was recovered at sea several days later. The man died of his injuries a short time afterward, but the ship's captain did interview him before he died. The board of inquiry dismissed his story because they believed it to be *the ranting of a delusional man.*" That's a quote. Anyway, the man claimed to have seen blue glowing objects floating in the air and moving in an erratic manner. The captain apparently assumed the man was delusional, and consequently, so did the board."

"So, what the man saw in 1944 and what I saw half an hour ago may be part of the same phenomena? But how do we know for sure they have anything to do with the satellite anomalies?"

"Yesterday, I got a message from Bennett." Jenkins continued. "We have some more information on the objects that were tracked by the RYNO satellite. The infrared sensor on RYNO couldn't capture the emission spectrum from the objects, but there was an analysis done on the images taken by another asset. It turns out, our objects were emitting radiation predominantly in the short wavelength end of the visual spectrum."

The phrase *"other assets"* was a euphemism for an intelligence source Kate did not have clearance to know about. Jenkins was saying that they have a picture of the objects and that they glow blue in color. Just like what the delusional man claimed to have seen over half a century earlier. And just like the object Kate just saw pass the stern of the ship 30 minutes earlier.

"Do you think what we are seeing is some sort of natural phenomenon? Do you think it's the same phenomenon that was also observed by this fellow back in the 1940s?" Kate asked.

"I don't know," Jenkins said. "Bennett has someone going through the minutes of the board convened over the loss of LST-563. He also has people looking for any information in the old Hellfire program documents. He will let us know if they find anything. So far, this is all we have. By the way, the only other people cleared for this information are Dr. Fulton and this fellow Geoffrey Fox. Apparently, both Fox and Fulton have backgrounds with the Hellfire program--Hellfire II, the newer one."

"With all you folks cleared for this information, wouldn't it be better to wait for my clearance to come through, before I look at the data on Hellfire II?" Kate asked. "Particularly, since you don't seem to think its relevant."

"Normally, yes, absolutely," Jenkins replied. "But we need someone from PACOM on Clipperton that knows all the background, and I won't be going with the landing party. As you probably surmised, Fox is CIA. What you probably didn't know is that Professor Fulton was also CIA. The *Company* has not been forthcoming with their interest in the island, other than its link to the loss of some of their satellite assets. But that doesn't explain why the Hellfire II people were sent along with us, rather than some of their satellite guys. The admiral doesn't trust them. You are to be his representative on the island."

"You're not going on island with the research team?"

"I've got more pressing responsibilities."

In the middle of the Pacific Ocean with nothing for hundreds of miles except the island that may be involved with major losses of satellite assets and the disruption of fleet communications, Kate couldn't imagine what could be more pressing. Knowing he would have told her if he wanted her to know, Kate was about to ask, anyway, when she heard a muffled announcement over the PA system. She couldn't quite make out what was being said. Jenkins, apparently, had the speaker turned off in his room.

"The ship is standing down from General Quarters," Jenkins said. "I'll run down the ship's tracking data for the object you saw, and we can compare it to the satellite tracking data for the objects that were picked up during the anomaly. We have a brief at 0700 this morning on the landing party preparations. All hands." He stressed the last point.

His inference about her not showing up at the team meetings did not go unnoticed.

"I'll be there."

"Good," he said. "We can go over your findings after the briefing. Go ahead and look over the Hellfire documentation in this folder. It covers both programs."

Sam Irvington was not present for the team briefing that morning. He was, apparently, under the weather––severely seasick. Kate made a note to look in on him after the meeting. For the moment, she sat listening to Marine Second Lieutenant Baker discuss camping equipment and wondered why she had agreed to be at this meeting.

The weather had changed. Several men that entered the wardroom during their meeting were in raincoats and were drenched. It was also obvious that the seas had built in the nine hours since her tour of the ship's bridge. *Fort McHenry* now rolled back and forth with a period of oscillation that Kate had timed at 19 seconds per cycle. Timing the roll period of the ship was something to do while the marine lieutenant went through a monotonic dissertation on how to set up a portable shelter. These were the shelters they would apparently be erecting on the island. Kate also studied the chart of the island on display, as part of the marine's brief. At first, she didn't understand why they were setting up camp on the western reef, while the area of interest was on the southeastern side of the island. Then she learned that the weather was going to continue to get worse––possibly much worse. The site on the western reef provided the most protection from the wind and seas. She also learned from the lieutenant's briefing that there was a sailboat on the reef just south of their planned campsite. The boat flew an American flag and had one person aboard. PACOM was, obviously, keeping an eye on the island.

The *Fort McHenry* was 320 nautical miles Northeast of Clipperton Island. The original plan was to take the ship in close to the island, then land by small boat, waiting for the weather if need be. Because of *other concerns* the group's plans had changed. The research team was now to depart as soon as they were close enough to reach the island by air. They would use a marine helicopter that was in the ship's small aircraft hangar. The aircraft, which was originally just cargo being transported to Okinawa, would be put into service for this mission. Irvington and Commander Jenkins would not be part of this first team on the helicopter but would join them later, after the ship arrived on scene.

Apparently, not all members of the research team were cleared to know what these other concerns were. Whatever they were, they seem to warrant sending Professor Fulton, Mr. Fox, Kate and three marines to the island as early as possible, forcing them to camp out on the island in bad weather for the night. She wasn't sure the idea made sense.

Lieutenant Baker was completing his camping and security briefing. Kate collected her notes and was about to take the podium, when Commander Jenkins stood up and made his apologies. There would not be enough time before the team left to discuss Kate's findings. Kate smiled. She wasn't disappointed. She hadn't gotten enough sleep and was feeling a little seasick. Mostly, she was frustrated. She had found the message from Bennett on her stateroom desk, when she returned from the Jenkins Hellfire program brief. The Hubble Project had been, for all intents and purposes, cancelled. The observatory assets had been redirected by the Air Force to another project of higher priority. Her team was disbanding, most returning to the Naval Observatory for reassignment. Kate would be joining them, when the Clipperton project was completed. All that time and money,…and, now, there was a higher priority. Hubble was to be scrapped.

And now this little expedition was turning out to be muddled and confusing. She was hoping to kick back, do a little analysis and be a team member on this trip, then get back to Maui and dive into her work. Exactly the opposite was happening. It was now looking like she would be responsible for PACOM interests in a situation where another agency, CIA, may be at conflicting purposes. The politics had the potential of being much worse than those on the Hubble Program--the ex-Hubble Program. The program she would not be returning to.

Kate took a couple of deep breaths.

"Get on solid ground," she told herself. "Get some sleep. Take a break and roast a couple of marshmallows on the campfire." What the heck. She had time now anyway. No impossible schedules to keep. No employees to prod. No irritating observatory commander who needs appeasing. She forced herself to smile. Smiling always seemed to help.

"We don't have a lot of time to get ready, folks. The landing party needs to be on the flight deck by 1300 hours." Commander Jenkins comments jarred her back to the present. He was wrapping up the meeting.

"Does anyone have any questions?"

"Are we bringing any marshmallows?" Kate asked.

11. The Shore Party

1430 30 March, 2007 Clipperton Atoll

Alan watched as the helicopter rounded the southern end of the island. Passing over the shallow water to his west, it turned north, flying at about 200 feet above the surface of the water. A few moments later it slowed, turned east and landed on a strip of open sand about 200 yards to the north of where *Wind Gypsy* was beached.

The storm he had seen on the horizon that morning was now upon them. His anemometer showed the wind at 30 to 35 knots from the southwest. It was raining…hard. From under his makeshift awning rigged over the cockpit, he could see people emerging from the helicopter. He reached down through the companionway hatch and retrieved his binoculars. He recognized the aircraft design. It was a CH-46, distinguishable by its twin rotors. It was dull green in color. *Olive drab* as he remembered it being called. US MARINES appeared in dark block letters at the rear of the fuselage. Several people were disembarking onto the beach. They were vainly attempting to protect themselves from the gale force wind and driving rain, as well as the sand kicked up by the helicopter's downdraft. They ran for the cover of a small stand of palm trees just south of the landing site. Meanwhile, three men in fatigue uniforms were unloading olive drab containers from the aircraft's rear cargo ramp. After the cargo was unloaded, the three men joined the others. Shortly thereafter, the dampened scream of the aircraft's turbojet engines elevated in pitch, and the helicopter rose off the reef. It dipped its front end to the east and headed directly over the lagoon. Moments later, it was out of sight in the downpour.

The military men went back to the landing site and began moving cargo, while the three passengers left the clump of trees and began walking toward the boat. Alan watched as the small group approached *Wind Gypsy* from her port side. One of them, a woman, was holding the hood of her raincoat out and over her face, trying to stay dry. Another, a man of average stature walked behind her. The third, a tall older man stopped at the port side bow of the boat and inspected Alan's repair job. The other two had, apparently, not noticed the damage. Alan waved them around to the starboard side, where the boarding ladder was still secured near the cockpit. The rope ladder was awkward to climb. The woman had little trouble reaching the cockpit. However, rainwater streamed off Alan's makeshift awning and flowed directly down and in line with the ladder. Not noticing it, Alan made no attempt to redirect the flow. The woman was drenched by the time she reached the cockpit.

"Alan Peterson. Welcome aboard *Wind Gypsy,*" he said, extending his hand.

Kate glared at him.

"Can't you redirect that torrent, so it is not drenching you when you come up the ladder." Exasperated, she shouted over the wind.

"I'm not coming up the ladder," he replied. "Perhaps, you would like to see if it is any better going down," he added sarcastically.

Continuing to glare at him, Kate moved to the back of the cockpit. She held up the edge of the awning, redirecting the runoff out of line with the ladder.

Geoffrey Fox negotiated the boarding ladder with little trouble. And Professor Fulton was unexpectedly spry, handling the ladder gingerly. He had hooked his cane over his arm just below his elbow.

By the time the professor was aboard, the wind had increased to the point where the noise of wind and rain hitting the awning was too loud for anything less than a shout to be heard in the cockpit.

"How about we go below where we can hear each other," Alan shouted, as he descended the companionway. He was followed by the three drenched members of the research team.

Once below, Alan glanced through the porthole in *Wind Gypsy*'s galley. The three military men were wrestling what appeared to be heavy equipment boxes south along the reef to the small stand of palms, where his three guests had taken refuge earlier.

Alan directed the guests to the settee. The booth-like bench seat and table sat three comfortably. And he was less concerned about getting the settee wet. Once the three were seated, Alan sat opposite them on the starboard side bench seat, which doubled as a bunk. He frequently used it and wanted to keep it dry. He didn't offer anything to his three guests and didn't want to initiate the conversation. He was sure they were there about the machine and was concerned that his entering the cave may have affected some type of experiment. He wasn't volunteering anything. Then again, for all he knew, they could be there for something entirely different. He doubted it.

Kate looked around the interior of the boat. It seemed bigger than it had looked from the outside. The walls were paneled with a dark wood. The floor was a combination of white and dark wood, the ceiling was painted white. The small windows were brass-framed with brass knobs. There were green curtains stretched between elastic bands at the top and bottom of each window. Although the curtains were open, the boat was dark inside. She noticed the kitchen. It was a tiny area past a small doorway and to the left as she came down the stairs from outside. The stainless-steel sink was small and deep and the counters white Formica with dark wood trim. There were a few cabinet drawers. There was also a small stainless-steel gas range, suspended on the wall to the left. A narrow hallway led to the front of the boat. There was a door on the left of the hallway and a dresser of sorts on the right, all dark wood. At the end of the hall, there appeared to be a cot built into the front of the boat. The booth at which she was now seated was comfortable, if a bit cramped. The table was white Formica, again with a dark wood trim lip around the edge. There was a stainless-steel pole from the floor to the ceiling through the center of the table, which held it in place. The booth had foam cushions on the seats and seat backs. They were covered with dark green velour. There was a built-in sofa on the right side of the boat across from the dining booth, also dark green velour. The sailor sat across from them on the sofa.

Kate noticed a faint smell that reminded her of being inside the emergency generator room at the observatory. Engine smells mixed with the smell of an ocean tidal pool. Deodorizer might help she thought.

"My name is Alan Peterson. As you might have noticed, I'm here for repairs." Alan interrupted Kate's inspection of her surroundings. He had become uncomfortable with the stares he was getting from the two men.

Professor Fulton responded first.

"This is an Anderson, isn't it? The Taiwanese know how to make a pretty boat. Lots of teak," he said. "Robert Fulton, University of Hawaii, Engineering." Professor Fulton extended his hand. "I noticed your repairs." he added. "Hit the reef?"

"No, torpedoed," Alan responded.

Fulton frowned. "I'm sorry. I am being quite rude. This is Katherine Harris, Naval Observatory, and Mr. Geoff Fox…ah, State Department," Fulton was not sure what Fox's cover was. They hadn't really talked about it earlier.

"Foreign relations," Fox said.

Professor Fulton had his glasses off and was attempting to dry the lenses with his wet handkerchief. Alan reached behind him and pulled a roll of paper towels out of the storage bin, tore one off and handed it to him. He then went forward to the bunk that Kate had spotted earlier and, taking his last two clean towels from the shelf, brought them back to the main cabin and set them on the table in front of Kate. Fox took the top towel and began drying his face and hair. The other sat on the table.

"Torpedoed?" Professor Fulton continued.

Alan ignored him and attempted to redirect the conversation.

"So, what brings you folks and the U.S. Military to Clipperton Island?"

There was an uncomfortably long silence, followed by a thumping on the hull of the boat that startled them all. Alan stepped aft to the companionway, and standing on the top rung of the ladder, stuck his head over the starboard rail.

"Permission to come aboard?" One of the marines was at the base of the boarding ladder.

Alan looked down at the man in uniform. The gold bar of second lieutenant rank was visible on his turned-up collar. He was also drenched. Alan stepped back to the location that Kate had found earlier and held the awning up, redirecting the water off the boarding ladder. He looked around the boat. The other two men were nowhere in sight. It was raining harder.

"Come up," he shouted to Lieutenant Baker.

The marine officer made quick work of the ladder, and Alan waved him below. In the main cabin, Lieutenant Baker ducked into the galley, allowing Alan to pass him in the narrow passage and reclaim his seat. The lieutenant remained standing, closest to the companionway, and exit.

"Mr. Peterson, this is Lieutenant Baker," said Professor Fulton.

The two men nodded at each other.

"Mr. Peterson, here, was just asking us why we were visiting Clipperton Island." The professor continued. "Perhaps you could help us answer his question."

They had been informed before leaving the ship that the marines were in charge of security while on the island. Also, that Lieutenant Baker would be responsible for dealing with the sailor, as his presence was considered a security issue.

"Research expedition," Lieutenant Baker said. "What brings you here?"

"Repairs," Alan responded.

"Mr. Peterson's boat was torpedoed," Professor Fulton added.

"I see," Baker said as he glanced around the cabin.

There were several books on the shelf behind the bench seat where Alan was seated. Baker scanned the titles as best he could from his location in the galley. They looked technical-- geology and mining.

The man was, obviously, not volunteering a lot of information about himself or what brought him to the island. But then, Lieutenant Baker doubted that he was a security risk, notwithstanding his claim to having been torpedoed. It appeared that the guy just wasn't that chatty. You had to be a little odd to be way out here in this little boat anyway, the lieutenant thought.

"So, what are you researching?" Alan asked.

The boat grew silent again.

Kate was getting irritated by the conversation. The sailor had originally irritated her by standing above and watching water come down on her earlier without even attempting to do anything about it. She had developed an instant dislike for the man. But still, he may be a source of information, and he has been hospitable enough since they entered his boat. She took the towel he offered and dried her glasses.

"Marine life," Geoff Fox answered the sailor's question with a lie, interrupting Kate's thoughts. Fox was jousting, trying to get information without revealing anything himself.

"Whale watching?"

The sailor was playing the same game. Kate decided there needed to be a little more give and take.

"We've seen some unusual events on the south east side of The Rock," she said, catching a glare from Fox. "High speed objects leaving the southeast side of Clipperton Rock. Was one such object your torpedo?"

Insight

12. The Capable Man

1930 30 March, 2007 Clipperton Atoll

Kate looked out the little window on the right side of the boat, just above the sailor's head. Night had fallen on the island. She once heard that twilight was shorter near the equator. It made sense as the sun's motion in the sky at lower latitudes is nearly perpendicular to the horizon. Therefore, it should take less time for the sun to go from fully above the horizon to completely set. Still, it seemed as if she had looked out the window one second, and it was daylight. The next second, it was darkness. She rose up in her seat and realized how tired and achy she was. She looked through the window, just above her head. There were lights on in the shelter the marines had finished erecting.

The initial almost hostile manner of the sailor had given way to what might even be called congenial, if reserved. The last hour of conversation could even have been called pleasant. The man was a mining engineer with what was, apparently, a good background in geology. Kate learned more about the island and its rock formation from the exchange of information between the research team and the sailor, than she had by studying the data Phil Beckman sent her while they were on the ship. And he had seen the objects on the satellite images up close. Both Fox and Lieutenant Baker took notes as the sailor described the entrance to the cave, the tunnels and caverns and the remains of what only could have been the original Hellfire investigators. The man's description of the caves and his encounters with the objects and the machine were thorough and articulate, as if he were giving a report--perhaps, transferring responsibility. He did seem a little irritated, when he asked the professor who was responsible for the machine and was unable to get an answer. It seemed that he believed the damage to his boat had been done by one of the objects from the cave, and he may have wanted to seek compensation.

Kate glanced back down from the window to the sailor--Peterson. Alan Peterson was his name. He was tall, maybe six feet two inches and thin. And he looked, well, scruffy. His hair was long, over his ears and unkempt. His beard was at least a week old, and there was what looked like a grease smudge on his forehead. His shirt was dirty and had a frayed collar. The hems of his shorts were also frayed. He was very tan with what looked to be some peeling skin and sunburn spots on his forehead and arms. He looked like he might have been marooned on the island for years rather than just two days, Kate thought.

Why was he out here in the middle of the ocean, floating around in this tiny boat? That alone put him in what Kate called her strange-bird category. However, even setting that aside, the sailor was still a strange bird. Her first instincts were probably right. He seemed more concerned about his boat than anything else--the objects he had described seeing near the cave, the human remains he had found inside and the machine buried in solid rock. None of that seemed to really interest him, nearly as much as getting his boat off the beach.

So, although the conversation had become much more relaxed, it was still clear that the sailor viewed the research team merely as possible manual labor for that purpose. Kate caught herself staring at him. She turned away, looking instead at the little desk near the back of the cabin. There was one other thing that the sailor did show interest in, she thought...the weather. He had gotten up earlier in the conversation and stepped back past the kitchen to the base of the companionway. When entering the boat, she had noticed on the right side just ahead of a narrow bed, a small desk with what appeared to be electronic instruments and a radar screen mounted to its rear. There was also a chart spread out in front of the electronic equipment. Kate remembered glancing at the chart when she entered the boat. It was a NOAA navigational chart with a group of inserts, different islands. One of the inserts she recognized was a small chart of Clipperton Island.

The sailor had turned on a radio and tuned it to a marine weather channel. At that time the announcer was talking about winds and atmospheric pressure in the Western Pacific. The sailor left the radio on and returned to his seat. Kate heard the announcer shift the coverage of the local region.

"...Weather for the eastern and central Pacific, as of 0030 Zulu, 29 March," the announcer began.

———————•———————

Alan stopped mid-sentence and stepped back to the boat's navigation station, turning up the volume on the single side-band radio.

"The tropical depression that formed in the wake of an atypically strong vertical sheer off the western coastline of Central America has deepened. It is currently located at latitude 09 degrees 20 minutes north, longitude 108 degrees 10 minutes west, moving westerly at 10 nautical miles per hour. Barometric pressure is assessed at 985 millibars and is expected to decrease to below 950 millibars within 15 hours. Designated Pacific Tropical Storm Alma, mariners are..."

Although he really didn't need to, Alan glanced at his chart and confirmed that Alma was headed straight for them. He picked up his dividers and spanned the distance between the storm's location and the island. He placed the dividers on the latitude scale of the chart, and read off the distance, 01 degree, 30 minutes, 90 nautical miles. At its current speed, the storm would reach Clipperton Island in nine hours, 0700 tomorrow. The tide should be flooding after 0400 but not yet high enough to float *Wind Gypsy* before the storm hit, even with the storm surge. He was going to have to ride it out on the beach.

The wider section of reef and the stand of palm trees to the east of the boat should help break the brunt of the wind and seas, but he needed to stiffen up the bracings in his makeshift boat cradle.

He was deep in thought about everything that needed to be done before the storm arrived, as he glanced forward to the main salon and realized everyone was staring at him.

"Can your shelter handle near hurricane winds?" he asked Lieutenant Baker.

"Yes, but it won't be particularly comfortable," the lieutenant answered.

Alan had seen the structure when he went topside earlier to invite the marine officer aboard. There would be some protection afforded them by palm trees to the east of the campsite, but the reef was low and narrow at their location. Depending on the barometric pressure and the storm track, they could be in trouble by morning.

The ocean level rises a bit less than ½ inch per millibar drop in barometric pressure. This effect can cause an extreme high tide, even though what is normally called storm surge would not be a major concern on an atoll. With its current barometric pressure, the ocean surface is approximately one foot above normal tide at the location of the storm center. It could easily reach several feet higher than normal before Alma's center passed over Clipperton Island. With the surf in the lagoon reaching several feet, the combination of normal tide, low pressure effects and storm surge, this surf could well break over the reef at the location of the campsite. That could be more than uncomfortable. It could be a disaster!

"How about your makeshift boat cradle?" Dr. Fulton asked breaking Alan's train of thought.

Alan frowned, turning back to Lieutenant Baker.

"Do you have any construction tools--saws, hammers--in those boxes? If so, I'd like to make use of them to brace the boat up a little better before the storm hits."

"Yes, we have a reasonably complete set of construction tools," Lieutenant Baker replied. "Talk to Gunnery Sergeant Thornton.

He's the one most familiar with the kit-out. I'll ask him to give you a hand, once we're set up on the beach."

Alan thanked the young lieutenant. Since finding the machine earlier that day, he had developed a deep sense of foreboding. The thing was...*alien*. The technology looked *alien* or, at least, what Alan thought *alien* technology would look like. And whatever equipment made the shafts and that room in that solid rock had to be *alien*. The objects, spheres, that were emitted by the machine-- the same objects that probably caused the damage to his boat-- looked *alien*. Now, he was finding out that the little research team sent here by the military didn't know what the spheres were or what the purpose of the machine was. Or did they? He had a sense that the fellow, Fox, knew something about the machine. He wasn't sure why, but the man gave Alan an uneasy feeling.

After leaving the cave that afternoon, Alan's first instinct had been to run. But after starting to tear apart the boat cradle, so he could pull *Wind Gypsy* off the beach, he came to his senses. There just wasn't enough water to re-float the boat that evening, at least not before the next high tide. And so, he told himself that he would leave the next morning.

Now this little research team has arrived wholly unprepared for the weather. It was a typical government SNAFU.

Alan was beginning to realize how much the deep sense of foreboding he had developed that afternoon in the cave was affecting him. He had spent most of the evening talking with the research team but not concentrating on their project. Rather, he had been concentrating on how to get away from this island as soon as possible. He was doing exactly what he had done when the mine explosion occurred. He wanted to get away as fast as possible and leave the problem to the bureaucrats and the military. They're the ones who caused it. Save yourself!

After all the second guessing and the rationalization he had done after the accident, he realized for the first time what was eating him up inside. *He had run.* He had run for his life from the mine, the project and his people. So many of his people had died or been injured in the explosion. What had become of the wounded and the families of the dead? He didn't know. He had run for his life and never looked back. But to stay at the mine would have been a death sentence. Is that the case here? As he realized, it wasn't, Alan Peterson became ashamed. "Time to do the right thing," he said to himself.

After being lost in thought for some time, Alan returned his attention to his guests, "I'm concerned about your campsite. The high water caused by this storm could very well submerge the low section of reef where your shelters are located. We should move you to higher ground. I would suggest either to the north, near the old structure, or to the south, nearer The Rock. We should do that before we worry about the boat."

Kate watched as the sailor turned down the volume on his radio. Maybe she was wrong about this guy. Coming from the Midwest, Kate knew little about the ocean and ocean weather. The sailor must at least have some idea about what he is saying. She was about to ask how high the water could rise, when Geoffrey Fox spoke the first complete sentence that Kate had heard from the man since they met on the ship nearly three days earlier.

"Is the communications equipment operational," he asked Lieutenant Baker?

"The MilStar terminal is set up. I haven't initialized it yet. HF is five by five with the ship," the lieutenant responded.

"I need to file a report. I'll meet you back at the camp." Fox passed by Alan, stepped up the companionway ladder to the cockpit and was gone.

Kate watched the man leave. "Someone started talking about work, and Mr. Fox suddenly had a report to file," she said to herself.

"We'll keep an eye on the tide, Mr. Peterson," Lieutenant Baker responded to Alan. "I don't think we can relocate any distance from where we are before the storm is on us."

"I suggest you secure anything you can't get along without to a palm tree…a sturdy one." Alan said. "And I'd hoist anything you don't want submerged in salt water up one of the trees as high as you can get it," he added. "Let me know if I can help."

"Thank you, Sir," replied the lieutenant. "We had better get back to the shelters and get our gear stowed," he said to the rest of the group. "Sounds like we're all in for a rough night."

The social call with the boat owner was breaking up. Baker and the sailor made their way up the ladder to the cockpit of the little boat. Kate noticed that Professor Fulton was inspecting the boat's interior. Although the conversation had not gone in that direction, Kate suspected that the professor would have liked to talk a bit about Mr. Peterson's sailing adventure. She watched as the professor got up from the booth and stepped into the hallway at the front of the boat, opening the door on the left side. "He's snooping," she said to herself and grinned.

As they moved toward the back of the boat, Professor Fulton stopped at the foot of the ladder and inspected the radar and other instruments, as well as the charts on the small table. Kate just couldn't understand the fascination with boats that so many people had. Most of her fellow scientists at the observatory, and, in fact, many of the residents of Hawaii, seemed to be involved with boats and sailing. This was the jet age, she thought to herself. Sailboats are just relics of the past.

———————•———————

About an hour after the lieutenant and the research team left the boat, Gunnery Sergeant Nate Thornton arrived with a chain saw and bag of hand tools.

Sergeant Thornton was in his mid-30s. He had made a career of the Marine Corps. Alan estimated that the man was about his same height, maybe a little taller, six feet two inches or so and solid muscle. His blond hair was cut Marine Corps short, and his eyes were dark and cold. He was menacing looking, except for the broad smile on his face as he approached the boat. In a few minutes of conversation with the sergeant, Alan learned that the man was a native of Oregon, that his entire family had worked in the woods for as long as the sergeant could remember, that he was adept at timber falling and rough construction. Although he was not a sailor, he understood rigging, block-and-tackle terminology and equipment handling. Alan also found out that he had been with force recon for a good percentage of his military career. He was no doubt a tough character.

The two of them spent some time inspecting the cradle that Alan had fashioned the previous day and that he had started to take down earlier. It would need to be stiffened. The sergeant had some ideas as to how it could be done. The marine also expressed a concern about the tree to which the bow line of the boat was attached. A good percentage of its roots were exposed on its windward side. There was a chance it may fall under the load of the storm winds. If it did, it could pull the boat along with it, possibly dragging *Wind Gypsy* off the cradle, or even worse, it might fall on the boat. In either case, something needed to be done. They decided that the tree needed to come down.

Alan switched on the spreader lights, running lights, cabin lights, anchor light and every other light he had aboard. He held the battery-powered searchlight illuminating the base of the offending tree, while the sergeant got ready to fall it. Thornton made an undercut on the northwest side of the tree, a couple of feet above the point where the bow line was attached. Alan couldn't help but notice the big grin on the man's face as he operated the chain saw. The wind was howling, it was pouring down rain, they were both drenched and the sergeant was thoroughly enjoying himself. Sergeant Thornton started the back cut. It was a big palm tree, perhaps three feet in diameter at the stump. If it fell on the boat, it would do a lot of damage, and the tree was leaning directly over *Wind Gypsy*.

Standing on the bow, Alan shifted uneasily on his feet. Maybe he should move just in case. The rain was now torrential. He protected his eyes with his hand just as Sergeant Thornton hit the saw's kill switch, silencing the noise from its un-muffled, two-cycle engine.

"Just like back home," the sergeant shouted over the wind and rain.

There was a loud snap. The tree fell alongside and to the north of the boat, right where Sergeant Thornton said it would fall. Alan realized he had been holding his breath. He let it out. He already liked this marine.

For the next three hours, the two men worked together, cutting up the tree and using various parts of it to shore up the boat cradle. Alan left most of the rigging and cutting to Sergeant Thornton and busied himself with aiding where he could. Mostly he just stayed out of the man's way. By the time they finished bracing up the boat, Alan had concluded that Sergeant Nate Thornton was a very capable man.

Alan adjusted the burner of the galley stove, as the pot of coffee began to perk. He then went back to the navigation station and glanced at the digital readout of the boat's anemometer. It was fluctuating between 45 and 55 knots. The wind was now from the east-northeast and was getting stronger. He stepped back into the galley. Out the porthole above the stove, he could see that lights were still on inside the two shelters to the north. Sergeant Thornton was seated on the couch across from the settee drying his hair with a towel. He still had a smile on his face.

"That's as much fun as I've had in some time," he said

"I don't know how to thank you for the help," Alan responded.

"Don't worry about it."

Although it was not cold, evaporation from his drenched clothing had given Alan a chill. It didn't even appear that the sergeant noticed any chill. However, Alan managed to talk him into a cup of hot coffee before returning to join his companions.

"Do you know anything about this thing your research team is here to investigate?" Alan asked as he handed the marine a cup of coffee.

"You mean the thing that's been disrupting comms and GPS for the last week?"

None of the research team had mentioned anything about GPS or communications outages earlier.

"You know, my GPS went on the blink a couple of days ago," Alan added.

"Yours and everyone else's on this side of the globe. Satcom's been dropping in and out, too."

"Do they think the satellite outages have something to do with those things I saw on the other side of The Rock?" Alan asked.

"Don't know," the sergeant said. "I think the navy is just eliminating possibilities. If they would have known for sure this was the problem, they'd have landed a battalion," he added. "You saw the things up close. Can you tell me what they look like?"

Alan described all that he had seen to the marine sergeant. He described the damage to the boat hull, explaining how it looked like a burn, and how he believed one of the spheres had caused the damage. He talked about the entrance to the cave and the caverns, the camouflage and the polished surfaces of the rock. The sergeant asked several questions about ingress and egress from the cave, the tunnel and cavern layouts, visibility, details about the spheres, the machine, the dispersion of the bodies and the weapons he had seen. The marine was, obviously, more interested in a tactical summary of the cave, than any technology related details about the objects themselves.

"Did you see any ammunition for the .30-cal?" Sergeant Thornton asked.

Alan thought. He pictured the cavern where the remains of the navy personnel and the machine gun were located.

"No, I didn't see any ammunition," he said.

The sergeant nodded.

"Cooked off," he said. "Like the hole burnt in your boat. Heat from a blue ball may have cooked off…made the rounds blow up and destroy themselves."

"Along with everyone in the cave," he added as he finished his coffee and stood. "Got to get back. Thanks for the coffee."

"I can't tell you how much I appreciate your help," Alan said again, shaking the sergeant's hand. "Anything I can do, let me know."

"Take me for a boat ride someday," the marine said with a grin. "You going to need some help getting this thing off the beach?" Sergeant Thornton was at the base of the companionway ladder.

"Probably," Alan said.

"Let me know. I'll get you some help. The ship's supposed to be here by this comin' mornin', but she may stand off in the rough weather and wait 'til it clears up. I suspect we'll see her late in the day," the sergeant said as he went through the companionway hatch into the driving wind and rain.

Alan watched through the galley porthole for several minutes. Eventually the lights went out in one of the shelters but remained on in the larger of the two. Shortly thereafter, Alan fell asleep watching the anemometer and listening to weather reports on the radio.

13. The Disaster

0700 31 March, 2007 USPACOM, Camp Smith, Oahu, HI

"I was caught with my pants down, Bill. This entire staff has been working on operation plans for the two years I've been here, and none of those plans address this issue. At this moment, we're operating in the blind on this thing. I'm not paid to work that way. How did we miss it?"

Admiral Wells was as mad as Bennett had ever seen him. He had been called into the admiral's office, as soon as he arrived at the PACOM facility that morning. The Commander and Chief of the US Pacific Command had just returned from Washington DC the previous evening. The Pentagon briefing that he had attended was his introduction to the calamity that was now called "Imminent Dawn".

"I'm sorry, Admiral. I found out about it at the same time you did. It looks like the boys at Cheyenne Mountain sat on it for two days before letting anyone know.

The Space Surveillance Center at Cheyenne Mountain, Colorado, was responsible for processing data from a collection of radars and optical sensors scattered all over the globe. They were used to detect, track and identify objects in space. Because a good number of these assets are located in the Pacific Region, they fall under the administrative control of PACOM.

Herein was the rub. An object was spotted by PACOM assets, the information transferred to the Airforce Space Command without the admiral's knowledge and he only found out about it two days later from his bosses at the Pentagon. Although, as the admiral pointed out, the real issue was not so much the way he found out about it, but rather that they had no plans to deal with it. If he would have had the two days warning beforehand, he could have done a much better job answering questions from his bosses in the Joint Chiefs of Staff.

Technically, Bennett, as the PACOM representative for these matters, should have been in the loop. The Maui Observatory was obviously within his area of responsibility. He realized, now, that Colonel Elder was trying to warn him about the object before the last Hubble Project meeting, just before he sent Kate off to the middle of nowhere. The colonel had said that there was something big coming down the pike, and his operational bosses at Space Command wouldn't let him release the findings.

On the other hand, he already knew about the comet. The problem was that the previous data, from his friend at the Wilson Observatory in California, indicated the object's trajectory was well clear of the earth. He hadn't paid much attention to it after that. The truth was, most of his energies were now focused on the satellite problems they had been dealing with since the original outages.

But regardless of all that, Bennett felt he had let the admiral down.

"With respect to the object, Sir, the data shows it has a very low-level albedo, it is very dim. And it has a trajectory well off the plane of the ecliptic. Only the big optical sensors are seeing it, and we couldn't pick it up from disturbances in the planetary orbits, because it's way out of the planet's orbital plane. This thing is just flying by, Sir. The path is retrograde. It's passing the sun in the opposite direction from the earth's rotation. That means it's closing fast. The reason we are seeing it at all with optics is that it is flickering from micrometeoroid impacts on its surface. You could say we're seeing a meteoroid shower on the comet."

"You're telling me we couldn't have seen it earlier?"

"No, I'm not, Sir. We should have had it earlier, but the fact is, we've had so many satellite outages in the last few days that most of the space surveillance assets are tied up tracking disabled spacecraft. And we still don't have a root cause for any of those anomalies. Frankly, the object is so dim optically, that it pretty much had to get in range of the big radars in order for us to pick it up. The thing is pretty much non-reflective in the optical range."

"OK, I know the Pentagon is working impact assessments. We are going to need all the information we can get, in order to come up with a realistic operations plan. What are the best estimates so far on projected damage?"

"Well, Sir, the good news is that its impact angle is quite small. It's going to just skim us, Sir. That means that instead of one big impact, there is a good chance this thing is going to break up in the atmosphere and spread over 20 or 30 miles. If it were a head-on collision, it would be a planet killer. The mass is nearly four million metric tons. It's half a mile in diameter, Sir. At its closing velocity and impact angle, it will be the equivalent of about a three-million-megatons' blast.

The impact point is off the western coast of South America, along the Peruvian coastline. Initially, we expect the resulting tidal wave to exceed anything ever seen here on Oahu, as well as the rest of the islands and the entire Pacific Rim. I would recommend the Operations Department look at moving as many assets as possible to high ground on the northern shore and leeward side of the island. My recommendation at the moment is to move all naval assets to the northeast of the islands and as far off the CONUS coastline as possible. Practically anything that can float should be underway. We can expect the weather to go to hell in a hurry after the event. We're developing the models for that now. But we know the first problem we will face is the tsunami."

"Any data on the long-term effects?" The admiral had been sitting quietly, taking in everything Bennett said.

"Not yet, Sir. But it will be bad. It's probably safe to say we can stop worrying about global warming."

Bennett's attempt at levity went unnoticed or at least unacknowledged.

"Do we know what this thing is? Where it came from?"

"No, Sir. It appears to be a rogue piece of galactic rock that has just happened by."

"OK. Tell the boys on Maui to keep us in the loop. Make sure ops has any new data you come up with. Prepare to brief the full staff on this thing at 1500." Admiral Wells signaled the end of the meeting.

"Yes, Sir." Bennett left the admiral's office. The meeting had gone better than he expected. He still had a job.

14. The Move

0800 30 March, 2007 Clipperton Atoll

"Keep this boat shipshape. When trouble happens, I don't have time to be lookin' fer somethin' that ain't stowed where it should be or diggin' flotsam out a the bilge pump inlet cuz stuff ain't cleaned up. Keep yer gear stowed proper and yer mess cleared up."

Alan awoke to the old sailor's admonition. He had been dreaming about his father. In the dream, he and his father were out in the old man's boat. The fishing had been poor, and the old man was grumpy. Alan remembered how he could always tell whether the fish were biting by his father's mood when he came home. But in the dream, the boat was on fire and sinking. He couldn't recall why…. It had been hit…by a blue object. They were on fire and taking on water, and the bilge pump inlet was fouled….

He opened his eyes and sat up. Every muscle in his body ached. He had a kink in his neck. His clothes were still damp. He smelled something burning,…

Alan jumped to his feet and scanned the interior of the boat. He had left the flame on under the coffee pot the night before. He stepped into the galley and switched off the burner. The acrid smell of burnt coffee was strong. He left the pot sitting on the burner to cool off and stepped back to the navigation table, grumbling to himself about paying attention to what he was doing.

The wind had increased in strength, reaching nearly 80 knots at 0530 before starting to ease. From the wind direction and speed, he could tell that Hurricane Alma had passed to the north of the island, less than 100 miles north according to the last weather report. The storm gained speed through the night, arriving several hours earlier than his original estimate. Now, the roar of the wind and rain had subsided. By 0730 that morning, the wind had dropped below gale force.

Alan glanced at the anemometer display. The instrument showed the wind speed fluctuating between 25 and 30 knots, near gale force. But compared to the previous evening it sounded like a summer breeze outside. He stood listening to the wind and rain for a few minutes. The boat felt stable. The mast had stopped its loud vibrating. *Wind Gypsy* was also no longer shifting in the cradle. At the peak of the storm, she had been bouncing back and forth quite a bit. He was glad that he and Sergeant Thornton had taken the time to set his other two anchors off the sides of the boat before the wind changed direction. There were hurricane force winds on the beam that night, and as strong as the cradle was, he questioned whether it would have held without the extra anchors. Now, fastened into the beefed-up cradle, secured on all four quarters, *Wind Gypsy* wasn't going anywhere.

Alan switched off the anemometer and checked the battery gauges out of instinct. Nearly all the lights had been on last night, while they were working on the cradle and rigging. The wind instruments and radio had been powered up the rest of the night. In all, there had been a heavy load placed on the batteries. They would need to be charged at some point. He flipped the meter through the three battery banks. So far, the charge on all of them was still good.

Through the galley porthole, he could see that the spray from surf breaking in the lagoon had let up and was only intermittently reaching the shelters at the research team's campsite. It had to have been a miserable night for those folks, he thought.

Alan turned and started up the companionway. Then he realized that something was missing. The radio! He had left the radio on. Why wasn't he hearing anything? Tuned to the weather frequency, he should be hearing a continuous weather report for the Pacific Region. He reached over the chart table and wiggled the volume control. Nothing. He flipped through several channels. Nothing. Maybe it blew a fuse? No, the radio's channel display light was on, meaning it was getting power. The problem is not likely to be the fuse. He switched the radio on and off several times. Still no signal. The antenna may have been damaged or disconnected in the wind; he hoped. Antennas were easy to repair.

Alan switched off the radio and went topside to the cockpit. As he stepped out, he traced the path of the antenna wire from where it left the stern just above a large porcelain insulator on the backstay, to where it was attached to the boat's mast rigging. Everything looked OK. Maybe the radio had died, he thought. His thoughts momentarily wandered through the implications of not having the side-band radio. His calculations wouldn't be as accurate, but he could still navigate. He didn't really need the satellite weather report; he knew how to read the weather. He made a mental note to start recording barometric pressure in his logbook twice a day. Then his thoughts returned to the present.

Looking up the beach, Alan had a clear view of the research team's campsite. One of the two shelters was partially collapsed; a number of its tie-downs gave way under the hurricane-force winds. The marines had tied off the big storage containers to palm trees the previous night. The containers were now all lined up to the southwest of the trees where they had been tied. They had, obviously, swung around to their current position while afloat. The reef must have been awash during the storm, he concluded. As he watched, Kate Harris left the partially collapsed shelter and made her way into the other structure.

Alan glanced at his watch. Four hours until high tide. It could be unusually high with the storm still close. The augmented tide could bring the water level above the reef again. These government folks may still want to think about moving their campsite. He glanced over the boat's railing. There were several feet of water around the boat. *Wind Gypsy* would be afloat before high tide. He went below and changed into dry clothing.

Working the kink out of his neck while scrubbing out the coffee pot, Alan decided he would put on some hot water for tea. This morning, coffee just didn't sound good.

Kate opened one eye. The walls of the tent were light. The sun had come up. She groaned. Although it seemed like she had been awake most of the night, her memory of events for the previous 12 hours was fuzzy. After leaving the sailboat, she recalled that Lieutenant Baker had joined Mr. Fox in the main shelter. They were trying to call the ship on the high frequency transceiver but weren't having any luck. From what Kate could make out, the third marine, Corporal Hansen, was a radio technician. He had, apparently, gotten the radios working earlier, but by the time they returned from the sailboat, the wind had knocked down the antenna.

After an hour of trying to reach the ship, they gave up on the high frequency link and switched their efforts to the MilStar satellite terminal. Kate had never seen a MilStar terminal but had heard about the system. It looked much too large and clumsy for a radio, but then, the MilStar system was designed to withstand a nuclear attack, so…

Kate had some familiarity with the issues involved with equipment survival in a radiation environment, from her previous work with the South Atlantic Anomaly. She knew most communication systems would not survive the radio-wave pulse associated with a nuclear detonation. She had watched with fascination and also dismay as the marines unfolded a dish antenna and aligned it to the satellite. It reminded Kate that some human beings, and, for that matter, at least some members of this small team were still designing systems under the assumption that such hideous weapons might be used.

Once Corporal Hansen had the terminal set up, there ensued a somewhat heated discussion about who would use it first. Mr. Fox won the argument.

Kate had hoped to get a message off to Jenkins or Bennett with the information the sailor had given them about his encounter with the blue objects. Unfortunately, it looked like Geoffrey Fox was going to be on the terminal most of the night. She remembered finding something to eat in an open storage container. She had sat down at the small table that was set up in a smaller compartment on the west side of the shelter, and a few minutes later, Professor Fulton joined her. They discussed the sailor's description of his encounter with the blue objects.

Then she went to bed in the little shelter the marines had set up for equipment storage, which now seconded as her sleeping quarters. The marines had moved all the equipment boxes out earlier and lashed them to trees. "We wouldn't want to lose any equipment," she said to herself as she looked around the now empty tent. "The astronomer, we can do without. The equipment, better lash it down."

Commotion of one form or the other continued for most of the night, heated discussions mainly. Kate remembered waking once to Lieutenant Baker and Mr. Fox having another argument about the MilStar terminal. The lieutenant needed to get a "Situation Report" to his commander. She awoke, again, somewhat later to another argument between the two. This time something to do with *command authority*. The chain saw noise and the wind howling through the palm bows directly overhead kept her awake for an hour after the second argument was over. When it seemed like she had just fallen asleep, there was another loud exchange between Lieutenant Baker and Sergeant Thornton. Something about weapons, she recalled.

And then there was the wind. The scream of the wind was frightening, and it seemed to last all night. There was also the surf crashing on the lagoon shoreline and the occasional sound of what must have been trees falling in the coconut palm thicket to the south of the camp.

Kate opened her other eye and looked around. The back of her tent was collapsed. It didn't matter. She was tired. She flopped over and tried to go back to sleep. Finally, she sat up in the cot and put her stocking feet on the ground. There was three inches of water on the floor of the shelter.

"Swell," she said as she took her socks off and wrung them out. She was still in the wet coveralls she had been wearing for, how many days now? She stood up and waded across the floor of the tent, poked her head outside and looked around.

The campsite was in shambles. Surf was breaking on the lagoon side of the reef 30 yards to the east. Water rushed around the palm trees between the camp and the lagoon. A palm tree had fallen near the rear of the shelter. The support lines had given way as the tree fell across them, which explained why the shelter was partially collapsed. A wire, probably the HF radio antenna, was lying across the top of the two shelters and trailing off onto the beach and out into the ocean. There were palm bows and coconuts piled up along the east side of both structures and along the many downed trees.

Kate ducked back into the tent and found her shoes floating in the corner. She was glad she had left her computer and personal items in their waterproof container the previous night. Otherwise, they would have been on the floor of the shelter, flooded and wet. She had only one change of clothing, another suit of blue coveralls. It would be a disaster if they became wet. She placed her wet socks so that they hung from the end of her cot and pulled on her wet shoes. She ran her hands through her hair and shrugging, made her way to the main shelter.

Sergeant Thornton passed Alan a copy of the last weather report they had received from Pearl Harbor the previous night. It was the last weather report before a big wave broke over the camp at the peak of the storm and ocean water entered the main shelter. The force of the wave knocked over the MilStar antenna and flooded both the MilStar and HF transceivers, rendering them inoperable.

Alan flipped through the weather report. It contained a weather satellite image, showing Hurricane Alma had already started to re-curve to the north and east by 0400 that morning. The storm track had, apparently, been altered by the development of another low-pressure system, which was forming to the east of Clipperton Island. Hurricane Alma's path, as well as the development of this new low-pressure system, were referred to as *atypical* in the report. That was an understatement, Alan thought. Although, the fact that these well-formed low-pressure systems actually had occurred, was proof that they were possible. Atypical seemed a bit weak as a statement of their likelihood. In Alan's years as a naval officer, he had educated himself on the subject of ocean weather systems––how, where and when they form, how they move and most importantly, where not to be and when not to be there in a small boat. The early months of the year, February through May, were the best times for transit from the northern hemisphere to the south because this period is before the hurricane season in the north and after the cyclone season in the south. March is far too early for hurricanes or even significant low-pressure cells to form in the Northern Pacific. But even ignoring that fact, this was the wrong longitude for such a storm. A Pacific Ocean storm needs more ocean waters between it and the Central American land mass to develop into a hurricane. Clipperton Island was too far east for such a weather pattern. These storm systems were *atypical,* indeed.

"From what I can tell reading this report, it looks like we may be in for another storm in the not-too-distant future, maybe six to eight hours from now," Alan said. "My side-band radio is out, so I have no way of updating the information you have here. But to be on the safe side, I'd recommend we move your camp to higher ground. As I said before, I would recommend either north near the old structure on the northern reef, or south near the west side of The Rock. South would probably be better, since you should get a windbreak from The Rock."

"It'll take some time to pack this gear that distance, but I tend to agree with Mr. Peterson," said Lieutenant Baker. "We didn't fair all that well last night," he added, looking at the communications equipment. "The *Fort McHenry* has moved to the south and east of our location to avoid the storms. Given this weather, it's not clear when she will be able to provide small boat support. We can assume, we are on our own, until the weather clears, or we see a helicopter on the horizon."

When Alan arrived earlier that morning, the entire population of the island had gathered in the main shelter. The entire population that is, except for the boobies, the crabs and Mr. Geoffrey Fox.

"Has anyone seen Mr. Fox this morning?" Professor Fulton asked the assembled group.

"He left the shelter about 0600," said Sergeant Thornton. "Right after the worst of the winds had passed. Probably headed for the caves Mister Peterson was talking about."

"Perhaps, I'll go look for him while you younger folks are moving equipment. Maybe I could talk Miss Harris into joining me."

————————•————————

After the majority of the heavy equipment had been moved, Lieutenant Baker put on an olive drab vest (Alan recognized as a flak jacket), a small backpack and a pistol belt. He spoke briefly to the sergeant, then left Alan and the two enlisted men to finish moving equipment and setting up camp.

"The lieutenant wants to check on the research team," Sergeant Thornton said, when Alan asked what was up.

The sergeant didn't seem happy. Alan didn't think it was because they had been left to do the work, while the lieutenant went exploring. It was something else that was making the man upset.

The two marines and Alan completed the move in relative silence with only occasional comments from Sergeant Thornton. The new campsite was approximately 150 yards to the west of Clipperton Rock in a small clearing surrounded by palm trees and undergrowth.

Although Alan had some concerns that the wind might knock a tree down on the camp, the sergeant judged such an event unlikely given the protection of The Rock. Alan was more than comfortable deferring to the sergeant's judgment, when it came to trees.

After all the equipment had been moved, Corporal Hansen set up the MilStar terminal again and retrieved five gallons of fresh water from the boat. *Wind Gypsy* had two 60-gallon water tanks that Alan kept full of rainwater. The corporal hoped that a good freshwater rinsing would revive the equipment. Both Alan and Sergeant Thornton were skeptical.

During an earlier exchange, Alan got the sense that there was some animosity between Sergeant Thornton and Lieutenant Baker. By his rank, Second Lieutenant Baker could not have a great deal of experience in the military. Less than a year or so, Alan guessed. Considering the situation they were now in, it seemed to Alan that the young officer could easily be in over his head. Being the senior military man on the island, the lieutenant was responsible for the success of their mission and the safety of the people in his charge. He probably believed that to include everyone on the island, except possibly Alan himself. And he probably didn't know the people in his charge that well, which made his job that much harder.

Sergeant Thornton had mentioned that the researchers joined the ship a short time before they were sent to the island and that all three marines were actually assigned to different units. They were together on the ship just for transit to Okinawa. Hansen was assigned to a communications unit, Lieutenant Baker to a marine air wing and the sergeant to a force recon unit. Without communications, Baker was isolated from any command authority, so he couldn't seek the counsel of his seniors before making a decision. This might be the first time in his military career he had been placed in such a situation.

Alan learned as a young ensign in the navy that an officer's success or failure hinged on his relationship with his senior enlisted people. Although he had no idea of the circumstances for the animosity he was seeing, Alan guessed that Lieutenant Baker was, at least for the moment, failing as a military officer.

"We had better go see how the group is doing in the cave," he said to Sergeant Thornton, as they finished moving the last storage container into the main shelter.

"Can't do it," the sergeant said. "I've been ordered to stay here and get communications re-established with the ship."

"I see," said Alan.

He was beginning to understand at least part of the problem the two men were having. Baker wasn't using his men properly. The sergeant had a background in force recon. He knew how to handle himself in the field...in a hostile environment.

The lieutenant should let Hansen, whose training was in communications, work the radio problems. Use the experience of your people where it is most needed.

Alan thought back to his six years in the military. He had made similar mistakes and suffered the failures and lectures of his superiors for them. But he had learned quickly the importance of knowing the job, having the right people work it and stepping back to allow them to work. His lessons in the military had served him well in his later mining career. He quickly reached a supervisory position, always having been considered more than competent and excellent with people. Before the incident in Indonesia, Alan was one of the most senior field managers with his company. Watching the interaction of this group of marines and researchers, Alan couldn't help but compare them to a small group of field engineers, any of a number he had been responsible for over his career.

Then he caught himself. He was slipping into his management mode. That was something he had decided he wasn't going to do anymore. He was the sailor, the outsider in this little group of people. That's where he wanted to be, he told himself. But he wasn't going to let them get in trouble, while he just sat back and watched.

"I think I'm going to catch up with the lieutenant and see what they've found," he said. "I have quite a bit of electrical tools and spare parts in the cabinet under the chart table, Sergeant. Help yourselves to anything you need."

"Thanks, I'll let Hansen know. Be careful."

Alan had retrieved his small pack from the boat during their last trip to the old campsite. It contained a flashlight, knife, long-sleeve shirt, a length of old halyard and a water bottle. He took a drink of water, put the pack on and started down the trail toward The Rock.

15. Higher Resolution

1530 31 March University of Hawaii

"…and your grade will be based on 25 percent each for the midterm and final, and 50 percent for the homework and weekly quizzes. Class time is important to me. It should be important to you. Use it, listen and take good notes."

Harold Thompson had been teaching Introductory Astronomy at the University of Hawaii for 12 years. He had originally considered it a waste of his time, something that should be done by a graduate student. But he had grown to enjoy teaching the class. So much so, that when it was suggested one of the non-tenured staff take it over, he had protested. "This class affords me the opportunity to see the undergraduate student body at their earliest introduction to the physical sciences. It allows me a useful gauge in future selection of exceptional students for graduate training," he had told the department head. Actually, he just enjoyed the younger students' enthusiasm for the subject.

Competition for a position in astronomy was stiff. It dominated the school to such a degree that the atmosphere of learning at the graduate level was being stifled by infighting, backstabbing and petty one-upmanship. Teaching had given way to preening and the polishing of image. He didn't like it. He liked teaching.

Professor Thompson looked at the wall clock at the back of the classroom--3:35 p.m.

"I see we have 10 minutes left in this session. I'll open the floor to questions, any topic…as long as it's astronomy," he said with a grin. "Please, precede your question with your name. It's the easiest way for me to associate names with faces."

Several students raised their hands. He picked the young lady in the second row.

"Amy Butz, Professor. Are you publishing your notes on a web page?"

"No, and that's not an astronomy question," he responded with a smile. The young man in the third row was next.

"Paul Johnson. Do you have anything to do with the SETI research being done here at UH? Do you think they'll find anything?"

"That's two questions. The answers are no, and not if they continue in the manner in which they are currently searching."

"What's the problem with the way they are searching?" The young man had not sat back down after his first two questions.

"That's three questions, Mr. Johnson." Professor Thompson said with a frown. He glanced at the clock again. "But let me see if I can answer you, in the time left to us." Professor Thompson sat down on the corner of his desk at the front of the classroom.

"SETI, the Search for Extra-Terrestrial Intelligence, as it exists today, is the fallout of the old NASA High Resolution Microwave Survey or HRMS program. They are now using two approaches. One looks at the entire sky over a narrow band of frequencies, the other at selected stars and a large number of radio channels.

There are several assumptions that form the basis for these two programs, many of which, in my opinion, have no foundation in observable fact. I think both approaches ignore some aspects of the one sample of intelligent life we do know about––our own.

But to your question, what's the problem with the way they are searching? To start with, it is grossly inefficient. If you are looking in a direction where you know the closest star is hundreds of thousands or billions of light years away, then it should be obvious that you're not going to find anything. No species would have a transmitter with the power to reach that distance. The decrease in signal strength over distance would make a signal from that distance undetectable. The all-sky program is spending all its time looking where there is nothing to see."

"So, you think just looking at selected stars will be more likely to succeed?" Mr. Johnson asked a fourth question.

"Yes, if they were looking at the right stars." But what are the likely targets for such a search? They are currently looking at solar type stars within 300 light years of earth and older than 3 billion years. They are using a broad frequency band in the search, but I don't believe the frequency is all that important, as long as you stay within a band where an artificial signal could be detectable above background noise.

On the other hand, I do believe that the selection of targets is very important. And I think the selections being made are, for the most part, wrong."

"Why do you say that? I'm sorry, I'm Sandy Dunkin. Why do you think we won't find intelligent life on the selected targets?" Ms. Dunkin was seated at the back of the room.

"Thank you for your question, Ms. Dunkin. I was getting to that. It turns out earth is rather unique in one very interesting respect. It's in the wrong place to have intelligent life on it."

The classroom became quiet. Professor Thompson liked it when he got the students' attention. Apparently, his last statement had done that.

"But to understand what I'm talking about I'll need to describe to you a bit about our galaxy."

"What do you mean we are in the wrong place?" Ms. Dunkin asked another question.

Professor Thompson looked at the clock again. There wasn't time to go into the subject of galactic mass distribution and collision cross sections.

"There is too much matter, stars and other objects in the region around the earth. As a result, there are too many stellar collisions.

They happen too often to allow intelligent life to develop. We are an anomaly. We can't expect there to be many more. The SETI search needs to look where the density of stars and interstellar debris is much lower than it is around our sun.

I'd say farther out from the galactic center. We are just too close to the center of the galaxy to have a stable enough environment for intelligent life. Except of course for the fact that, here we are."

"I don't think we're all that intelligent," came a voice from the back of the room, followed by laughter.

The bell rang and the commotion of students leaving the room filled the air.

"We'll finish up this discussion on Wednesday. Read chapter one for next class," the professor shouted over the noise.

The room emptied. Professor Thompson picked up his notes and walked down the hallway a short distance to his office. He flopped into his overstuffed chair. Day one of the new quarter was almost over. One more class. What was it? Ah yes, Graduate Optics. He closed his eyes as the phone rang.

"Hello, Harry, this is Bob Bennett. How's Janet doing?"

Captain Bennett had been a classmate of Thompson's at Columbia. They had kept in touch these many years. Thompson was pleased when Bob was transferred to the islands and their families now met socially on regular occasions. Bob, however, rarely called him at his office. "She's doing fine, Bob. How are Mary and the boys? Have you contracted island fever yet?"

"I've got a favor to ask," Bennett cut off the small talk. "I need the folks at Keck to do a search around Right Ascension 22 hours 28 minutes, declination minus 01 degrees, and I need the data on what they see."

Harry Thompson scratched the coordinates down on a scrap of paper. He wasn't sure how to respond. He had some privileges at the observatory, but he certainly didn't set the schedule for the telescopes.

On the summit of Hawaii's dormant Mauna Kea volcano, Keck Observatory's twin telescopes were the world's largest optical and infrared instruments with the highest resolution available from any telescope on earth. They were in constant use; telescope time was scheduled months in advance.

"What's this about Bob?"

"There's not enough time to go through channels with this Harry, and what I'm telling you probably won't come out in the news for several days. Please, keep it to yourself. We believe there is a comet approaching from the coordinates I gave you. Its trajectory will bring it very close to earth."

Harry Thompson thought about what Bennett was saying.

"I'm pretty sure I can't talk them into doing what you're asking, Bob. The schedule is…"

"How about if I offer them funding for one year of operation. I can have a check cut this week."

Bennett was lying. He knew the annual budget of the observatory was over $10,000,000. That big an expenditure would have to go through the finance department, assuming he could even get it approved. In any event, it would take more than a week.

He also knew that, like all other observatories, Keck operated on a shoestring. If anything was going to get their attention, it would be the money.

"I'll get back to you today," Professor Thompson said and hung up the phone.

He needed to make arrangements for someone to take over his Graduate Optics class.

16. Confusion

1300 31 March, 2007 Clipperton Atoll

Alan made his way around the southern end of the island and along the shallow water on the seaward side of The Rock. From this perspective, he could pick out long thin vertical structures that extended up from the face of Clipperton Rock near its top. These dikes, as they were called, are a common feature of a volcanic plug. As he reached The Rock's southeastern side, the two channels through the reef that he found the previous day became visible. He felt antsy, and he wasn't sure why. Nothing seemed to have changed since the last time he had been at the cave entrance, other than changes resulting from the previous night's weather. A high sand berm had formed along the base of the trees overnight. Other than that, the area looked much the same.

The research party was nowhere in sight. They had, apparently, found the entrance to the cave and gone inside.

As the sheer face of The Rock's eastern side came into view, Alan realized what was bothering him. It was nearly the same time of day that he had seen the objects appear on the previous two occasions, a little before noon. He waded through the shallow water to a point closer to the face of The Rock, approaching the sandy beach area near the cavern entrance.

As if on cue, a blue sphere emerged from the rock face and, at high speed, hit the water with a tremendous splash and disappeared from sight to the east, trailing a large wake. Alan's eyes followed the object only momentarily and then went back to the rock face in time to see the second object appear and repeat the scene he had observed the day before. He waded cautiously out of the water and onto the beach, just as a wave of nausea came over him, as it had the previous day. He sat down in the sand and leaned his backpack against the rock face, waiting for it to pass. Before it was completely gone, Alan forced himself to stand. He felt his way along the face of The Rock to the edge of the cavern opening. Steadying himself against the edge of the opening, he entered.

"...need help," he could hear Kate Harris shouting.

He made his way quickly to the back of the cave. "I'm on my way down," he said, easing his way as fast as he could down the polished floor of the shaft to the long cavern, he'd found the previous day.

As he approached the junction of the two shafts, he could see a bright lantern sitting on the floor of the cavern and Kate bent over someone lying next to it. The injured person was Lieutenant Baker. Alan glanced around the cavern, as he entered. He couldn't see any of the others, but in the bright light of the lantern, the skeletal remains he'd found the previous day seemed more...gruesome.

Kate was holding a folded shirt against Baker's right hip. It was saturated with blood. Both the lieutenant's right hip and leg were bleeding. The remnants of Baker's pistol lay on the floor of the cavern next to him. The magazine had apparently exploded while the gun was in its holster. The rounds had *cooked off.* Alan remembered the term Sergeant Thornton had used the previous night. It also appeared that the chambered round had fired, hitting Baker in the right calf just below the knee. Kate was holding pressure on the man's hip. Meanwhile the calf wound was bleeding profusely.

"I need help with the bleeding," Kate said as he approached them.

Alan removed the shirt from his pack and ripping off one of the sleeves, tied it around the lieutenant's calf where the bullet had entered. The man yelled out when Alan tightened the cloth firmly around the wound. He was still conscious and in a lot of pain.

"Sorry, Lieutenant. We've got to get this bleeding stopped," Alan said.

A few minutes later, they had a bandage around Lieutenant Baker's waist holding compression on his hip wound. The bleeding was now significantly reduced. Alan put his raincoat over the lieutenant and propped his head up with his pack. He was resting, but still in significant pain. With the blood loss and the pain, the major worry now was shock.

"It hit him," Kate said. "The thing came up from the lower shaft and hit him on his right side. Then kept going. There was an explosion…"

"Are you hurt?"

"No. I'm OK."

"We'll need some help to get him out of here," Alan said. "Where are the others, Professor Fulton and Fox?"

"Professor Fulton was here with us," Kate said looking toward the back of the cavern. "We had just reached this opening…"

"Professor Fulton…Professor Fulton can you hear me?" Kate shouted. "He was back there," she indicated the end of the cavern farthest from the entrance shaft.

Alan switched on his flashlight and walked toward the back of the cavern scanning the walls and floor with the light's beam. There was no one there.

"Professor Fulton," he shouted. Nothing.

He returned to where the lieutenant was lying. Kate was still kneeling next to the wounded man.

"How about Fox?" he said. "Did you find him?"

"No. He must be farther down in the tunnel. Down the lower shaft. We called for him, but he didn't answer."

"We need to get help. We need the sergeant's and the corporal's help and something we can use as a stretcher. If you'll go after the sergeant, I'll go down to the lower cavern and try to locate Fox and the professor."

"What about the lieutenant?"

"I'm OK," Lieutenant Baker said. His teeth were chattering. "Go. Go find the others and get help before those things come back."

"I'll be back as soon as I can," Kate said as she started up the shaft to the surface. Alan made his way down the lower shaft, both of them moving as rapidly as they could. They left the lantern with the lieutenant.

Alan's flashlight batteries were starting to lose their charge by the time he reached the lower chamber. He called out to Fox and Professor Fulton several times with no response. Easing his way along the southern wall of the room, he slid his hand along the smooth rock to steady himself in the dim light. As he came to the eastern corner, his hand disappeared into the rock wall just as had happened the previous day. Again, locating the camouflaged doorway, which blended with the solid rock surface of this section of wall, he stepped through and into the little *control room*. Fox was standing in front of what Alan could only describe as a *control panel*. The panel protruded out from the southern wall of the small triangular shaped room. All three walls of the room had a metallic appearance. They were smooth and mirror-like. And they glowed with the same blue light of the larger opening. The *control panel* had what looked like a display screen and some switches and knobs on its surface. Although, Alan couldn't be sure that the small protrusions were in fact switches and knobs. Fox was making a sketch of the room, the control panel and its controls in a notepad.

"You failed to mention this room last night," Fox said.

"You failed to mention why you were here on the island last night," Alan responded.

Both men stood staring at each other for a few moments. Alan noticed that the panel before Fox was lit up. There were red characters on what appeared to be a computer screen. He stepped closer and looked at the display, surprised that he recognized the characters. They were Cyrillic! Alan followed the lines of text picking out a few words:

He searched his memory of high school Russian.

"Welcome?…alert?…emergency?…soil?" He thought out loud. "This thing is Russian!" Alan was astonished.

"Can you read Russian?"

"No, no, high school. I don't remember any of it."

"Does this look Russian?"

"It's Russian. I just can't remember enough to read it. Listen! Lieutenant Baker has been hurt. He's in the cavern above us. I need a hand getting him back to the campsite."

Fox put his notepad in his pack. Then both men made their way out of the control room and across the larger room to the base of the shaft.

"Have you seen Dr. Fulton?" Alan asked.

"No."

"He's here somewhere. There must be another shaft, probably camouflaged like the control room entrance. We'll look for him after we get Lieutenant Baker out."

They worked their way up the steep shaft to the long cavern where Lieutenant Baker was lying. The lieutenant was holding pressure on his hip wound.

"It started bleeding again," he said as Alan and Fox knelt down beside him.

"We'll get you out of here," Alan said.

As he started to examine the wound, Alan heard talking-- including a female voice-- coming from the upper shaft.

"Are you down there, Mr. Peterson?" one of the voices called out. It was Sergeant Thornton.

"Yes."

"We'll be right down."

At the top of the upper shaft, Kate watched as Sergeant Thornton surveyed the cave and shaft entrance. Then they both peered down the shaft to the cavern. The light, from the lantern near where Lieutenant Baker was lying, illuminated the cavern at the bottom of the shaft. They could make out Alan and Fox kneeling next to the injured man.

A few moments later, Corporal Hansen took a bright searchlight out of his pack. As he held it, illuminating the walls of the cave, Sergeant Thornton found a small fissure in the rock surface near the shaft entrance. With three powerful blows from a hammer, he drove a piton into the hairline crack. Then, in what looked like one continuous motion, he snapped on a carabiner and climbing rope and secured it to a loop in his harness. Without a word, the sergeant then turned, and to Kate's amazement, literally ran down the upper shaft, paying out the climbing rope behind him as he went. The entire process took less than a minute; it was an impressive show of prowess.

"You were right, Sergeant. I made a stupid mistake," Lieutenant Baker said, as the sergeant knelt beside him. Thornton lowered his pack and removed a first aid kit and a collapsed canvas cot.

"We'll get you out of here, Sir," he said.

As Alan and Fox assembled the cot, which also doubled as a stretcher, Sergeant Thornton took several field dressings out of the first aid kit, tended to the lieutenant's wounds and administered a morphine syrette. Once the stretcher was assembled, Alan tied the sergeant's rope to one end. The lieutenant was then strapped in, whereupon the sergeant and Alan picked him up and started up the shaft.

At the top of the shaft, Kate held the searchlight as Corporal Hansen pulled on the rope and aided in the ascent.

As they reached the top, Alan could see through the cave opening that it was raining, and that the wind had increased in strength. Foam was now being blown off the top of the waves to the south of the island, an indication that the wind was at least gale force. The weather had definitely deteriorated from what it had been earlier in the day.

They set the stretcher down near the cave entrance. The young officer now appeared to be resting. The morphine was working.

"We're going to get him back to the shelter and get these wounds cleaned and dressed properly," Sergeant Thornton said, as Corporal Hansen took Alan's end of the stretcher.

Covering the Lieutenant as best they could, the two marines carried the stretcher out into the now torrential downpour and howling wind.

"Where's Mr. Fox?" Alan asked upon returning to the cavern.

"He went back down the shaft," Kate replied. "I still don't know where the professor went. He must still be in here somewhere."

"I'll go back down and look for them."

"I'm going with you," Kate said.

Alan stopped at the entrance to the lower shaft.

"You mentioned that the professor was in the cavern with you and Lieutenant Baker when the blue spheres came through. Is that when you last saw him?"

"Yes. I don't think he went down the lower shaft, but I'm not sure. He was having enough trouble with the slope of the upper shaft. He said he had trouble going down slopes with his knee."

"Then he may still be in this cavern, maybe farther back. I must have missed him earlier," Alan said.

Kate picked up the lantern and began searching around the rubble near the two shafts. Alan moved to the back, nearly 100 feet from where Kate was searching and shined the searchlight back toward the entrance, illuminating the back side of the larger rocks in the cavern.

"Any sign of him?" Alan shouted.

"No."

Alan turned the light on the far end of the cavern.

At the very back of the opening, the rough walls gave way to what looked like the same smooth rippled surface as the walls of the two shafts and the lower room. He moved his hand along the smooth surface. For the third time in two days, he watched as his hand unexpectedly disappeared into what looked like solid rock. And for the third time, he jerked it back reflexively.

The opening was narrow, perhaps two feet across by seven feet high. The floor of the opening was covered with rubble, which spilled out and onto the floor of the cavern where he stood.

Alan stepped through. He was in a tunnel, much like the shafts that connected the lower chamber to the surface. It was approximately 10 feet in diameter with the same smooth walls. It was completely blocked by rubble to his right. He stood for a moment looking at the rubble, trying to get his bearings. Was he facing north? He noticed something new mixed with the rock. There was a wooden plank, its end sticking out of the rubble pile. "Shoring," he said to himself. He searched the rock around the splintered piece of wood. There was a scrap of cloth and another skeleton, perhaps older than those of the men in the cavern he just left.

A tap on Alan's shoulder made him jump.

"Ah, Mr. Peterson, you've joined us. I've found something remarkable. Let me show you." It was Professor Fulton.

17. Imminent Dawn

1900 31 March, 2007 USS *Fort McHenry*
Eastern Pacific

The weather was again deteriorating. The latest weather satellite images showed Hurricane Alma had started to dissipate. These images from the old Defense Meteorological Satellite weren't all that clear but still clear enough to show a new storm, designated Boris, south and east of the *Fort McHenry*'s position. Boris had evidently originated at the same location as had Alma and had already been upgraded to a hurricane. From what the captain could tell, Boris would be growing to something very powerful.

Captain Tom Arthur sat in his at-sea cabin and studied the weather satellite images. He needed to change course and move the ship out of the dangerous quadrant of this new storm. But at this point, no matter what they did now, they were in for a rough ride. He sat back in his chair and relaxed into the motion of the ship. *Fort McHenry* was pitching and taking on a bit of a roll. He knew that a good number of the marines and the few passengers aboard were probably already seasick. It would get worse.

Captain Arthur knew he had made some mistakes in the last day and a half. Hopefully, those mistakes wouldn't cost any lives. The helicopter had returned and been restored to the small hangar on the port side of *Fort McHenry*'s flight deck. Since then, the winds had been at least force nine, severe gale, too strong to bring the aircraft out of the hangar, let alone send it to retrieve the shore party. Then Hurricane Alma! Alma was little more than a tropical depression when the shore party was sent in, an oddity this far east at this time of year. There was no reason the weather should have deteriorated so rapidly and become so severe. Nonetheless, he had made an error in allowing the CIA man, Fox, to talk him into releasing the shore party before the ship had arrived on-site. And now, the small team has been ashore for more than 24 hours without radio contact. Nothing, since their original radio check, shortly after they arrived on the island.

The last message from PACFLT had put him in a real bind. He took the red folder from the small safe below his desk and re-read the message.

```
OTTSZYUW RULSWCA0001 0870008-SSSS--RHMCSUU.
ZRN SSSSS
O 0114Z 01 APRIL 2007
FM CINCPACFLT//N2//
TO USS FORT MCHENRY//OO//
INFO COMTHIRDFLT SAN DIEGO CA//OO/N3//
BT
S E C R E T //N00000//PASS TO CDR JENKINS
SUBJ IMMINENT DAWN {S}
REF {a} CINCPACFLT INST 5135
1. {C} PROCEED NAVAL STATION PEARL HARBOR HI
   IAW REF {A}; URGENT ACTION REPEAT URGENT
   ACTION.
2. {U} AWAIT FURTHER ORDERS.
BT
```

Captain Arthur knew the referenced document by heart. He had drafted the current revision, while on staff at PACFLT during his last assignment. The phrase *URGENT ACTION* meant that this order was his highest priority. Pearl knew he had a shore party on the island. They were telling him to leave the shore party in the middle of a hurricane and immediately make way for Pearl Harbor. Because of something called *Imminent Dawn*? What was that important?

He had responded to the message requesting clarification. It would take something more direct than this reference to a general fleet instruction, however unambiguous it might be, for him to leave people behind in these circumstances.

As the captain sat staring at the message, he could feel the ship's roll becoming more pronounced. The wind speed was increasing. He put the folder back in his safe. His first duty was always the safety of the ship and right now that meant changing course to avoid the brunt of Hurricane Boris. He picked up his phone to call the bridge.

As he did so, there was a knock on his cabin door. It was the radio room watch with flash traffic. He replaced the receiver and opened the folder that the man handed him.

```
ZTTSZYUW RULSWCA0001 0870012-SSSS--RHMCSUU.
ZRN SSSSS
Z 0147Z 01 APRIL 2007
FM CINCPACFLT//00//
TO USS FORT MCHENRY//00//
INFO COMTHIRDFLT SAN DIEGO CA//00//
BT
S E C R E T //N00000//PASS TO CDR JENKINS
SUBJ IMMINENT DAWN {S}
REF {a} CINCPACFLT INST 5135
1. {C} FORT MCHENRY URGENTLY NEEDED PEARL
   HARBOR. DEPART IMMEDIATELY.
ADM CUMMINGS SENDS
BT
```

Captain Arthur read the short message twice.

"God help the people on that island." He picked up his phone and rang the bridge.

"This is the Captain. Put on the OOD please."

A moment later; "Yes, Sir." It was Ned Carson, the ship's operations officer.

"Ned, we're ordered to Pearl immediately. Have CIC plot a course. Flank speed. Give me an ETA as soon as you have it." He paused. "Get Commander Jenkins and Captain Parks to my quarters as soon as possible." He hung up the receiver.

Captain Arthur needed to tell the Marine detachment commander and the research team leader in person that he was about to leave their people behind on that little speck of an island in the middle of a major hurricane.

18. First Assessment

Alan and Professor Fulton met Geoff Fox at the opening to the cave.

"Have you seen Miss Harris?" Alan asked.

"She left a few minutes ago. She was looking for you," Fox said.

The CIA agent had gone back to the machine's control room and had finished making a copy of the Cyrillic message he had found earlier. He was now eager to get back to the campsite and use the communications equipment to report to his bosses. It seemed to Alan that he was completely indifferent to the fact that Professor Fulton had been located and was not hurt.

The three men stood for a moment looking through the cave opening at the small section of beach in front of them. It was nearly dusk. Large surf now broke across the entire southeastern reef. The weather had clearly deteriorated further, since Alan last looked out of the cave entrance. Heavy rain was falling horizontally outside, oddly blocked from entering the cave by the camouflage curtain.

"It's quite remarkable how this barrier blocks rain while allowing us to pass through," Professor Fulton said. "I have no idea how it does that."

The three men turned up their collars and stepped through the curtain to the outside. Alan looked around to the south of The Rock. The tide had risen significantly, and the big surf he could see from inside the cave, broke heavy against the rock's base. The path they had used earlier to get around The Rock on the ocean side, was now impassable. Alan guided the others around to the north, along the route he had used when he originally found the cave. Getting through the palm thicket, they stopped at the shore of the lagoon. The water level in the lagoon was also higher than it had been that previous day. They would have to stay close to The Rock face and negotiate the rubble that covered the bottom. With luck they wouldn't have to swim. He glanced north along the eastern reef of the atoll. Big surf was breaking along the entire eastern side of the island, flooding over into the lagoon at the narrower section of reef. It looked like the old ship may have shifted in the heavy seas of the previous night. It would probably shift more before this storm was over.

Alan recalled something he had read about atolls during his trip planning. It's not uncommon to have a constant ebb tide in the passes between the lagoon and the ocean on these islands. In the Tuamotus, a cluster of atolls in southern French Polynesia, the southern trade winds force a constant line of surf to break on their windward reefs. At narrow sections of reef, a good percentage of the surf spills over into the lagoon, filling it to above sea level. This overflow of water moves out of the passes, resulting in an outgoing or ebb current. Even when the natural tide is at flood stage, some of these island passes may have ebb flow. And when the natural tide is ebbing, the combination of the two effects can cause an out-flowing current in excess of six to ten knots, much too strong to be navigated by small sailing craft.

Although there were no passes into Clipperton's lagoon, the low section of reef on the southern and western sides of the island may have water flowing over and out of the lagoon before the night was over. It's funny what pops into your head, when you're tired and scared.

Picking their way along the base of The Rock, the three men sloshed through brackish lagoon water, stumbling occasionally on the submerged rubble that lined this section of The Rock's base. With effort, they reached the western side without encountering water above waist deep. They were all now totally drenched, as they trudged up onto the higher ground near the new campsite. The large shelter Alan had helped move earlier in the day was visible through the trees. Although it was still raining heavily, The Rock provided good shelter from the brunt of the wind's force.

"It certainly didn't take long to move the camp," Fox said when he saw the shelter. Alan held back a sarcastic comment. He had spent the better part of the morning helping move the camp to the new site, while Fox was off exploring. He wanted to mention that for those that had done the work, it seemed like it took quite a while.

As they approached the shelter, Professor Fulton stopped and inspected the new campsite. Alan stopped next to him, noticing that the professor had a confused look on his face.

"Are you OK, Professor?"

"How could you have done this so quickly?" The professor looked very confused.

"We spent all morning moving, Professor."

"But it hasn't been long enough...."

"Let's get out of the rain," Alan said. He was becoming concerned about the older man. It had been a long day, and Alan was sure Fulton hadn't had anything to eat. He was showing signs of fatigue. Alan led him inside. Fox had already gone in.

The shelter was partitioned into three compartments, along the length of the structure. The entryway was at the middle of the side wall and led into the center compartment, where there were two folding tables and several folding chairs. On either end of the structure were two other compartments accessible from the central room. The compartment to the right was for sleeping; the other was a kitchen and eating area. The entire structure and its furnishings collapsed to fit into two rigid, watertight containers that were approximately four by four by eight feet. Alan knew from his morning workout that the containers were quite heavy.

As Alan and the professor entered the shelter, Fox was standing next to Corporal Hansen at one of the tables where the communications equipment had been set up. He was asking about the status of the MilStar Terminal.

"We're not receiving a sync signal from the satellite, Sir," Corporal Hansen said.

"Is the satellite down?"

"No, Sir. We've got the downlink signal. It just looks like the receiver isn't syncing. We can't get a lock, Sir. I've tried resetting the key several times. No joy. It doesn't look like the transmitter is working either. I'm not showing anything on the SWR meter, when I try an uplink signal. Probably, the output stage of the amplifier is blown. The transceiver case had salt water in it from the big waves last night. I tried rinsing it in fresh water, but it's not looking good. I don't think I can fix it, Sir."

"How about the HF gear? Can we reach the ship?" Fox was sounding irritated.

"That rig is fried, Sir. The local oscillator is history. Can't transmit or receive on it either."

"I need to talk to Langley," Fox snapped. "ASAP! What am I supposed to do, put a message in a bottle?"

Alan could see Fox's frustration level increasing over the period of the conversation. His face was red, his fists clinched. His last comment was nearly a scream.

A moan came from the compartment to the right of the entryway. Professor Fulton lifted the flap, and he and Alan entered the smaller compartment. Lieutenant Baker was lying on a small cot. Alan realized it was the same cot that they had used as a stretcher earlier. Kate and the sergeant were tending to the wounded man. The lieutenant sounded delirious.

"I screwed up. I screwed up my first assignment," the young officer kept repeating.

"Take it easy, Sir. You did OK. No one died." Sergeant Thornton's approach to calming down the lieutenant left some room for improvement.

"How is he?" Alan asked.

"The sergeant had the wounds cleaned up and the bleeding stopped. But he is already developing a fever," Kate said. "There are oral antibiotics in the medical kit. Hopefully, it's just a matter of getting them down him and keeping him hydrated."

They could all hear Mr. Fox's voice from the next compartment. He was quizzing Corporal Hansen as to how he knew, *for sure,* that the communications equipment was not repairable.

"And he needs rest," Sergeant Thornton said as he lifted the door flap and entered the center compartment.

"There's no magic here, Mr. Fox. Our communications are down," the sergeant said, moving across the room to the table where Fox and the corporal were standing. "It looks like we won't have an operational radio until the *Fort McHenry* gets here. Meanwhile, Lieutenant Baker needs rest, so *hold down the noise.*" The sergeant now stood directly in front of Mr. Fox, their faces less than four inches apart. Thornton towered over the smaller man. He was not smiling.

"I agree with Professor Fulton," Kate said. "It can't be Russian."

A strange conversation had ensued after Sergeant Thornton laid down the rules concerning noise level, or at least Alan thought it was strange. The professor had more or less regained his bearings after having something to eat. Corporal Hansen had gone in to attend to the lieutenant, while Kate, Professor Fulton, Fox, Alan and Sergeant Thornton settled into chairs surrounding the larger table in the central compartment. Fox kept glancing across the room at the defunct communications equipment on the other table. They were talking in near whispers, leaning over the table to be heard. Their efforts to "hold down the noise" made the conversation seem almost conspiratorial. And the three Hellfire-cleared members of the group were making it seem even more so. They were attempting to discuss the machine's likelihood of being part of that classified program without divulging the program itself. In attempting to do so, Alan could see they were using a great deal of unspoken communications. He smiled to himself.

Alan had dealt with enough classified information during his years in the navy to know what was going on between the members of the research team. The researchers were doing a bad job of concealing their secret mission. If he and the sergeant were not to be cleared for the subject, then this discussion shouldn't be taking place with them present. Besides, he didn't want to be part of the conspiracy he told himself.

"The technology we are seeing here is far too advanced for the 1950s and '60s. In fact, it's more advanced than anything I've ever seen," Kate continued.

"What if you're wrong?" Fox said glancing back and forth between Kate and Professor Fulton. "What if it is Russian, and it's activated?"

"Nothing I have seen would suggest that is the case," Professor Fulton said.

"You haven't seen the controls. The sailor here says this writing is Russian. I can't afford to be wrong in my assessment of this risk," Fox said.

"Wrong about what?" Alan was becoming tired. He was also becoming irritated by the conversation. He was not really part of the discussion, and he knew that he probably shouldn't be. At the same time, he was frustrated by not being able to understand the concern of the researchers. Then too, the little research group was starting to rehash the same arguments for the third, maybe fourth time.

At Alan's question, the table became quiet. Kate, Fox and Professor Fulton exchanged glances.

"Mr. Fox is concerned that the machine might be Russian," Kate broke the silence.

"I can see that," Alan said. "Is there a U.S. diplomatic issue with the Russians having a machine on a French island, or am I just missing something?" Alan was now teasing the researchers. He knew Fox wasn't a diplomat.

"There might be," said Fox.

"I see. So, you're out here in the middle of a major storm on a diplomatic mission then." Alan had lost his patience. "Look, here is my two cents worth. The shafts that run between the three chambers we have found in The Rock, the upper cave, the middle cavern and the lower room, as well as the lower opening itself, were not made by any tunneling equipment that currently exists. And I'm familiar with such equipment."

"The writing on the screen in what you might call the *control room* is Cyrillic, and the language is Russian." Alan pushed his chair back and got up from the table.

"One last thing, the occurrence of the events or the appearance of the blue spheres, whatever you wish to call these phenomena, seems to be happening at regular intervals. They have appeared shortly before 12 o'clock every day I've been on the island. That's all I have. I'm going back to my boat. Good luck."

Alan crossed the room and left the shelter, before anyone could even respond. Sergeant Thornton followed after him, catching up to him just north of the campsite.

"Is that a side-band radio that I saw on your boat?" Sergeant Thornton asked, putting his hand on Alan's shoulder to get his attention.

"Yes, but it quit working last night. It must have been damaged in the storm. Might be just the antenna, but I don't know."

"Mind if Corporal Hansen takes a look at it? He may be able to do something. We really need to contact the ship."

"Send him over," Alan said. "Maybe he can at least get the receiver up, and we can find out what's going on with this crazy weather."

The sergeant nodded at Alan, then turned back into the wind and began trudging through the downpour towards the shelter.

Alan headed back down the trail, kicking himself for not getting his boat off the beach that afternoon, while he had the chance.

Steven C. Golly

19. Approaching Storm

0900 31 March, 2007 Clipperton Atoll

Corporal Hansen arrived shortly after Alan had returned to the boat. Within a few minutes, he had fixed the side-band radio. As Alan suspected earlier, the problem turned out to be the antenna. The corporal tuned the receiver to the Pacific weather channel. Within a few minutes, they learned about hurricane Boris.

Alan plotted the location of the storm, 105 nautical miles east of Clipperton Island moving west at 20 knots. On its current track, Boris would pass directly over the island in less than six hours as a force-four hurricane with winds in excess of 130 miles per hour.

He considered his situation, as well as that of the research team. Hurricane Boris was not the little blow that had gone through the previous night. This was a killer storm. Alan had been through two typhoons aboard ships during his time in the navy. He could still feel the motion of the ship in the enormous seas and still see the view from the bridge at the height of the storm. He shook his head. Aground on this little island in a little boat was a lethal place to be in a force-four hurricane.

He glanced out the porthole above *Wind Gypsy*'s navigation station. He could see the lights of the campsite. The island was not on the normal tropical storm track, so the winds in the region would normally only be weak Northeastern Pacific Trades and, perhaps, an occasional squall. Force-four hurricane winds could bring down a significant number of trees, trees that would otherwise grow fine in the light winds of the region. As the wind strengthened with the storm's approach, Clipperton Rock would no longer provide the wind break it now did at the site. The trees around the shelter would carry the brunt of the wind's force. There will be trees downed by the winds of this storm…perhaps, many. And the storm surge from this hurricane will be significant. It will bring the ocean level above the reef, flooding the campsite.

There was really only one option…run. Get the boat off the beach and run as far and as fast as possible from the storm. The only chance of survival was to get out of the storm's path.

"I think we can contact the ship using your side-band radio," Corporal Hansen said, interrupting Alan's thoughts.

"How close do you think they are?" Alan asked.

"Don't know. They should be close, I guess. I'll need to get the ship's frequencies from my notebook. I'll let the sergeant know we're up and running with your radio. That should make Mr. Fox very happy."

"So, it would seem," Alan said. "I hope that ship is close. Regardless, we need to get off this island…tonight! I'll go back to the camp with you. I need to speak to Sergeant Thornton."

The two men left the boat and headed back to the camp. They had to wade ashore through several feet of water from the point where the boarding ladder was lowered. At near low tide *Wind Gypsy* was all but afloat in her makeshift cradle. The effects of the storm were already upon them. At flood, *Wind Gypsy* may well be bouncing off the tops of the cradle's uprights, a good way to punch holes in the hull. Another reason to leave, he thought. No matter what, *Wind Gypsy* needed to be off the beach before the brunt of the storm hit. The best option for the safety of everyone was to run south southeast, as far from the storm's dangerous quadrant as possible. And as soon as possible.

———————•———————

Sergeant Thornton was in the sleeping area on the northern end of the shelter tending to Lieutenant Baker. With the help of Professor

Fulton, who had been a corpsman in the service many years earlier, Kate and the sergeant had managed to finish cleaning and dressing the lieutenant's wounds. Most importantly, they had stopped the hemorrhaging that had restarted from the man's thigh.

Meanwhile, after another personal inspection of the defunct communications equipment, Geoffrey Fox had gone off to the equipment storage shelter. Kate could occasionally hear what sounded like crates being opened, over the noise of the wind and rain, as he rummaged through the equipment. It was clear now to Kate that Fox was convinced the machine was a threat. In her view, if the machine was in fact Russian, which she deemed highly unlikely, the best course of action was to contact the Russians and find out what its purpose was and what, if anything, needed to be done. In any case, there wasn't much that could be done until the ship arrived, and the team had access to communications again.

But Kate wasn't at all convinced that the machine had anything to do with the Hellfire program, and she was concerned that the expedition seemed to have turned solely in that direction. As Commander Jenkins reminded her before she left the ship, the research team was sent to the island to determine whether the events they had observed there were associated with the satellite outages and the anomalies seen by her project team on Maui. It wasn't a hunting expedition to look for old, cold-war artifacts. In fact, it was inconceivable to her that an ancient cold-war machine could have anything to do with the telescope observation errors or the satellite anomalies of the last several days. There was no physics to support how a cold-war atomic device could cause such effects. Besides, in her opinion, the technology in the cavern was much too sophisticated for a machine of the cold-war era...much too sophisticated. And there was something else....

"I saw something remarkable in the tunnel," Professor Fulton said. Kate and the professor had been sitting at the table in the central common room, where the team had met earlier.

"You mean the tunnel where Alan found you?"

"Yes. It was quite strange. One end was blocked by a cave-in, but in the other direction, the tunnel ran for 50 feet or so and then made an abrupt turn to the left. After another 100 feet or so, it terminated at a, I'm not sure how to describe it,...a *partition*. On one side of the partition was the tunnel where I stood. On the other side was the ocean. It was like looking into an aquarium, as if the end of the tunnel was a wall of glass holding the ocean out. But it wasn't glass. In fact, I could pass my hand through it. Remarkable!"

"This isn't 1950's technology, is it?" Kate asked.

"No. What we are seeing here is much more advanced than Hellfire hardware, than any 1950's hardware. And the physics! It is quite beyond me. I'm not sure what it is. This technology doesn't exist...well except here. I believe this machine to be...*alien*."

There was a long pause in the conversation as the two scientists stared into each other's eyes.

"I'm glad you said that first," Kate finally replied. "It sounds more convincing coming from you."

Professor Fulton smiled. "You need to be more sure of yourself," he said.

"I've heard that before," Kate paused. "Fox and the sailor say the display is in Russian. What do you make of that?"

"I'm not sure....It could be....I'm not sure."

Kate decided to change the subject.

"I didn't get a chance to go over my findings, while we were on the ship. I'd like to know what you think."

"Now is as good a time as any," he said, leaning farther forward in his chair. "It doesn't look like we're going anywhere for a while."

———•———

"That could be consistent with the time discrepancy I noted this morning, or should I say afternoon," Professor Fulton was saying as Alan and Corporal Hansen entered the shelter. Kate and Professor Fulton turned to greet them. The corporal stepped immediately into the north sleeping compartment where Sergeant Thornton was looking after the lieutenant.

"You need to move camp," Alan said.

"I thought we just did," said Kate.

"You need to move camp again."

"I don't understand why we..." Kate started to say as Sergeant Thornton entered the center compartment.

"Hansen says your radio is working," the sergeant said.

"You're more than welcome to use it, Sergeant, but it may entail going on a boat ride. There's a hurricane headed straight for the island, and it won't be safe on this reef for much longer. I'm recommending that you move aboard the boat, and that we get underway as soon as possible."

"Hansen mentioned the storm. He said it's big."

"Yes, force four and it looks like it will pass directly over Clipperton Island. I would expect the entire island to be awash, except The Rock." Alan said.

"I've heard stories of the South Pacific islanders riding out such storms by tying themselves to palm trees," Professor Fulton said.

"Not a bad idea for your equipment, but I wouldn't recommend it for your person." Alan answered.

"How is the lieutenant? Can he be moved?" Kate asked the sergeant, wondering how they would get the wounded man up and onto the boat. He was definitely not ambulatory. He would have to be moved by stretcher. They all looked at Sergeant Thornton.

"He's resting OK. Looks like we've got the bleeding stopped, but we could open his wounds back up if we move him now. How would we get him aboard the boat?" Thornton echoed Kate's thoughts.

"We can hoist the stretcher aboard, using the main boom and topping lift," said Alan. "That won't be a problem. I think we're going to have to risk it. He won't survive the storm on the island. Getting the stretcher down the companionway might be a little trickier, but there's enough of us to do that. We need to move quickly though."

"This is very unusual, very unusual," Professor Fulton said. "Force four you say. The latitude here is too low for a storm of this magnitude and this early…it's too early for such weather."

"Fact is, it's here, and we don't have a lot of time," Alan responded.

"Shouldn't we consider the caves? That might be a better place to ride this out than the boat, particularly if the camouflage curtain holds the water out like Professor Fulton says it does. He discovered it in the tunnel," Kate said.

"Perhaps," said Alan. "I wouldn't risk it if I were you. In any case, I'm taking the boat off the reef and as far south as I can get before the storm arrives. You're welcome to come along. It's your decision."

At that moment a wave of nausea came over everyone in the shelter. Alan and Sergeant Thornton fell to their knees where they stood. Kate placed her head on the table, holding back becoming sick. Professor Fulton tilted sideways in his chair and fell to the floor. They all heard a loud crack, and moments later a crash as a large tree fell on the equipment shelter.

"What the…what was that?" Sergeant Thornton was the first to speak as the wave of nausea passed.

Alan glanced at his watch. It was 11:41 a.m.

"The machine," he said. "Right on schedule."

20. Executive Order

1830 31 March, 2007 Clipperton Atoll

Mister Geoffrey Fox knew that few people took him seriously, something he had learned at a young age. The second son in a family of "old money," Geoffrey grew up spending summers in Nantucket and winters on the slopes at Aspen. He received a degree from Harvard in French, after having been accepted as a legacy student. The degree required nearly six years of effort. Well, if not effort, six years of presence at the venerable institution. The fact was, Geoffrey was quite intelligent, just unmotivated. And why should he be? He wanted for nothing, except, perhaps, to be taken at least somewhat seriously.

After his school training, and through his father's connections in the government, Geoffrey secured a position with the CIA. As it would turn out, an old school chum of the elder Fox was rather well placed in the agency. Geoffrey wanted a posting in the Operations Directorate. That, after all, was where the real spies worked. But instead, he ended up in a support position for the Diplomatic Corps. His father thought it was a good fit for his talents, such as they were. Geoffrey thought the position boring.

After six months of training with the Diplomatic Corps, he found a way out. That way out was Hellfire. The old program was gearing down. Most of the original members had long since retired. The younger talent was moving on to more current efforts, such as counterterrorism and other Middle Eastern and Asian programs. The Hellfire Program needed field personnel. His application was accepted.

Geoffrey didn't do well at The Farm, the CIA's field agent training center. He didn't have the temperament. He lacked technique, and most of all, he had none of the social skills of even a mediocre field agent. He did, however, excel at tradecraft, and he became an excellent explosives man. The Hellfire Program office, now desperate for people, accepted Geoffrey in a conditional status after his field training. He was transferred to the Honolulu Field Office, under Diplomatic Corps cover, to be sent into the field only when accompanied by a qualified field agent.

Then the Clipperton incident occurred. Geoffrey's associate and field counterpart in Honolulu was on leave at the time, "stateside," as they called it in the office. True to the guidelines of their conditional acceptance, Geoffrey would not be allowed to handle the incident alone. After some coordination through CINCPACFLT, Professor Fulton, an experienced field agent with a long history in the Hellfire Program, was recruited to *accompany* Geoffrey on the Clipperton assignment.

The old man hadn't been much help. There was no attempt to do any pre-mission coordination, while they were aboard the ship. Getting the plan worked out before they arrived on the island would have been helpful. Then, where was he when he was really needed? The old man had gotten lost in the cavern, that's where!

Geoffrey was convinced it had been a mistake to bring the professor out of retirement and assign him to this mission. He didn't need supervision for this little job. The mission was obvious. They had found a Russian Hellfire machine, and it had to be deactivated. The only useful thing the professor could have done was to identify the function of the controls Geoffrey had found. But it didn't really matter. He would take care of it himself, even without the old man's support. Again, as in the past, his opinion was not being taken seriously. But he would change that. He would take the necessary action himself.

But first, he would try to check in with the program office at Langley. He had been given an Iridium telephone before he left Honolulu. It was to be a means of last resort for communications. He had never used one of the devices before. Iridium was a bankrupt, private, telephone company that had been taken over by the government several years earlier. Initially designed, built and marketed as a global satellite telephone service, the demand turned out to be much less than expected based on the company's initial market analysis. The Iridium Corporation went quickly into Chapter 11. That's when the government stepped in. The little expedition to Clipperton Island was an excellent example of where Iridium had a market. The problems were, it's a tiny market and a costly program. And that is why the concept turned out to be commercially unviable, but then commercial viability is never a problem for the government.

None of that was Geoffrey's concern. His only concern was that he wasn't sure how to use the Iridium phone. But then, how hard could it be?

With some guidance from Corporal Hansen, he found his equipment where the marines had stored it earlier, in one of the waterproof containers in the equipment shelter. With some effort, he found and retrieved the phone in its gray metal case from the bottom container at the back of the shelter. He should have started looking there he thought. He hadn't opened the case before now and was surprised by how bulky the thing was. He had expected something like his cell phone. The Iridium phone looked more like an old-time, World War II walkie-talkie with a fat antenna. He found the switch and turned it on. A few moments later there was a dial tone. He was right. It was simple to operate. But then, how hard could it be?

Geoffrey decided to make contact without Professor Fulton's involvement. The professor would only hinder the mission. He found and put on his raincoat, tucking the bulky phone into the inside pocket. He made his way to the western face of The Rock, far enough away from the shelters, so that his phone call could not be heard by the others on the team. It would also be somewhat protected from the wind by The Rock. He dialed the number and got a busy signal. He checked the number and dialed again. He had transposed the last two digits.

"Hello."

"Hello, have I caught Mister Trenton at a bad time?"

"Is this about the subscription?"

"No, this is Hal Carmichael." Fox used Professor Fulton's cover name. He had gotten it from the professor's old file and verified it was still current while on the ship.

The bona fides had gone quite well, he thought. No trip-ups. What exactly was so hard about this field work anyway?

"Just a moment please." The line went silent. It took several minutes for the next response. Fox moved closer to The Rock hoping to get a little protection from the wind.

"This is Trenton. How can I help you?"

"I have your order ready."

"Could you hold it until I arrive?"

"Yes, I believe we can. You will need to make a deposit. There are others interested."

"I see. Just a moment."

Using the silly code that he had learned in training, Geoffrey told them he needed authorization to secure the site. It was several more minutes before the next response. Even with the raincoat, he was completely soaked and was starting to get a dreadful chill by the time that Langley finally responded.

"OK, Mr. Carmichael. You'll have our deposit in less than a week. Go ahead and put the item in storage, if you would."

"Very well, thank you for your business."

The line went dead.

Geoffrey made his way back to the storage shelter. His mission was now clear. He needed to secure the machine, so that it could not be disturbed for the next week. That's when Langley would have people on the island to take over. He had already decided the best way to do that. He would use the marines' explosives he had found while looking for the Iridium phone, and he would seal off the entrance to the cave.

He knew how to do that.

21. Sea Legs

1600 01 April, 2007 Eastern Pacific

Wind Gypsy's auxiliary engine had run nearly wide open for over 12 hours. Alan attempted to hold a course of 165° as best he could in the confused seas, occasionally getting a brief break from the helm when the autopilot managed to hold the boat's heading for a short time. These rare respites didn't last long, as the autopilot was unreliable in the big seas generated by the storm. Inevitably, a big wave would slap the bow off course, so far that the rudder response wasn't quick enough to compensate. The usual outcome was that the rudder was forced into a stall, and the boat would be out of control. As a consequence, Alan had for the most part, been at the helm the entire time since leaving the island.

The only other person aboard with any sailing experience was Professor Fulton, and the older man was still suffering fatigue from the previous day's exertion. The professor had been able to help at the helm for the short time it took Alan to raise what little sails he could in the strong winds before leaving the island. With this combination of sails and the auxiliary engine, the boat was moving at its fastest possible speed through the water.

And considering the weather, *Wind Gypsy* rode pretty well under this sail plan. That being said, it had not been a pleasant ride.

The seas were quite large. At the worst of it, Alan estimated 30 feet of ocean swell with 10-foot wind waves that frequently broke into the cockpit. That, along with the howling wind, blowing spray and torrential rain, made it particularly uncomfortable topside. Alan was feeling the effects. His body ached from fatigue. He was exhausted.

The good news was that they had gotten out of the storm track early and, therefore, were missing the worst of it. Hurricane Boris had formed so quickly that the seas didn't have a chance to build as high as they could have, had the storm built more slowly.

They were now over 100 miles south of the hurricane's track, and the seas were subsiding. The wind had died down to a little more than a gentle breeze by late afternoon. Alan cut the throttle back to an idle and released the autopilot. At the crest of a swell, he turned the helm hard and tacked the boat around to the reciprocal course, 345°. He then re-engaged the autopilot on the new heading. As he did so, the companionway hatch slid forward, and Professor Fulton poked his head out.

"You've changed course," the professor said.

"I think we can head back. The weather is well past our longitude by now."

"I agree. You must be exhausted. Can I relieve you for a while? I've done a lot of sailing. If you could just show me the operation of the autopilot, I'll be quite able to manage."

"I'm going to take you up on that offer, Sir," Alan said. "There's some rain gear hanging in the forward stateroom you'll want to put on. I'll set a bit more sail. We can carry more sail now that the wind has died down. There's an extra harness hanging down below to the right of the companionway. Put it on before you come up, if you would."

Alan retrieved a winch handle from the port-side cockpit locker, snapped onto the port jack line with his harness pendant, and stepped out of the cockpit, making his way forward. He was reminded, again, how achy and stiff his body was and just how dead tired he was.

———•———

They had been lucky. The timely decision to leave the island was made shortly after the first tree fell on the supply tent. Two other large trees had fallen near the camp before Lieutenant Baker was hoisted aboard the boat and moved to the small cabin at the bottom of the companionway.

They had been lucky that the lieutenant's wounds hadn't reopened. After he had been moved aboard and was resting as comfortably as possible, the marines had returned to the island and been able to stow a good percentage of their equipment in watertight containers. The containers were secured to trees before they left the campsite.

They had been lucky that after knocking the braces off the makeshift boat cradle, it turned out to be relatively easy to re-float *Wind Gypsy*. With the high tide and the island breaking the brunt of the then nearly hurricane-force winds, they cleared the coral heads off the island's southeastern side and got under sail without incident.

And they had also been lucky because, although the winds were stiff and the seas large, they escaped the brunt of the storm, and the boat was never really in danger from the weather.

But there was some bad news.

Geoffrey Fox was missing.

As the marines and Alan moved the lieutenant to the boat and secured equipment, Kate and Professor Fulton looked for the government agent. They couldn't find him. At first, they were concerned that he had been hit by one of the falling trees, particularly after the first tree hit the storage shelter. Kate was sure that Fox had been in the smaller tent most of the evening. But their search of the shelter and the area surrounding the campsite came up empty. After they secured all the equipment to trees and moved essentials aboard the boat, Alan and Sergeant Thornton did one last check of the area for Mr. Fox. The sergeant felt sure that the government man had gone back to the cave, so they made their way around The Rock, wading through now chest-deep water and building surf on the lagoon side. They reached the cave entrance and called out for Fox several times from the upper cave. But there was no answer, and there was no sign that he had been in the cave. Dripping wet when they entered, they both left trails of water wherever they went in the cave. Except for these signs of their presence, there was no water in the cave, and no water in the upper shaft. Convinced that Fox had not come back to the cave that evening, they returned to the boat. After a short conference, they made the decision to leave. It was a matter of survival. No one was happy about leaving Fox, but there was no choice.

Then they received other bad news. After *Wind Gypsy* was underway and on her southerly heading, Corporal Hansen used the side-band radio to contact the *Fort McHenry*. That's when they found out that the ship was enroute to Pearl Harbor and had left them behind!

They were given no information as to what could be so important that they should be left on the small island in the middle of a hurricane. The only response was that *Operational Exigencies* had forced the ship's departure. Whatever the crisis was, it was apparently more important than the welfare of the research team. After the initial shock wore off, they settled into the realization that, as Sergeant Thornton put it, "Somethin' serious must be happnin'." As it was, they were all too exhausted to put a lot of effort into getting upset. Escaping the storm was the top priority, and as the storm subsided, they were all just glad they had survived.

———————•———————

The seas had continued to subside through the night. The ocean swell was now at less than 10 feet and the wind waves were less than three feet in height. The boat was sailing nicely, moving under a steady breeze. *Wind Gypsy* was rising over the crest of the swell with only a slight pitching motion.

Kate came up the companionway and stepped into the cockpit. It was early evening, and the air was fresh, significantly less humid above deck than it was inside the cabin. The southern sky was partially overcast. Professor Fulton was seated on the right, that is, the *starboard* side of the boat. He was looking at the horizon through binoculars. The professor had been teaching her proper boat terminology earlier, before he had gone up to relieve Alan at the helm. He lowered the binoculars as she sat down across from him, still staring at the horizon. Neither of them said anything for a few minutes.

This had been Kate's first real boat ride. She was on a boat only once before when she was a teenager. A group of kids had gone fishing in several small boats on Lake Erie. She remembered getting sunburned. It hadn't been particularly fun.

The storm was terrifying. The boat's motion reminded her of the Twist-O-Wheel ride she had once taken at the county fair as a kid. The ride made her sick. She was convinced that the only reason she didn't get sick during the storm was because she hadn't had anything to eat for the 20 hours preceding their leaving the island. She still wasn't all that hungry, but the boat's ride was a lot more comfortable now, and topside it was, well, almost pleasant. Maybe she could eat something, she thought.

"Where are we?" Kate broke the silence.

"I would estimate we are still 60 miles south of the island," Professor Fulton said. "The boat is making quite good headway. We should be back by morning. Are you hungry? I'm famished."

Alan popped his head out of the companionway. He had awakened when Kate brushed by him on her way to the cockpit.

"I've got canned chili, tuna, no bread, beef stew and canned chili. Oh, and some crackers. There may be a little cheese left, if you want to scrape off the mold."

"I would be delighted to have some of the chili," Professor Fulton said.

"And you, Miss Harris?" Alan noticed that both marines had gotten seasick during the storm and were still looking under the weather. He had talked them into drinking as much water as they could. At the same time, he was impressed by the astronomer. It was easy to see that she wasn't a sailor by her lack of knowledge of the boat, but she came through the storm like a trooper. And now, she seemed to be enjoying the ride.

"Kate. Please, call me Kate," she said. "Maybe, I could join the professor in some chili. Is there anything I can do to help?"

"Nope. Thanks. Got it. The galley is only big enough for one. I'll put on some coffee, too. Be back in a bit." Alan ducked back below. He opened the door to the port cabin. The lieutenant appeared to be resting comfortably. He entered the galley and took a couple of cans of chili from the cupboard. In the main cabin he could see that Sergeant Thornton was asleep in the settee bunk, the make-shift bed that was formed by lowering the table to the level of the settee seats and placing the seat-back cushions on the table surface. Corporal Hansen had emerged from the forward stateroom and was stretched out on the couch seat to starboard of the settee. He was also asleep. Alan put a pan on the stovetop and lit the flame. Neither marine stirred.

———————•———————

Kate, Alan and the Professor sat in the cockpit sipping hot coffee. The autopilot was now handling the helm with little effort, freeing them to enjoy the afternoon. Kate and Professor Fulton's conversation had returned to the machine and also to Kate's findings concerning the satellite and telescope data. Alan listened to the two scientists' discussion. It was technical and he could only understand about half of what they were saying. Kate brought up the stellar positional errors the research team at the observatory had found that first day. Alan began to wonder how, with all the GPS errors and the celestial observation errors, he had managed to find Clipperton Island, when the boat was first struck by one of the objects. He asked the question. Kate pointed out that the angular errors in stellar observations they had seen on Maui were much too small to cause any measurable error in his sextant measurements.

Actually, she was impressed that the man even knew how to use the old navigational equipment, or how to reduce a sighting. The mathematics of the spherical triangle was an ancient mystery to most modern sailors. The science now belongs to satellite constellation architects, orbital dynamics professionals and the occasional astronomer; like Kate.

"The acceleration would have to be significant to produce that large of a displacement in your observations," Professor Fulton said, "particularly if the displacements are centered on the GP of the island. That might explain the temporal effects we were talking about earlier."

"Temporal effects?" Alan was becoming more confused.

"Yes, Alan. Both Mr. Fox and I noted it yesterday. In fact, I found it quite confusing. When we first came back to the camp, Mr. Fox and I perceived that it had only been a few minutes, maybe half an hour that we were in the tunnel. Yet the day had gone by. You had moved the camp, the lieutenant had been hurt and the weather had turned, all in what we thought to be a very short time. My wristwatch confirmed it. There was a five-hour discrepancy between my watch and your ship's clock. I set my watch to your clock the day we arrived on the island. I checked it again last night. I lost five hours and 33 minutes. The acceleration would have to be extremely large to account for that."

"Are you saying the thing in the caverns is a time machine? I don't understand what you mean by acceleration?"

"No, Alan; not a time machine. I don't believe that is its purpose. But it, apparently, is affecting local time. I guess, the best way to explain is to fall back on the basic tenants of special relativity. You're familiar with time dilation? You know, it's like when the clocks on a spaceship leaving earth advance slower.

"You mean time is relative, as they say."

"Yes. Two people see time progressing at different rates, if they are moving relative to each other. In this case, for Mr. Fox and I to have experienced a time dilation, we must have been *accelerated* to a different velocity. With respect to the normal processes of living, the physical laws if you will, relative motion is not significant. But acceleration…" Professor Fulton's voice trailed off. He appeared to be concentrating.

"Do you suppose this machine generates gravity waves, Miss Harris?" He finally said.

The two scientists were now back in a complicated discussion of local acceleration, propagation, focal length and timing. Alan glanced at the horizon. It was dusk.

Earlier he had decided that dead reckoning would be good enough to bring the boat back to within radar range of the island. He had gotten a good radar return off The Rock at 15 miles out, when he first approached the island three days earlier. Now, he wasn't so sure. He hadn't been able to hold heading very well in the confused seas of the previous night. He adjusted the course assuming a one and one-half knot set to the west. But that was really just a rough guess.

As it turned out, it would be more than 30 hours before they reached the island again. A half knot error in his estimate of set, or a few degrees off in his heading would put the boat out of radar range of the island. He remembered he was really tired when he made the decision not to update his position. He knew better. What would the old sailor think of him missing his landfall?

The northern sky was completely overcast. Alan glanced to the south. Off the horizon he could see what was probably Suhail, to the southeast, Antares just above the horizon.

"Excuse me folks," he said during a lull in the conversation. "I need to attend to some chores."

He went below to retrieve his sextant and tablet.

———•———

With the cloud cover still heavy to the north, Alan could find only the two usable selected stars he had seen earlier. At least, the separation was good, and the two lines of position crossed at nearly a right angle. As plotted, their position was nearly 20 miles west northwest of his dead reckoning track, and 40 miles southwest of the island. He laid out a new track line on the chart and adjusted the autopilot, using the controls at the navigation table. Then he went topside to trim the sails. As he came back up the companionway, Kate was talking about the blue spheres.

———————•———————

Kate explained to the professor what she had determined on the ship. The displacement anomalies they had observed with the telescope on Maui occurred in a nearly triangular region of the sky. All the stellar positional errors and, remarkably, all the satellite anomalies were within that triangular region. What she had realized was that this region of the celestial sphere corresponded to the triangular sector of the earth surface described by Clipperton Island and the termination points of the two objects picked up by the RYNO satellite.

"It would be good to verify your observations with the data from the later events, the ones that have occurred since we left the ship," the professor said.

"Is there someone you could call to get the data?" Alan was listening in to the conversation as he trimmed the jib sheet.

"Yes, but my cell phone doesn't work in the middle of the ocean." Kate's answer had just a hint of sarcasm. At the same time, she had the hint of a smile on her face. She hadn't noticed that Alan had come back topside. She was intrigued earlier when he appeared with his sextant and climbed out onto the small platform at the very back of the boat, the *boomkin*, as Professor Fulton referred to it, and started taking sightings.

"Are you thinking we'll pass by a phone booth?" She asked.

"No, probably not, but you could always use the ship-to-shore radio channels."

———————•———————

"Hello, Kate…?"

"You will need to say *Over* if you want her to respond, Sir." It was the marine operator.

"Oh yeah, I remember. Kate, this is Phil.…Over."

Alan had reached the Honolulu marine operator and placed a call to Phil Beckman, the systems engineer that worked with Kate at the Observatory. Phil was having trouble with ship-to-shore radio protocols.

"Phil, I need the information on these last few events. Same data as you sent me earlier and anything unusual. Any data you can get me.…Over." Kate learned quickly from Phil's mistake.

"…Kate, I just found out about it this evening. That's why they closed down our program. The entire facility has been dedicated to tracking the comet. Its trajectory is hyperbolic." Phil had been talking over Kate. "It's traveling at a very high velocity. Kate, it looks like it's going to come close. It may hit us.…Over."

There was a long silence.

"Do you wish to terminate your call?" It was the marine operator again.

"No, no…what comet, Phil?…Over."

"O'Conner-Thompson. They just spotted it. I don't have any data on it yet, Kate. Its trajectory is converging on that of Haley's comet, along the Eta Aquarid meteorite stream. It's flickering in the visual range, probably meteorite impacts. It's moving a lot faster than the stream. And it's big. Maybe a planet killer, Kate.…Over."

Everyone onboard was now listening intently to the conversation. Sergeant Thornton and Corporal Hansen were at the settee drinking coffee. Professor Fulton was standing near the galley entrance. Alan was seated in the companionway, his feet on the companionway ladder. And Kate was seated at the navigation table. The door to the aft cabin, directly behind her, was open. Lieutenant Baker was propped up on his left elbow, also listening to what was being said on the side-band radio.

"What…what's the albedo look like? Absorption spectra? Can… Will you get us the data on this comet too, Phil?…Over."

"OK, Kate. I'll head back up to the observatory, now. See what I can find out from Stevens. I'll call you back in a few hours. Over… and Out." "Hello, marine operator, I'm finished.…Over."

"Thank you for using the Honolulu marine operator, Sir."

The signal went dead.

22. Sabotage

2030 31 March, 2007 Clipperton Atoll

Geoffrey Fox watched as the two men waded through the chest-high water of the lagoon, the beams of their flashlights playing off the white foam of the surf and the vertical surfaces of The Rock. He had managed to get two cases of high explosives, as well as the other blasting equipment he needed through the same water some 45 minutes earlier. With the wind and heavy rain in his face, he thought it had been a heroic accomplishment. These demolition supplies were now hidden behind a large, downed palm tree and dense undergrowth 200 yards from The Rock's northeastern face. With everything he needed moved to the site, Geoffrey had been surveying the rock above the cave entrance, when he spotted the flashlights of the two men. He had, of course, been watching for them, thinking they might come looking for him once they realized he was missing. It was important that his plan not be found out before he had the chance to execute it, as he was certain his idea wouldn't have been taken seriously by the other members of the research party.

He now eased back into the underbrush at the edge of the trees and watched the marine sergeant and the sailor wade out of the lagoon and make their way through the palm thicket to the eastern side of The Rock. They passed just in front of him, but he was well hidden, staying behind the trees until they entered the cave. Then, keeping his flashlight off, he made his way in the darkness back to where he had stashed the explosives.

Geoffrey was faced with a dilemma. Although he knew a lot about the specialized explosives used by the CIA and the military, and a great deal (at least he felt it was a great deal) about precision and kitchen-table demolitions, he knew little about rock blasting. But then, how hard could it be? The plastic explosives he had found in the marine's equipment pack weren't the best choice for moving rock. The brisance was too high for this application he suspected. He needed to move the rock, not shatter it into gravel, which is what these plastic explosives would tend to do. But then they should work OK, if he could get them properly placed. What would be ideal for placing the charges would be a rock drill, which of course he did not have. Actually, he wouldn't know how to use one if he did have a drill, he told himself in a rare self-critical moment. But then he was good enough with explosives not to need one, he reminded himself. He recovered quickly from his self-critique and smiled at his own cleverness.

Still, there weren't a lot of explosives. Charge placement would be important. In his cursory survey of the rock face, he found some small fissures above the camouflaged cave entrance. One fissure looked rather deep and ran nearly vertical above the center of the cave. There were also several horizontal fractures, perhaps 15 feet above the top of the opening. These defects in the rock were not significant in the sense that there wasn't any danger of a cave-in occurring in the near future from any natural causes. But he knew how to help such an event along.

Tucked in behind the downed tree and foliage, Geoffrey inventoried his demolition supplies. The marine's explosives kit had been limited and quite conventional. What he did find was in one of the smaller watertight crates in the storage shelter. It contained a metal cap holder with several packages of electric caps, all in individual wrappers and all with zero-time delay. There was a small wooden box with non-electric caps, a spool of time fuse and a handful of fuse lighters. There was a 10-cap blasting machine, a galvanometer and a reel of firing wire. There were three crates of M5A1 Composition C4, plastic explosives, each crate weighing 45 pounds, and a spool of detonating cord. There were other specialty explosives in the container, mostly small, special-purpose shape charges. It wasn't a very good selection Geoffrey thought, but with his knowledge of explosives, he would make do.

He had taken two of the heavy crates of plastic explosives, one at a time, around The Rock to his hiding place. That process alone was exhausting and while on his way back to the storage tent for the remaining equipment, he thought about calling the entire effort off, the task being so *manual*. Perhaps, he could talk the lieutenant into having the enlisted men do it in the morning, if the marine officer was still alive. No, that would probably not work. The others in the research party would surely argue against him. They didn't understand the global picture.

He had listened earlier through the tent wall as the men talked to each other. They had been talking about the weather. Quite boring, but it gave him a chance to rest up. Revived, he decided to complete his mission. After all, it wasn't that hard.

After studying the stash of explosives, he noted that there were two options for initiating the C4––use electric or use non-electric initiators. It was a difficult decision, but he went with the electric caps, even though doing so required packing more equipment around to the cave. He wouldn't have to worry about keeping the fuses dry. And timing the detonation of separate charges would be easier. That decided, on his final trip around The Rock and through the waters of the lagoon, he brought a pack containing the blasting box, firing wire and electric caps. He knew how to twist wires together with a "western union" splice. It was one of the tricks he had learned at The Farm.

Geoffrey spotted the two men leaving the cave, when their flashlights instantaneously appeared at the face of The Rock. He watched them make their way back through the palm trees, following the same path they had used earlier. They waded back into the lagoon and a few moments later, disappeared around the northern face of The Rock.

After waiting to make sure they weren't coming back, he dragged one of the explosives' crates out from behind the brush and through the 200 yards of sand. He found the entrance to the cave and noticed how quiet and dry it was behind the camouflage curtain. It was much more comfortable inside the cave and out of the wind and rain. The storm had been building all evening. It was now quite miserable outside, and he thought about just staying in the cave until the weather cleared a bit. No, they would find him and stop him. He needed to complete his mission and show his superiors that he was someone to be paid attention to. He pulled up his collar and went back after the second box of explosives. This couldn't be that hard anyway, he thought.

———————•———————

Actually, it had been a ghastly job. Just reaching the locations where the explosives needed to be placed had become a monumental problem. He managed to scavenge enough driftwood from the beach to erect a makeshift ladder. Really, it was just a bundle of limbs and flotsam leaning against the face of The Rock, in such a way that he could climb up high enough to get a foothold on a small ledge that ran above the cave entrance.

Geoffrey estimated that 40 pounds of Composition C4 plastic explosives placed as deep as possible into the vertical fissure at two locations would work--one five feet above, the other five feet below the horizontal fissure. The charges would need to be tamped as best he possibly could and detonated at exactly the same time. He pictured the blast in his mind. The shock waves from the two detonations would, hopefully, cause the large section of rock at the top of the cave to break loose and fall. That large rock and other smaller fragments loosened by the blast should be enough to close the cave opening, at least until Langley could get some equipment on the island to deal with the Russian Hellfire machine.

It had been a truly unpleasant job getting the explosives placed in the fissure, particularly in such dreadful weather. Then the tamping. The explosives would need to be well tamped. But the only obvious material was the sand from the beach. It was not particularly good tamping material, but it was what he had. So, he tried it anyway.

It didn't work. The torrential rain washed it off the explosive charges faster than he could carry it up the face of the rock and pack it on.

That's when he remembered the dark silt mud along the beach of the lagoon. Rather than being light and porous like the coral sand, this dark sand was the remnant of the volcanic materials in Clipperton Rock. It was much finer and much more dense.

Geoffrey used the strong canvas haversacks that held the C4 explosive blocks to carry volcanic sand from the lagoon to The Rock and up to the charges. Filled with this material, the bags were heavy. Although it would make good tamping, the task of moving it to the cave was very laborious. He almost had talked himself into not tamping the charges, after dragging the first load from the lagoon to the cave, but he knew better. What would happen if the explosives weren't effective enough to collapse the cave entrance? What would the others think? What would his superiors think? No. The charges had to work. He made three more trips carrying the heavy loads of sand from the lagoon. After he had tamped the charges, he used the other empty haversacks to protect the sand from being washed away by the rain. It was an exhausting task, but necessary, he told himself. His mission must be a success.

———————•———————

With the explosive charges placed, tamped and capped off, Geoffrey Fox stood in the protection of the cave's camouflage curtain looking out into torrential rain and hurricane-force winds. The palm tree thicket to the northeast of the cave was awash. Water appeared to be running over the reef from the lagoon side and into the ocean. Although he could hear nothing, he knew the wind was howling. He waited a few more minutes, collecting his thoughts and his courage. He would blow the cave entrance then get back to the warmth of the shelters. He wouldn't tell anyone what he had done, except Langley, of course. Let the rest of them find out on their own.

Smiling at that thought, Geoffrey picked up the firing wire reel, the blasting box and the Iridium phone he brought along to report his success to Langley. He then stepped out into the weather. The force of the wind knocked him to the ground. After a few moments, he braced himself against The Rock and made his way along its vertical face to the modest protection of the tree line, unreeling firing wire as he went.

Two hundred feet from the cave, he wrapped the wire around a tree to secure it. The wind now seemed to be coming from all directions. Geoffrey crouched down next to a tree where he had some protection from the wind, the rain and the blast. He untwisted the wires of the firing reel and tightened them onto the blasting box. He inserted the handle into the actuator and wiped the rain from his eyes. He counted to three. "Fire in the hole…and all that," he said to himself in a singsong voice, mocking the ritual he had learned in demolition training. "Why do you have to say that anyway?" he thought as he twisted the handle.

Above the howl of the wind, he heard the cracking sound produced by 84 pounds of high explosives detonated just above the opening to the cave. Moments later, the last thing Geoffrey Fox heard was the cracking sound of a palm tree trunk fracturing under hurricane-force winds.

23. Obstacles

Clipperton Rock was visible on the northern horizon. He estimated it was 15 miles out. Alan adjusted the autopilot to steer a course toward the southwestern reef.

After Kate's conversation with Phil Beckman the previous evening, it had remained quiet on the boat for some time. The following morning, Alan helped Kate place a call to Captain Bennett at his PACOM number, but he was not in the office. That was not surprising as it was 5 a.m. in Oahu. Kate left a message. She didn't have his home number, which was apparently unlisted. And she had no luck after trying again to reach him at his office number. Frustrated, she took up a position on the starboard side of the cockpit next to the companionway. Alan left the side-band radio on the marine operator channel, so that they would receive Phil's return call when it came. Sensing Kate's frustration, Alan left her to her thoughts, as best as one could on a 38-foot boat.

Sergeant Thornton had spent a good percentage of the night with Lieutenant Baker, tending to his dressings and discussing their plans for the possible long stay on the island. Corporal Hansen had returned to the forward stateroom and slept sporadically through the night. Seasickness, which he had a little trouble with on the *Fort McHenry*, had significantly affected him during the storm. He was still weak but beginning to hold down liquids. Professor Fulton was sleeping on the starboard side bench seat in the main salon.

Kate had spent the evening in the cockpit with Alan, although the conversation was only occasional. She watched the night sky slowly emerge from the clouds and busied herself counting stars that she recognized and trying to remember the shapes of the constellations. It was a game that she and her father played when she was a child in Ohio.

"*Wind Gypsy, Wind Gypsy,* this is the Honolulu Marine Operator calling the vessel *Wind Gypsy,* Over." The voice from the side-band radio speaker broke the silence of the morning.

Alan reached under the starboard side of the companionway hatch and retrieved the radio microphone from its clip. "Honolulu Marine Operator, this is the *Wind Gypsy,* Whiskey Yankee Juliet Seven Zero Six Two....Over." Alan still used his station call sign, although he was no longer required to do so under the new international communications protocols.

"Roger, Skipper. Please hold."

A few moments later; "Thank you, Skipper. May I please speak to Ms. Kate Harris? Over."

Alan handed the mike to Kate as she approached the companionway. She recognized the voice of Captain Bennett.

"Hello, Richard," she said. "Over."

"Hi, Kate. First let me apologize for getting you into that mess down there. It looks like the machine you folks found on the island is causing an odd weather phenomenon. The storms we are seeing are apparently being created by that thing. That last cell turned bad quickly. I heard via *Fort McHenry* that Fox was missing, Lieutenant...Baker, was hurt and the rest of you were riding it out on the boat. What is it, the *Wind Gypsy*? Did you get through the storm all right? Over."

"We are OK, Richard. Phil said something about a comet. Over."

"I talked to Phil a few minutes ago. He said you were right. All of the events we have seen effect the same region of the sky, and that region corresponds to the triangle described by the island and the two objects. Good work, Kate. They're working on the issue now at the observatory. That is, the few folks who aren't focused on the comet are working on it. The comet's name is Thompson-O'Conner. It was first spotted by the fellow O'Conner, an amateur in Arizona somewhere, then confirmed by Professor Harry Thompson at the University of Hawaii. The observatory on Maui had it last week, but Space Command sat on it for four days. They wouldn't let Colonel Elder release the information to us. He knew about it before our last meeting. Had I known, Kate, I'd have put you on it. I'm sorry. Over."

"Thanks, Richard. So, what do we know about the comet? Over."

Bennett gave them the most current data. It appeared to be composed of mostly iron. It was moving very fast and the current predictions indicate it will strike the atmosphere off the coastline of Peru, although the prediction was subject to some error.

"The Keck Observatory is seeing some perturbations in the trajectory," Bennett continued. "Something is changing its orbit slightly, every so often. They are not sure what's causing it, and they haven't worked the timing out yet. That's all we know so far. PACOM and everyone else on the islands, in fact the entire Pacific Rim, are moving to high ground or to sea. They needed the *Fort McHenry* to evacuate the low islands, Kate. The decision was that the evacuation took priority. I'm sorry, but it looks like you're stuck there until it's over. Projections show impact on April 5. Over."

Kate had been thinking about her situation all evening. The biggest astronomical event of the century was occurring, and she was on a little boat in the middle of the Pacific Ocean. Soon she would be back on an isolated little island in the middle of the Pacific Ocean, cut off from any means of being involved. She had to focus on something besides the comet or she was going to drive herself crazy. Right now, the only thing to focus on was the job she had been sent there to do.

"Fox said the machine had a display panel that was in Russian. Could we find out whether this thing is Russian? I thought this was a French island. Over."

"OK, Kate. I'll look into it. How about I call you back this evening, say 1730?" It would be just before he went home to help his family finish packing up the household. "I can let you know if there is anything new then. Over."

"All right, Richard. Thanks for getting back to us. We'll be expecting your call." She handed the mike to Alan, and he completed the call.

"This is the vessel *Wind Gypsy*, Whiskey, Yankee, Juliet Seven Zero Six Two. Out."

———————•———————

The skies had become overcast again. It was actually a mixed blessing. Glare from the sun made it difficult to see coral heads in shoal water. With the cloudy sky, Alan had little trouble negotiating these hazards, as he approached the southwestern shore of the atoll where there were many coral heads. He realized how lucky he had been when he first brought the boat onto the island reef. He could have just as easily gone aground on a coral head and sunk.

Once in close, they had little trouble picking up the fenders that they had used as anchor buoys. Sergeant Thornton and Professor Fulton helped with the boat hook and windlass. They made quick work of getting the boat securely at anchor on the big storm hook used to pull *Wind Gypsy* off the reef previously. With the big anchor set, *Wind Gypsy* rode comfortably…her bow bearing to the northeast and into the slight swell.

Everyone aboard anticipated the nausea they experienced the previous day at the 1145 time frame, but it didn't happen. They wondered if the machine had stopped activating or if the time frame for its activation had changed. Were the blue spheres still appearing, or had they stopped? Whatever the reason, they were all glad it hadn't happened, especially Corporal Hansen.

Alan scanned the shoreline with his binoculars. The havoc from the storm was evident. There were many trees down––either gone completely, cluttering the shoreline or wedged against those still standing. He could see several trees that had been broken off part way up, 10 to 15 feet of splintered trunk was all that remained. There were palm fronds and other foliage piled up against downed trees or wrapped around the trunks of standing trees. Partially uprooted trees stood at precarious angles here and there on the reef.

Alan looked across the southern end of the island at The Rock. It appeared unchanged, if a little darker, more ominous. He frowned, then realized the storm's rainfall had probably washed a little of the gray bird guano away, exposing more of the dark basalt rock beneath. He wasn't imagining things.

"Any sign of Fox or our storage containers?" It was the sergeant.

"Can't see anything over where the campsite was, Sergeant. There's a lot of debris on the ground." Alan handed the binoculars to the sergeant. "I'll get the dinghy in the water."

The sergeant scanned the shoreline quickly with the binoculars, then lowered them. "I'll give you a hand," he said.

———————•———————

Alan shuttled Kate and Professor Fulton ashore and was now back at the boat to pick up the marines. He was glad that he had decided to restow the dinghy before the first storm. It would not have survived the second. As he approached *Wind Gypsy*, it was clear that there was no one topside. Alan tied the dinghy off and climbed aboard. He opened the porthole between the cockpit and the aft cabin, allowing a small amount of fresh air into where the lieutenant was resting. He reached through the porthole and swung a small fan around to the opening, switching it on. Lieutenant Baker was sitting up in the aft cabin bunk. He thanked Alan for the fresh air. The lieutenant was attempting to convince the sergeant that he would be OK, while the remainder of the team was ashore searching for Mr. Fox and surveying the damage to their equipment.

"I can get along here on my own. You need to find Mr. Fox, Sergeant. Take Corporal Hansen along with you. I'm all right." He reiterated his concern about finding Mr. Fox. The man hadn't lost his sense of responsibility for the members of the landing party, including the CIA agent. And, considering his wounds, the young officer was doing quite well, although still weak from loss of blood.

After a couple more reassurances from the lieutenant, they boarded the dinghy and motored around to the southern end of the island, just west of The Rock. Alan could see Kate and Professor Fulton searching through the debris where the campsite had been as they approached the beach. They greeted Alan and the marines as he landed the dinghy.

"I'm afraid the campsite is shambles," the professor reported. "Some of the equipment boxes are buried under fallen trees, and it looks like some may be missing."

"Hansen and I will dig them out and do an inventory. I would appreciate it if the rest of you would search for Mr. Fox." Sergeant Thornton was surveying the damage as he spoke.

———————•———————

They all agreed that the most likely thing for Fox to do as the storm surge flooded over the island reef, was to seek high ground on The Rock or shelter in the cave. They headed for the cave first. The path, which they had used earlier, was blocked in several places by fallen trees and uprooted brush. In one place, downed trees had formed a small dam, and the ocean current had piled a huge mound of coconuts against it. Crabs scurried around the pile, and Alan noted, with perhaps a little dismay, that the booby birds had already returned.

With a bit more effort than needed in their earlier visit to The Rock, Alan, Kate and Professor Fulton again rounded its southern end in ankle deep water and approached the cave entrance. To the southeast, the channels through which the blue spheres traversed earlier were again visible. But something was different. Alan was the first to realize what they were looking at. The face of The Rock, at the site of the cave entrance had given way. A large pile of rubble from the cave-in now stood where the cave entrance had been. Professor Fulton started to step forward. Alan held him back by the arm.

"A moment please, Professor." Alan used his binoculars, which he had strapped around his neck, to inspect the sheer face of newly exposed rock above the pile of rubble. He saw nothing to suggest that it was unstable. There didn't appear to be any signs of another imminent rockslide. Alan released the professor's arm.

———•———

They searched with their hands, prodded with sticks, screamed at the top of their lungs. Fox was not there and neither was the cave entrance. Kate stumbled out of the rubble pile and walked up the beach to the east of The Rock. She sat down on a tree trunk, took her small pack off and set it down in front of her. She reached in for her water bottle. Her eyes caught a small bit of red color in the fronds of another fallen tree near where she was seated. She left the pack where it was and walked over to the other downed tree. Visible through the palm fronds was the body of Geoffrey Fox, almost completely buried in coral sand. Only the side of his face and part of the collar of his red shirt were exposed. She called to the others.

Alan was bent over looking at the surge from the breaking surf rush up the sand beach along the edge of The Rock. He thought, maybe, he might catch it as it disappeared into the sheer face of the outcropping and, so, disclose the camouflage opening, they had been looking for during the last hour. He was having no luck. Then he remembered the camouflage deflected water like a rock-hard surface. "That won't work" he said to himself. He was frustrated. Kate's call broke his self-critique. As he started to stand up, he noticed what looked like a black rope or wire become partially exposed, as the receding water washed away some of the sand at the base of The Rock. He thought it may be a strand of kelp, although he hadn't seen any kelp since leaving the mainland coast. Maybe, it washed up on the island's southern reef by the storm. He glanced over in Kate's direction. Professor Fulton had already joined her. They were looking at something under the fronds of a downed coconut palm. Alan reached down and grasped the strand of material. He pulled gently, exposing several feet in both directions. It was buried just under the sand. He wiped the sand off the section in his hand and inspected it. It was wire, and he recognized the type immediately.

Kate and Professor Fulton watched as Alan walked toward them, pulling the wire out of the sand as he came. It led him to the base of a tree near where they stood. The wire was wrapped once around the tree trunk and tied off. The loose end was attached to a black object with a handle. Kate didn't know what it was and had no idea why Alan was so interested in a piece of debris that appeared to have been washed up on the beach, probably part of an old fishing net.

Alan removed the blasting box from the firing wire and put it in his pack as he walked to where Kate and Professor Fulton stood over Fox's body.

"He collapsed the entrance to the cave with high explosives," Alan said to the others as he walked up. "Not an easy thing to do without some form of rock drill and the right explosives. Any idea why he would do this?"

Kate shook her head. Alan followed her gaze to the body under the tree.

"He was, apparently, a man of strong convictions," said Professor Fulton.

24. Hellfire II

1730 02 April, 2007 Clipperton Atoll

After helping dig Fox's body out from under the fallen tree, Alan took Kate and Professor Fulton back to the boat in the dinghy.

"What did you mean by a man of strong convictions?" he asked the professor as they approached the boat.

"I mean that he stuck to his assignment, despite the adverse weather and contrary opinion."

"His assignment was to blow up the machine?" Alan asked.

"Not necessarily. His assignment was to protect United States interests. He was convinced the machine was Russian and that it had activated," Professor Fulton replied.

"Activated to do what?" Alan asked as he maneuvered the dinghy alongside *Wind Gypsy* and tied it off. The professor didn't answer.

Alan helped the two scientists aboard, then stepped down the companionway and checked the bilge. A small puddle of water sloshed around the bottom of the submersible pump. The hull patch was doing its job. He replaced the bilge access cover as Kate stepped out of the aft cabin where she had checked on Lieutenant Baker. "He's resting," she said. "He hasn't heard the radio. Bennett hasn't called yet."

Kate went back up to the cockpit, while Alan pulled three Mexican sodas out of the ice box. Then he joined her and Professor Fulton.

"Activated to do what?" he repeated the question as he handed a soda to the professor.

Professor Fulton still didn't answer.

Kate, who had only been half listening to the conversation between the two men, was now becoming frustrated. Since finding access to the machine blocked by the cave-in, Kate had been feeling what she could only describe to herself as a profound sense of loss. Something important had been taken from her. Kate needed to be doing something, now. She needed the mystery of the machine to solve. She needed to do the job she was sent to the island to do. The rest of the world was engaged in the most important astronomical event of the century, and she couldn't participate. All she had was the job she was sent to do, and now Fox had taken that from her. She hadn't spoken on the trip back to the boat. In fact, she had said very little since finding the blocked cave entrance. She broke her silence.

"He was working on the Hellfire II program, wasn't he, Professor?"

Professor Fulton's eyes flashed quickly at Kate. Hellfire II was a *black* program. Even the name was classified. "I really couldn't comment on that subject," he finally said.

"Professor Fulton, I'm cleared for the program, but that doesn't really matter. In less than a week, a week we will spend on this island. In less than that week, we will all be dead. So please, tell us why Fox destroyed the machine."

A smile came over the professor's face. An ironic smile. He wasn't happy.

Robert Fulton had a good life. He had a wife whom he adored, three bright and successful children and a challenging career. He had his health. At 72 years, he had accomplished a great deal. His parents were not well to do. After his stint in the navy as a corpsman, he put himself through school, studying physical chemistry and completing his undergraduate work in three years. Rather than continue on with graduate school, he had joined the CIA as an analyst in the chemical weapons research department. He enjoyed the puzzle, trying to figure out what the Russians were doing with their weaponry, from the information that was being gathered by field agents and early air and satellite reconnaissance. But the big concerns back then were nuclear weapons, and that's where the major efforts of the intelligence community lay. He attended graduate training at MIT. This time he studied nuclear physics. As with his undergraduate training, he completed his graduate work early and returned to the CIA to do nuclear weapons research. He completed a 30-year career with the Agency, the last 15 of which were field work. Still a young man, he went to work for the navy at the nuclear reactor prototype lab in Atomic, Idaho, until he found the position in the physics department at the University of Hawaii. He and his wife had wanted to live in Hawaii since their 20th anniversary cruise to the islands.

Still doing consulting for the navy at the nuclear sub-base in Pearl Harbor, now, Professor Fulton was thoroughly enjoying academia. He was completely surprised with the visit to his office on the UH campus by the PACOM representative and taken aback by their comments concerning the old Hellfire program. He had debriefed out of that classified compartment 20 years earlier. But the little field research team was forming, and they needed help, now. So, he joined them a few days before the new semester was to start. And now, here he was, thousands of miles from home with imminent disaster about to fall. He worried for his wife and children.

"Professor Fulton, are you all right?" Kate broke him out of his introspection.

"Yes, yes, I'm fine. Just worried about my family," he said.

They all sat quietly for a few moments. Then Kate asked her question again.

"Did Fox talk to you about his findings? Do you have any idea why he would want to blow up the machine?"

Professor Fulton made the decision. After all those years of government secrecy, his response to inappropriate questions was force of habit. "I can't comment on that."…"I have nothing to say about that."…"I can neither confirm nor deny that." Now, the reasons for security were gone. What possible difference could it make who knew what about a cold war program from half a century ago, given the current global situation. Kate was right. Professor Fulton decided to answer the question.

"He was concerned that it was a Russian doomsday machine."

"Doomsday machine? That's just science fiction," Kate responded.

"I thought you said you were cleared for Hellfire." Professor Fulton's eyebrows were raised.

"I am. I just haven't gotten the brief yet. I was briefed into the initial program, Hellfire I, but there wasn't anything about doomsday machines involved. I didn't have time to look over the Hellfire II information before we left the ship."

"Hellfire I was before my time," Fulton said. "As for Hellfire II, after the first test weapon was detonated in Nevada, then the detonations over Hiroshima and Nagasaki, the theory of a spontaneous global chain reaction was believed to have been disproven by demonstration. Then the Streltsovsk event was discovered by the Russians."

"I'm sorry. I'm not familiar with the Streltsovsk Event," Kate said.

"Few people are," the Professor continued. "The Streltsovsk Mines are in southeastern Siberia. The Russians found a natural nuclear reactor, much like the one found by the French at Oklo, Western Africa."

"I remember studying the Oklo Mine," Alan broke into the conversation. "The French were extracting rich ore from that find. Then they started to see decreases in U235 yield and increases in reaction byproducts in the ore. It's clear now from the acoustic survey and analysis of the strata formation, but they weren't expecting it before it was discovered."

"They should have been," said Professor Fulton. "The Russians knew about the phenomena back in the early 1950s. They found a much more recent natural event at Streltsovsk back then and pieced together what it was, long before anyone else even had an inkling."

"What are you talking about?" Kate asked? "What kind of *natural event?*"

"A natural nuclear reactor," Alan answered her question.

"Come on. How is it possible for a nuclear reactor to occur naturally? Nuclear physics really isn't my subject, but doesn't it require high concentrations of the right isotopes, U235 as I remember. Doesn't it require high concentrations of U235, confinement, a moderator, an active control system to create and maintain a nuclear chain reaction? How could a reactor occur naturally?"

"By combining the right isotopes in the right concentrations and in the presence of a moderator with sufficient natural thermal control and containment." Professor Fulton answered her question. "You are quite correct, Kate. It is not trivial. The biggest issue is the isotope concentration. But then, nothing about a natural reactor is a trivial matter. It is very unusual to see a natural reactor occur now. But two billion years ago...two billion years ago. Back then the percentage of U235 in uranium ore was higher, high enough to support a chain reaction. The Oklo reactor is 1. 7 billion years old. Back then, the percentage of U235 in uranium ore was quite a bit higher than it is now."

"But you said, what was it, Streltsovsk, the Streltsovsk Event was more recent?"

"Three hundred years ago."

"Then I still don't understand," Kate said.

"You're not alone on that, Kate. It took us more than eight years at CIA to understand the significance of the Streltsovsk find. Streltsovsk was not a uranium reaction. It was plutonium. Streltsovsk was a natural breeder reactor. You see...."

"What does all this have to do with doomsday machines and Fox's mission?" Alan had gone below and retrieved the last bag of crackers. He could now see that the conversation was about to go off into the technical hinterland. He wanted to anchor it to current events.

"Quite right, Alan. I apologize for lecturing. Let's stay on track."

"The Russians realized, shortly after the discovery at Streltsovsk, that it was possible to trigger chain reactions at any sufficiently rich uranium deposit with the right neutron source. And so, with the nuclear arms race in full stride and realizing that they were losing, they started sinking a lot of resources into developing a doomsday system. It would be a system that would trigger chain reactions not only in natural ore deposits, but in uranium stockpiles and even existing warheads. They figured out how to do it, and we--ah--appropriated the design."

"Are you saying the Russians...and the Americans built doomsday machines back in the 1950s?" Kate couldn't believe what she was hearing.

"No, it wasn't until 1961 that the Russians started to deploy their system. We were right behind them."

"What nature doesn't do to us, will be done by our fellow man." Alan quoted an old protest song.

"There was a secret treaty signed in 1962 banning further development and calling for the disassembly of any existing systems," Professor Fulton continued. "Some say the treaty had something to do with why Kennedy was shot, but I doubt it. But then, there were a lot of extremists back then." The professor's voice trailed off.

"Professor, if the systems were disassembled back in the 1960s, what was Fox doing?" Kate asked.

"Yes, well, the treaty was signed in the early 1960s, but there really was no means of verification established. And then the French got involved, with their big breeder reactor development-- their Phoenix Reactors on the Caspian Sea. The technology started to proliferate. Hellfire II evolved into the verification program for the old treaty and the centralized program for tracking the technology of the old doomsday devices. It, apparently, is ongoing." The professor took a drink from his soda.

"So, Fox was convinced that the machine is part of a Russian doomsday system left over from the early 1960s." Kate said, nodding her head.

"But you weren't," Alan said.

"No, the technology is wrong. Fox was new to the program, and unfamiliar with the Russian hardware. This machine is not Russian.

I told him that the night before we left the island. He said he would rather err on the safe side."

"You knew he was going to blow up the machine?" Kate could not hide her shock.

"No, Kate, I didn't know. I had no idea he even had the means of doing the damage that he, apparently, has done. I thought he would just get in contact with Langley and have our little expedition terminated. They must have directed him to take this action."

"Your communications were out, and he didn't use my radio, how could he have communicated with CIA headquarters?" Alan asked.

"The communications weren't completely out. Fox had an Iridium phone with his equipment. He must have retrieved it and called Langley, after Hansen told him the radios were down. He wanted to make sure Langley made the decisions on how we would proceed, not Pearl."

"So why would the CIA tell him to blow up the machine rather than just call off the expedition?" Alan asked.

"They wouldn't. If Langley believed this machine was part of the Russian Hellfire system, the last thing they would want to do would be to blow it up," Professor Fulton replied. "These systems yield particularly dirty bombs. I would think the State Department would nix any plan that had the potential of causing a detonation on a French island, particularly a dirty bomb."

"So, do you think Fox just went crazy and did this on his own?"

"Perhaps," Professor Fulton said. "It's more likely that he just wanted to close off any access to the machine until CIA could take control. My guess is that the machine is unharmed. He just caved in the access tunnel."

"From what I can tell, it looks like Mr. Fox was successful. I'm going back in to pick up Sergeant Thornton and the corporal," Alan said.

The professor nodded. Kate just sat staring at the ocean with the same blank expression she'd had since they found the cave entrance blocked.

There was nothing else they could do.

25. Revelation

1845 02 April Clipperton Atoll

Alan and the two marines were just arriving at the boat when the single side-band radio squawked on.

"*Wind Gypsy, Wind Gypsy,* this is the Honolulu Marine Operator calling the vessel *Wind Gypsy.* Over."

Professor Fulton answered the call, then passed the mike to Kate, as Alan climbed aboard. Captain Bennett was on the other end of the link.

"Sorry, I'm late, Kate. It's hard to get a telephone line on the island, let alone off. Oahu has turned into a madhouse. People are scrambling for higher ground. Over."

"That's OK, Richard. We're not particularly busy here. Any word on the comet? Over." Kate couldn't hide her frustration.

"Some estimates. Right ascension is 22 hours 28 minutes, declination minus one degree. It's right on top of the Halleyid meteorite stream. The estimated closing speed is 498 kilometers per second; it's definitely a hyperbolic trajectory. We still don't have a good assessment of the perturbations we were seeing. SPACECOM estimates the last one occurred at around 2100 Zulu yesterday. There still doesn't appear to be a correlation with the spin rate of the object. They don't know what's causing it. Maybe a dark companion object, although we're not seeing anything with Haystack or the big radars on Kwajalein. They don't know yet. We are still estimating impact near the west coast of South America on the fifth. Over."

Kate was doing the calculations in her head. 500 kilometers per second closing is five times 10 squared kilometers per second sun relative, three times 10 to the fourth per minute....She worked it out. The comet was somewhere near the asteroid belt, and somewhat off the plane of the ecliptic.

"Could it be interacting with the asteroid belt? Over." Kate was sick that she wouldn't have a chance to work this problem.

"I hadn't heard that as a consideration, Kate. I'll see what I can find out. There's another issue that we need to address, though. You are to cease all activities on Clipperton Island. That direction is from Washington..."

———•———

Bennett's instructions to the research team were that no one was to approach Clipperton Rock within a distance of 500 yards, and that all further efforts regarding their findings in the caves were to cease. The investigation was being taken over by higher authority. After the radio conversation, Professor Fulton pointed out that 500 yards was the standard distance established for cordoning off Hellfire equipment. The military's authority regarding activities on Clipperton Island had been usurped by the CIA, and they were now to play by the CIA rulebook.

Fox obviously had made contact with CIA Headquarters at Langley, and CIA obviously believed Fox's story that they had found a Russian doomsday machine.

"So, are you working for CIA, or the military?" Kate asked Professor Fulton as he returned the side-band microphone to its mount.

"I was sent here to accompany Mr. Fox."

"CIA then."

"I was to be the senior agent on this mission. Apparently, Mr. Fox thought otherwise. I have no idea why Langley would take this action without my input. Fox must have deceived them."

"Either way, Professor, this investigation is coming out wrong. The technology in the cave is much more advanced than 1960's

Russian, and it appears that the machine is the cause of our satellite and stellar observation anomalies."

"I'm not sure what we can do about it now, Kate."

Professor Fulton's eyes told her what he was really thinking. Regardless, of whether the machine was some unknown technology hidden on the island by some advanced civilization or whether it was an old time Russian cold war terror, it didn't really matter. World events were moving too rapidly for it to matter. In less than five days, it wouldn't matter.

Kate could also see in the professor's eyes that the old man was tired.

"You look like you could use some rest, Professor." Kate reached out and took his hand.

"I'm a bit tired," he said. "I believe, I'll lie down for awhile."

Professor Fulton made his way down the companionway and to the starboard settee bunk. Kate looked down the porthole into the aft cabin. Lieutenant Baker was sleeping. Maybe she should try to get some rest, too, she thought, as she sat back in the cockpit seat and watched the seabirds fly over the treetops on the reef to the northeast. A cooling breeze was coming over the bow of the boat. She put her feet up on the bench seat and got comfortable. She could see a narrow channel that had formed on the western reef between the lagoon and the ocean. It was, no doubt, caused by storm surge overflowing out of the lagoon at a low point in the reef. A pass, Alan had called it. Kate realized she had learned a great deal about islands and ocean weather in the last few days, mostly from the sailor. She still believed Alan was an odd fellow; he was out in the middle of the ocean in quite a small boat. He seemed intelligent, and he seemed to be comfortable, fending for himself here in the middle of nowhere. She hadn't met anyone like him before. All her friends were, what she would call well-adjusted, mostly science and technology types. When she pictured them in her mind, they almost always were seated at a desk working at a computer. The closest she had seen the sailor to technology was with a sextant and a pencil. He actually knew how to use the antique instrument....A handsome man...but peculiar, he was nothing like her father....

———————•———————

She glanced over to the southern end of the island, realizing she had fallen asleep. How long had she been sleeping?

The dinghy was beached at a sandy section of the shoreline. Alan and the marines were moving equipment farther away from The Rock, per Washington's direction.

She glanced up at the boat's mast. The jib halyard was oscillating in the breeze, slapping the mast rhythmically and causing the hollow aluminum spar to ring like the pipes of a church organ. Her thoughts shifted to the conversation with Bennett earlier that evening. 2100 Zulu Bennett had said. That's when the comet's perturbations had occurred. It was following the Eta Aquarid meteorite stream in the constellation Aquarius. Kate could feel herself falling asleep again. She remembered staying up late with her father, when she was a child, to watch the Leonid meteor shower. It was named after the constellation, Leo, from which the meteors appeared. Leo was in the northern sky; Aquarius was in the southern sky....

And then it clicked.

Kate sat up in the seat. The constellation Aquarius was right in the middle of the affected region of the sky, the region where they had found the satellite anomalies and the stellar observation errors. The machine was sending a *signal* in the direction of the comet at around 2100 Zulu or noon local each day. The comet's trajectory was being affected just after the machine activated. The delay was the travel time for a signal emanating from the earth to reach the comet. There was no question in her mind. The machine on Clipperton Atoll was affecting the orbit of a comet approaching the earth and, currently, at a distance of over 2.5 astronomical units, over 240 million miles away.

"Oh my God!" Kate blurted.

No one heard her.

Resolution

26. The Plan

Kate double checked her calculations. Several of the stars, which formed the constellation Aquarius, were in the field of view of the telescope, when the positional errors were first seen at the observatory back...when was it? It seemed so long ago, now. She forced herself to concentrate. She picked three of the stars and reexamined their positional errors, calculating the magnitude and direction of the apparent displacement from their true positions. With a bit of work, Kate verified that for each star, the displacement was, in fact, along the line between the star and the comet's position. She did similar calculations for several other stars in the triangular region of the sky over the island, the region she had identified while aboard the ship. There was only one conclusion: The optical disturbance they had seen at the observatory, the disturbance that was clearly caused by the machine and its blue projectiles, was centered at the comet's position in the sky.

Kate closed the cover of her laptop. In the waning daylight, she could see Alan and the two marines getting into the dinghy and preparing to return to the boat. The occasional flashes from their lights were illuminating palm trees on the beach. She realized that she was sitting in near darkness.

There was a small light hanging from a hook just above the companionway. She recalled that Alan had brought it out before going ashore earlier. Kate reached over and flipped the switch on the side of the light. A dim light filled the cockpit. She glanced aft to see a booby bird sitting on the boomkin railing at the back of the boat. It was staring at her with its head cocked slightly to one side. Kate stared back, surprised at its presence. She hadn't heard it land. As she sat gazing at the bird, Alan brought the dinghy alongside *Wind Gypsy* and tied it off. He looked up and followed Kate's gaze to the stern rail where the large bird was perched.

With an annoyed look on his face, Alan reached up and plucked the upper safety line, like one would the string of a bass fiddle. The line vibrated, imparting a similar motion to the stern rail. The bird turned its head and spotting Alan, squawked and took off.

"I see you've met my buddy," he said to Kate.

"You two don't seem all that friendly," Kate answered.

"We share a mutual respect and understanding. He doesn't destroy the boat, and I don't let him."

"How do you know it's a he?" Kate asked.

"You're right; it's probably female." They both smiled.

———————•———————

Alan heated up several cans of stew in his biggest pot and passed out bowls and sodas. After serving everyone, and having run out of bowls, he ate directly from the pot. They were all gathered in the cockpit, except Lieutenant Baker, who was sitting up in the aft cabin bunk eating a bowl of stew and looking out the porthole between the cabin and the cockpit. He could hear everything that was being said.

"I've checked it against the offset errors we were seeing with several other stars. The correlation is there. Displacement error is always in the direction of the comet, and inversely proportional to angular distance. It's as if the stars in this region of the sky have all moved closer together, closer to the point in the sky where the comet is located."

Kate's description of her work up to this point, although technical, was easy enough for Alan and the rest of the non-scientists in the group to follow.

Professor Fulton had been listening intently to Kate and asking frequent questions. He was trying to unravel the physics of the machine that could cause the effects Kate had seen at the observatory. Alan understood few of Professor Fulton's questions.

"So, you think the machine is sending a signal to the comet?" Sergeant Thornton asked. "Why?"

The professor was the first to respond. "It appears that the purpose is to affect its trajectory."

"You mean, it's guiding the comet towards earth?" The sergeant continued.

"Or away from it," Kate responded.

"If we had more data on the disturbances in the comet's trajectory, we would quite possibly be able to tell," said the professor. "I would suggest that we contact Captain Bennett and determine whether anyone has looked into these disturbances of the comet's trajectory more closely. He needs to know what you have found, Kate."

———————•———————

Alan and the two marines tried for several hours to contact the Honolulu Marine Operator without success. Then they tried San Francisco, New Orleans and San Diego. No luck. Corporal Hansen retuned the radio and tried raising NAVCOMSTA Hawaii. He knew the likelihood that the old frequencies were still being used by the Naval Communications Station was low, but all agreed, it was worth a try. He had lost his frequency listing in the previous storm, and without the MilStar link, he had no way of finding out what the new frequencies were. He couldn't get through.

Alan, finally, raised a fellow sailor, Dutch, the man called himself. He was on the vessel, *Halcyon,* at the Ilikai Marina, Honolulu. They were on the maritime hailing frequency. Dutch informed him that the Honolulu Marine Operator had stopped service, in order to move their transmitter to higher ground, as had the folks at the Coast Guard facility. Coast Guard, as well as navy and commercial vessels, were all in service transporting people and supplies to the mainland or the big island and higher ground. He said that Honolulu was in chaos, with everyone boarding up and leaving. His cell phone had given him a busy tone all day. As a live-aboard, he had decided to take his boat to sea. Alan wished him luck and Dutch, apparently, got back to his preparations for getting underway. At 2:30 in the morning, Alan and the marines gave up for the night.

———————•———————

Kate was up early. She figured out how to operate the cookstove and put on a pot of coffee. Then she made her way to the cockpit, where she sat with her fresh brew and watched the sunrise over Clipperton Rock. The morning sky was clear. Through the palm trees she could see the brilliant colors of the sunrise--red, magenta, gold and shades of blue. It looked like a postcard from paradise.

What would the sky look like after the comet's impact, she wondered? The thought broke her away from the little respite she had allowed herself.

Alan poked his head out of the companionway hatch. He had a cup of coffee in his hand. "Good morning," he said. "Want some breakfast?"

"What are you having?"

"I have beef stew, chili, crackers or tuna. No more cheese, but I do have juice-flavored, Mexican soda."

"Ah!…Juice-flavored soda. That must be the breakfast menu. May I have some crackers please?" Kate asked with a smile, pleased by the distraction from her morose thoughts.

"Right." Alan grabbed a box of crackers and made his way up the companionway. He handed the box to Kate and glanced toward the island, taking in the sunrise.

"Looks like we're in for some good weather for a change," he said.

"Captain Bennett said the machine was causing the local weather systems we were seeing. It seems that Mr. Fox has, if nothing else, improved the weather." Kate smiled and took a stale cracker out of the box, as Alan sat down in the cockpit across from her. "So,

Captain Peterson of the good ship *Wind Gypsy*, what do you recommend we do?" The sailor's company had definitely helped bring Kate out of her funk.

"The way I see it, we have three options," Alan began. "We can stay at anchor here. If we move a bit north along the reef, we'll be on the lee side of the island from the comet impact, so we might get some protection from the biggest seas. We may be able to ride it out.

Or we could run for the coast. Our best bet would probably be heading back to Mexico, to Acapulco or maybe Puerto Escondido. At full throttle, that's about three days to the northeast. Then we could head for high ground. There are several issues with this option. If we have any problems, we may not make the landfall before the comet hits. It would be close anyway, and we would be heading into the shallower water of the continental shelf, where the wave effects of the comet's impact may be worse than they are here. If we did make it, we may have avoided the seas, but we would probably be dealing with harsher atmospherics, and the panicking local population."

Alan was certainly not shying away from the coming disaster, Kate thought. He was facing it straight on. "A pragmatist," Kate said to herself, just like her father.

"What's the third option?"

"Run. Run as fast and as far from the impact as we can. Run to the northwest. Put as much distance between us and the impact point as possible. There's no landfall in that direction that we could make before the fifth, so, we would be riding it out in open water. But, unless you think there is a pressing need to stay here, I believe it's our best option."

Kate thought about what Alan was saying. She remembered back to their first meeting the night her group had arrived on the island; how he had given her the impression that all he was concerned about was his boat. Now, he seemed to tie his thoughts and his resources to the group, "If *we* do this," or "*we* will encounter that." Had he changed, or were her first impressions that far off?

"I don't think I thanked you for saving us from the storm," she said.

"You're welcome," he smiled.

They both sat watching the sunrise for a few minutes. Kate took a sip of her coffee. It had gotten cold. As she stood up to get a fresh cup, Professor Fulton stuck his head out of the companionway.

"More coffee anyone?"

"I could use a warm-up," Kate said.

"And I," said Alan.

"I'll put on another pot," Sergeant Thornton said coming up behind the professor. Fulton joined Kate and Alan in the cockpit, while the sergeant dealt with the coffee.

"Alan thinks our best bet may be to run for it. Sail as far away from the comet's impact point as we can." Kate brought the professor up to date with the conversation, as he sat down on the port side of the cockpit next to Alan. "What do you think we should do, Professor?"

"I think we should attempt to repair the machine," Professor Fulton said without hesitation.

Both Kate and Alan sat staring at the older man for a few moments. Alan was the first to speak.

"Without at least some form of heavy equipment, I don't think we have a chance of clearing the cave opening."

"We need to find a way," the professor responded.

"You believe the machine's purpose is to divert the comet?" Kate said.

"Without question. And I think our problem is more extensive than just clearing the opening. The machine is, apparently, degraded or malfunctioning in some manner. It needs to be repaired…quickly."

Sergeant Thornton stepped up through the companionway.

"We have orders to stay clear of The Rock," he said taking a seat in the cockpit. "They were specific. There is no way we can disregard them. Why do you think we should, Doc?"

"I base my conclusions primarily on Miss Harris's efforts," Professor Fulton began. "And on my own experience. First, and foremost for you, Sergeant, the artifact at the base of that Rock is not a Russian doomsday machine. I know this, young man, because I've seen them. They look nothing like what is in that cave. Mr. Fox was in error when he reported to Langley that it was such a device. Your orders are based on his misinformation. Second, from our direct experience here on the island, as well as the astronomical and satellite anomalies that occur whenever the machine activates, there is clearly a gravitational effect associated with its activation. Furthermore, as Miss Harris so cleverly deduced, this gravitational effect is focused on the comet, if that is what it is."

Alan interrupted. "What about the warning message, or what-ever it was? The controls are definitely Russian. I recognize some of the Cyrillic Russian words on the display panel that Fox found in the lower chamber."

"Yes, a good question. It is most peculiar," Professor Fulton responded. "I don't have an answer, other than to say the technology demonstrated by the machine is far too advanced to be Russian, or human, for that matter. No one knows how to generate gravity waves, and you yourself said that there is no known equipment that could produce the shafts and tunnels that we saw in The Rock. What of the camouflage, the illusion at the cave entrance and elsewhere in the caverns? Our military would love to have such a capability. It does not exist anywhere other than here. What I can say is that I have been privy to a great deal of technology and intelligence about technology in my career. This machine is far more advanced than anything man has made."

Now, Kate interrupted. "Professor, did I hear you question whether or not the object approaching us is a comet? Are you sug-gesting it could be an alien spaceship?"

"No, but neither am I dismissing that possibility. As Captain Bennett said, the object had an unusually low albedo and an unusu-ally high closing velocity. It could very well be just a cometary body with those characteristics. All we really know is that there is an alien machine here on this island sending gravitational waves in its direction." The professor paused.

"I heard that term, *albedo*, mentioned by Captain Bennett the other night. What does it mean?" It was Lieutenant Baker. He was sitting up in the aft bunk with a cup of coffee, listening to the conversation through the porthole.

"Ah, Lieutenant Baker, glad you're feeling better. Yes, albedo. It's a measure of reflectivity. In this instance it refers to the amount of sunlight that is being reflected back to earth by the comet's surface, measured as a percentage of the incident light. What did the captain say it was, less than .01 percent? I believe that's quite dim, isn't that right, Miss Harris?"

"Very dim," Kate replied. "Comets are typically around one percent albedo. The dimmest, Halley's Comet, is about .03 percent."

Everyone sat silently for a moment absorbing what the professor had said.

"So, why would we want to help aliens land on earth?" Sergeant Thornton broke the silence.

Professor Fulton smiled. "Well, I don't think we could be all that much help, but, hypothetically, if it were an alien ship, and I am skeptical about that, helping beings with such advanced technology probably couldn't hurt our standing with them. As the existence of the machine attests, they have been here before, apparently, without malice toward us. I would prefer to keep it that way."

"The geology of The Rock suggests they could have been here before us, before humans arrived on earth," Alan said. "Maybe they are coming here to get rid of a pest that is disrupting the operation of their machine. Maybe, this machine is just a channel marker in the galactic seaway, and we are just pesky sea life disrupting its operation."

"I suppose that could be the case," Professor Fulton responded. "But if that is the case, then the outcome would be the same as it would be if the object were in fact a comet with the energy described by Captain Bennett and allowed to impact the earth. In either case, humanity is finished."

Professor Fulton continued. "My conclusion that we must repair the machine, derives from this simple observation: Based on everything we have seen and so far, discussed, if we do nothing or just seek higher ground, as it were, our civilization will be destroyed. If the purpose of the machine is to cause this collision, and we repair it, our civilization will be destroyed. The outcome is unchanged. If the purpose of the machine is to deflect the comet, as I believe to be the case, repairing it will improve our chance of survival. It is the only action we can take that stands to improve our odds."

The group fell silent again. After several minutes, Lieutenant Baker spoke.

"Sergeant, it sounds like we need to clear the entrance to the cave, so that these folks can get in and repair the machine. I'm countermanding the order we received from PACOM."

"What order was that, Sir?" the sergeant asked innocently.

Alan noticed that Sergeant Thornton had his big grin back.

27. The Tunneling Approach

1000 03 April Clipperton Atoll

The situation still looked grim to Alan. "I'm not sure we have much of a chance of getting the entrance cleared in time to do any good without heavy equipment," he repeated.

"It's amazing what you can do with a little H.E." Sergeant Thornton responded. "At least Fox left us something to work with."

"We have high explosives?" Alan's face brightened a bit.

"Some," the sergeant responded. "Not a lot but some. A few haversacks of C4 and some small, shape charges. Not a lot."

"Well, it's something," Alan said. He was thinking. "It may be worth a shot," he said, after a few moments. "What do you say we get to work? I'd like to take a look at the explosives, Sergeant, and any other digging tools you might have."

A few minutes later the boat was alive with activity. Alan took the dishes down to the galley basin and then started loading the dinghy. Kate and Professor Fulton filled backpacks with sodas, water bottles, crackers and a few canned goods. The marines put their equipment together and helped with the dinghy. They all seemed to be working in unison for the first time since arriving on the island.

When the marines and Alan finished with their preparations, Alan poked his head down the companionway.

"We're ready to go," he said, noticing Kate standing near the galley basin washing the dishes. She was smiling.

Lieutenant Baker opened the aft cabin door and stepped out.

"I'm afraid, I'm not going to be much help on shore." He had gotten out of his bunk and was standing on his good leg. "If you'll check me out on this radio, I can at least monitor communications and try to raise Pearl Harbor, while you guys are busy ashore."

———•———

Corporal Hansen stayed aboard with the lieutenant and went over the operation of the two radios installed in *Wind Gypsy*'s small navigation station. With the remainder of the group aboard the dinghy, it was somewhat overloaded, and Alan had to ease back on the throttle to keep from flooding the small boat. They all got wet going through the surf at the beach. But then, in the already hot sun and high humidity of the island, the sea spray and splash of water felt good.

Once ashore, they started moving equipment that might be needed for digging, as well as what explosives were left by Fox. They placed the explosives in a safe location on the eastern side of The Rock near the cave. The move took two trips. Alan and Sergeant Thornton carried the explosives and blasting equipment. Kate and the Professor took hand tools and containers that could be used for moving debris. As Kate, Alan and the sergeant inspected the cave entrance again, with the purpose of assessing how best to clear the opening, Professor Fulton took the dinghy back to the boat and picked up Corporal Hansen.

"Why don't we just load all the explosives here, behind the majority of this rock, and blow it out to sea?" The sergeant had made his way up to the top of the rubble pile. He was standing above the others and near the undisturbed rock face above where the entrance had been.

"That might be a good idea if we had black powder or ammonium nitrate," Alan responded. "But I don't think we would get the effect we're after by doing what you are suggesting with C4."

The sergeant thought about one of the old demolition problems he had been assigned in special operations training.

"You're right," he replied. "Too high a brisance. What's your recommendation?"

"I'd say our best bet is to move as much of the small rubble as we can by hand and then shatter the bigger rocks into small enough pieces, so that they can also be moved by hand. I think that's the best way to use the explosives we have. There are plenty of blasting caps and fuses. We'll just have to stretch the explosives as far as we can."

The sergeant thought for a moment.

"Makes sense to me," he said, looking down from the rubble pile.

"Looks like the best bet is to move this stuff off to the left of where the opening was, off to the ocean side and out of the way." With that, Sergeant Thornton jumped down off the pile of rock. In two leaps and a bit of sliding, he was on the beach next to Kate and Alan. Without pausing, the sergeant then picked up a large rock, perhaps 80 pounds, and heaved it down the beach to the left of the cave opening. It rolled a short distance in the soft sand and came to a stop in the surf. He had another one in the air before the first had stopped rolling.

"Come on, come on, let's *do it*," he said sounding like a drill sergeant, only drill sergeants don't have grins on their faces.

With some minor grumbling in jest, Kate and Alan began moving rubble.

———————•———————

After 30 minutes of manual labor in the heat and humidity of the island, Kate was beginning to realize how big the task was that lay ahead of them. She liked the idea of one big blast to clear the opening. Then they could just walk through and into the cave.

"What was the matter with the idea of moving this stuff with explosives? What's 'brisance,' and what does it mean for it to be too high?"

"It wouldn't move much of this rock, just bust it up," Sergeant Thornton answered. "It's the wrong powder for movin' stuff."

"The sergeant's right. Brisance is a measure of the shattering ability of an explosive. Plastic explosives have a relatively high brisance. Their detonation rate is high. They create an energetic shock wave that tends to shatter materials they are in contact with when detonated, rather than move them. Black powder or nitrates have a much lower brisance. They tend more to move objects they are detonated next to, rather than shatter them.

Kate started to ask Alan how he knew so much about explosives, then realized, given his experience as a mining engineer, who had apparently done a lot of field work, he probably knew quite a bit about them. She realized again how much different he was than anyone she had ever met.

A few minutes later, Professor Fulton and Corporal Hansen came around the south end of The Rock and beached the dinghy near where the others were working. The professor had brought the boat through the channel where Alan first saw the blue spheres pass into the ocean.

Alan helped pull the dinghy up onto the beach, and then, they all decided it was time to take a break and get out of the direct sun. They made their way to the shade of the palm tree thicket just east of The Rock. The corporal was carrying half a case of cold sodas in a collapsible cooler. He passed them out, before sitting down beside the sergeant.

"How is the lieutenant doing?" Kate asked.

"He seems to be recovering quite nicely," said the professor. "I advised him not to overdo it."

"Did you pick up any news on the radio?" The sergeant asked.

"Talk of the comet is on all the ham bands. Lieutenant Baker was going to listen in on the long-wave broadcast channels, after he tried raising Pearl. All I heard was a lot of talk about the comet," Corporal Hansen replied. "Looks like you're making progress with the cave entrance. Have you uncovered the camouflage screen yet?"

"No, I would estimate that it's at least another 20 feet in from the face of the rubble. We've got a lot of digging to do yet, but we are starting to uncover some of the bigger rock. It's looking like, we'll need to set charges by late afternoon to break up some of the bigger stuff. We will probably need to set some shoring by this evening or early tomorrow."

"I'm not sure...I don't believe we brought *shoring* materials with us. Did we sergeant?" Professor Fulton was sitting in the sand, resting against a palm tree. Although quite spry for his age, the heat of the noonday sun and the high humidity was taking its toll.

"No, Sir," Sergeant Thornton said. "We're going to have to scavenge."

"The old shack on the north end of the island will provide what we need. I had a good look at it when I raided it for material the other day; that's where I got the stuff that I used to construct the boat cradle. There's plenty of lumber in the lean-to shed on the western side of the shack, or at least there was before the storm."

"Why don't Miss Harris and I go after the shoring and leave you gents to the digging," Professor Fulton said.

———————•———————

Kate and the professor collected hammers and a hand saw from the tool supplies. After Alan gave them an inventory of what would be needed for shoring material and after the group's short lunch break, they set off with the dinghy, leaving the three men to move rock.

Alan had suggested beaching the dinghy on the northwestern side of the island and walking the short distance to the shack, avoiding the larger surf to the north. The professor maneuvered the dinghy back through the narrow channel and past the surf without incident. They rounded the southwestern side of the island and passed near where *Wind Gypsy* was anchored. Lieutenant Baker had made his way to the cockpit and was stretched out on the port side, resting in the sunlight. He waved as they went by. Kate smiled. It was good to see that the young officer's condition was improving. She remembered the encounter with the blue object, and a chill went up her spine. We actually don't have any idea what we are dealing with or what makes it work, let alone how to fix it, she thought. How would we repair it, assuming we are successful in clearing the cave opening?

"It may be a better approach to use this channel into the lagoon, then beach on the northern end of the island on the lagoon side." Professor Fulton's comment brought her back to the present.

The previous day, Kate had noticed the pass that had formed between the lagoon and the ocean in the narrow section of reef on the western side of the island. The professor was now navigating the dinghy to a point just seaward of the pass. From this location they could see that the channel was perhaps 50-feet wide and ran due east, straight through the reef. The professor brought the dinghy in closer and inspected the shallow water of the opening with Alan's binoculars. There was a slight ebb current flowing, but other than that, the water looked deep enough to be navigable with the dinghy.

"Let's try it," he said.

"OK."

Kate could see the smooth water of the lagoon on the other side of the pass, as the professor turned the bow of the dinghy into the ebb current and started through. Negotiating the narrow channel turned out to be relatively easy, like going upstream in a calmer section of river. Just a little more throttle on the outboard motor to overcome the current.

Once through the pass, the water surface was, in fact, considerably smoother than on the ocean side of the reef. A much more pleasant ride, Kate thought. On the other hand, the water itself was not nearly as clear and the bottom was covered with predominately dead coral and sand. There were a few tropical fish, but nothing compared to the marine life surrounding the reef on the ocean side. The water depth increased gradually, as the professor maneuvered the dinghy away from the shoreline. At about 20 feet in depth, the bottom was no longer visible. As they motored farther out into the lagoon, the sulfur smell became stronger.

From their location near the pass, the old structure was clearly visible on the northern reef of the island. The professor headed the dinghy in its direction, maneuvering around several coral outcroppings. A few minutes later, they were on the beach directly south of the shack, perhaps 30 yards from the structure. Aside from a small amount of underbrush, they had a clear path between the dinghy and the shack.

It was apparent that the eastern and northern walls of the structure had collapsed inward. Most of the thatched roof was missing. Palm fronds and sand formed a berm on the eastern side of the structure where the walls should have been, remnants of the recent storm. The shed that Alan had described earlier was missing, except for the western wall, however, there were a few remnants of what had been stacks of lumber scattered about. Anything else that might have been there was apparently carried off by the seas during the storm.

After surveying the area, both Kate and Professor Fulton concluded that the few remaining scraps of lumber were not enough; they would also need to tear apart what remained of the building, in order to retrieve sufficient lumber for shoring.

————————•————————

They started by salvaging the rough-hewn flooring from the northern end of the building. Actually, the structure was little more than a small cabin. One room with four window openings, one on each wall. It didn't appear that the windows ever held glazing. The framing of the structure was rough-hewn from the indigenous palm trees. It had been originally fastened with wooden pegs and ties. There were wire nails here and there, suggesting that more recent repairs had been undertaken at some point. What remained of the original structure looked to be quite old.

Using a claw hammer and pry bar, they removed the old flooring, separating the sound boards into a pile just outside the entrance. Within 30 minutes they had worked their way through half the floor. They sat for a moment in the shade of the western wall and inspected the remainder of the structure. The southern end of the eastern wall had slid off its sill and across the floor, apparently moved by the force of the seas across the reef. It was now leaning against the opposite side of the building, resting on top of the remaining flooring. It would have to be moved before they could continue, and it was, obviously, too heavy to move in one piece. They would have to tear it apart, in order to move it out of the way.

Before starting that task, they decided to move the lumber that they had retrieved so far, down to the boat. It took several trips. As Professor Fulton picked up the last board, Kate surveyed the task of moving the wall out of the way. She ran her hand along the base of the wall, brushing sand out of the way and looking for a good spot to insert the pry bar. At one spot, a section of the inner wall paneling was missing. Kate reached through the small hole and cleared the sand out of the opening. There was something wedged between the inner and outer wall panels. Actually, the section of wall was unusual, as it was the only wall that had been finished on the inside. Kate pulled the object out of the hole. It was a small box, perhaps four by six inches on the sides and two inches high. It appeared to be made of a white material, which, based on the intricate carvings on the lid, was probably ivory. It looked like any number of such items she had seen in the shops in Honolulu. It had the look of Chinese craftsmanship, like a jewelry or knickknack box. The hinged-lid fell open as she removed the box from the opening, and a small piece of cloth, or maybe hide, wrapped with twine fell out. Kate inspected the interior of the box. There was nothing else inside. She untied the twine and opened what looked like a leather pouch. Inside was a five-sided object, approximately two inches across and about three-quarters inch thick. It was smooth and dark with a faint multicolored luster, like mother-of-pearl. She held it up to the sunlight. It seemed to lose its color, becoming a dull black. Kate noticed the edges of the object were precision cut and slightly rounded. It looked like a polished stone and, at least to the unaided eye, appeared to have been cut very accurately to the shape of a right pentagon.

"Have you found the buried treasure?" Professor Fulton had returned to the structure from the beach. Smiling, and perspiring heavily, he fairly collapsed in the shade of the old structure's western wall.

Kate handed him the object. He held it up to the sunlight.

"Looks like polished basalt," he said. He inspected the edges. "Nicely tooled," he added. "Was it in that box?"

Kate handed him the box.

"Yes. Inside what appears to be a leather pouch."

The professor inspected the box for several moments.

"That object was all that was in it," Kate added.

"It would appear, you have discovered the treasure of one of the Chinese miners here sometime back in the 18th century," he finally said.

As he handed the box and stone back to Kate, they both heard a faint cracking sound from the south. Kate stood and shading her eyes from the sun, scanned the southern reef of the island some three miles away. She thought she saw a puff of smoke rise above the trees to the east of The Rock.

"Looks like they've started blasting," she said.

Professor Fulton stood up beside her. "I think, we have all the materials we can handle in one trip," he said. "We should probably return to the excavation with what we have."

———•———

Their first thoughts had been to return to the southern end of the island along the same path they had used to reach the old structure. After getting all the materials tied off and strung behind the dingy, Professor Fulton realized it would be easier to drag their cargo down the relatively quiet waters of the lagoon. In fact, it would be much easier than attempting to negotiate the narrow pass and the rougher ocean water on the other side with the lumber under tow.

With some initial adjustments to the towline, they set off, making their way south along the eastern shore of the lagoon, where the water was protected by the eastern reef and the surface chop was much lower. In fact, the surface was glassy. Halfway down the lagoon they passed the rusted remains of an old ship, grounded on the eastern reef. Kate could just make out the hull numbers, *563*, a darker patch of rust red on the ship's forward hull.

As Professor Fulton maneuvered the dinghy around a pile of downed palm trees floating along the shoreline, Kate noticed the water on this side of the lagoon was clearer than it was near the pass on the western side. There were small patches of live coral and schools of tropical fish here, as opposed to what they had found on the opposite reef. Kate attributed the difference to the supply of nutrient-rich seawater carried over the reef on this side of the island by surf and prevailing ocean current. Intrigued, she donned a face mask that she found in the forward section of the dinghy and bent over the dinghy's flotation tub, putting the face mask in the water. For the remainder of the trip, she watched sea life go by as the professor coxswained the boat south, avoiding the occasional coral head or partially submerged palm tree.

———•———

Kate was enjoying her view of the seascape along the inner side of the eastern reef as they approached Clipperton Rock from its lagoon side. Then, just ahead of the boat, she thought she saw a faint blue light at the edge of her visibility.

As he maneuvered the dinghy closer to The Rock, Professor Fulton noticed the rocks and rubble that spread out into the lagoon from its base along the lagoon shoreline. He remembered wading through this rocky section of shore in the darkness and bad weather of their first day on the island. The area close to The Rock would not make a good place to land the rubber dinghy. He slowed the outboard, looking for a suitable landing spot farther north and to the east of The Rock. As he backed off on the throttle, the towline slacked, and the load of lumber gained on the boat, nearly colliding with its stern. The professor gunned the outboard and turned left, dodging the advancing tow. Kate sat up and looked around, startled by the sudden motion and the increased pitch of the outboard motor.

"We had better put in here on this sandy section of shoreline and avoid the rocks down the way," the professor said. He struggled a bit with the outboard motor, redirecting the lumber's motion toward the beach. Kate put the face mask back in the small bag and, as they approached shallow water, jumped over the side and helped direct the load of lumber onto the beach.

After securing the dinghy and maneuvering the lumber to shore, they separated out a small stack and each picked up an end. The professor led, as they made their way through the palm thicket to the ocean side of the reef, emerging onto the beach about 100 yards from The Rock.

Alan saw them come out of the trees with the load of lumber.

"Your timing couldn't be better," he shouted.

28. The Alternate Path

It took Alan and the marines 20 minutes to pack the remainder of the lumber from the lagoon site, where Professor Fulton had landed the dinghy, to a location near the cave entrance. The temperature had dropped considerably where the three men had been working, once the sun passed down behind The Rock. But even in the shade of the late afternoon, it was still hot. Alan had worn himself out, trying to keep up with the younger--and much more fit--marines. But it wasn't just the heat. He was out of shape, and he knew he would pay for his overexertion the following day.

They had cleared most of the smaller rubble by the early afternoon. After setting charges on the bigger rocks, they spent a bit of time searching for suitable tamping material, eventually finding the silt-laden sand in the shallow waters of the lagoon just north of The Rock. It made good tamping. The first explosion shattered three of the big rocks that were blocking the cave opening. The rest of the afternoon was spent moving the rubble from the explosion.

Alan had been watching the loose stone above where the men were working, concerned it might slide down on them at any moment. They needed to set shoring. As the marines moved the last load of lumber down the beach, Alan stood studying the excavation and the lumber pile, determining the best placement of the timbers.

Sergeant Thornton glanced at his wristwatch as he came up alongside Alan.

"I'd like to check on the lieutenant before it gets much later. We'll bring some chow when we come back. I'm going to have Hansen break out the rations from the containers at the old camp-site, and we'll move them out to the boat. We must be running your supplies low by now. We'll put a meal together and bring it back in. It looks like we've got several more hours of daylight. We might as well use them."

Alan agreed, but at the same time thinking how tired he was. If they were going to do any good, they would have to clear the access and repair the machine as soon as possible.

He studied the excavation. A lot of work remained to be done. It didn't look promising.

"I'll get started on the shoring," he said. "The portable generator and work lights are in the cockpit storage locker. Might as well bring them in with you," he added. "We'll need to make a night of it, if we're going to get through in time."

The marines headed back to the dinghy. Kate followed them and retrieved the small bag with the snorkels and face masks from the bow. She pointed out the pass through the western reef that the professor had used to get into the lagoon. Then she watched as the marines eased the dinghy out into the open water and sped off.

———————•———————

Kate walked back through the palm thicket, meandering her way along the waterline back to the excavation site. Alan and Professor Fulton were hoisting some of the lumber across the trunk of a downed palm, getting ready to cut it to length. Alan noticed the snorkel and mask in her hand.

"Going swimming?"

"I thought I saw something in the water as we were approaching the shore in the dinghy earlier," she said. "It looked like it was glowing blue."

Professor Fulton placed his end of the lumber stack on the ground.

"I wonder...Do you suppose that the opening we found in that isolated tunnel I came across that first day...Do you suppose that opening is passable from seaward? Could it be found from the outside?" The professor was thinking out loud more than addressing the others.

Alan recalled looking through the round aquarium-like opening that the professor found the day Lieutenant Baker was hurt. He remembered sunlight showed through the opening. He also remembered sticking his hand through the barrier *wall*, which, apparently, held the ocean water from flooding the tunnel and shafts. How eerie it felt. On the other side of the barrier, the surroundings looked much like any other location along the reef---sand, coral and tropical fish. If it were camouflaged in a similar manner as the cave entrance, it would be very difficult to find from the underwater side.

In his head, Alan traced his steps from the cave entrance to the barrier. He estimated the elevation of the opening to be perhaps 20 to 30 feet below sea level. He looked at The Rock and tried to remember, more accurately, the layout of the caverns and shafts he had seen. The cave entrance extended back about 15 feet to the north of the opening they were now trying to uncover. The shaft at the back of the cave dropped perhaps 30 feet and ran to the west...no, maybe west northwest, perhaps 60 to 80 feet. The upper chamber, where Lieutenant Baker had been injured, was, what, 80-feet deep running to the south...approximately. The tunnel Professor Fulton found at the back of the chamber ran east and west, no, maybe northeast and southwest. Then it turned and ran maybe north and south to the barrier, perhaps 80 feet from the back of the upper chamber.

Alan bent down over the pile of lumber and sketched the layout of the caverns, tunnels and shafts in the sand. Glancing back at The Rock, he estimated where the underwater opening might be in relation to features on its sheer face. It would be around the corner and to the south and west of where they had been working. He leaned over and tried to see features on the south face to use as landmarks, then noticed that Kate and Professor Fulton were staring at him.

"Is it going to take that much calculating to cut each board?" Kate was joking, and she had that beautiful smile on her face again. Alan looked at her and smiled back.

"I…no…I was just thinking about what Professor Fulton said. The barrier we saw in the tunnel, the one holding the ocean out of the caverns. I was just wondering if we could find it from the ocean side. Even if we could, though, I don't know how we would get through it. I was just…" Alan's voice trailed off.

"I think there's a chance we may be able to gain access, if we can find the opening," Fulton said. "Do you have any idea where to look? I must admit I was quite turned around in the caves."

"Well…yes," Alan said. I was just thinking it would lie off the beach just below that fissure on the south side of The Rock," Alan pointed to the left of the excavation site. "In about 20 to 30 feet of water," he added.

"I thought I saw something on the lagoon side," Kate repeated. She wondered if Alan had his location correct. She saw something in the lagoon, and he wanted to search the outer reef.

"What the professor and I saw would be on the ocean side," Alan said. "I would estimate that all the caverns we were in to be under The Rock, or to the south, on the ocean side of the reef. If there is a way into the machine on the lagoon side, it enters at a place we have not seen."

Kate pictured in her mind the layout of the caverns and shafts she had seen. Alan was right. The cavern where Lieutenant Baker was hurt would be just below the ocean surf on the south side of The Rock. The lower shaft turned north and toward the lagoon, but she didn't know how far it went. She had never been down to the lower chamber where the machine was.

"All I'm saying is that if we're going to look for alternate ways into the cavern, what I saw may be worth checking out," she said. "It may not be an entrance, but I definitely saw a blue light on the lagoon side of The Rock."

Steven C. Golly

Alan studied the excavation he had been working on all day. It was not at all promising he concluded. Although they had made good progress, there just wasn't enough time to reach the cave entrance, not in the time that remained before the comet impact. There had to be another way.

"Assuming we can find the entrance, Professor, what makes you think we will be able to get through the barrier?"

"Observations and wishful thinking, I suppose," Professor Fulton responded. "Can you find it?"

"Maybe," Alan said.

————————•————————

They decided to try looking for the opening that Professor Fulton had discovered from inside the tunnel first. Then, if they were unsuccessful on the ocean side of The Rock, they would move to the lagoon side and look for the light source that Kate had seen earlier that day.

Leaving the lumber propped on the log, they waded around the southern side of The Rock to a point just inland of where Alan had estimated the submerged opening should be. At this location, the sheer face of The Rock dropped into two feet of water. They stood on the sandy bottom and looked seaward. There were two rows of coral growth running parallel with the shoreline; one was about 30 feet out from the bluff and the other about 80. Several feet of surf broke on this outer reef. Alan wasn't sure how far out the opening was. It could be between the two rows of coral or seaward of the outer row.

He pictured in his mind the scene in the tunnel. The tunnel entrance was nearly vertical, and round. Seen from the outside it should look like a near vertical area on the sea bottom, 10 or more feet in height, 20 to 30 feet below the surface.

They started wading out into deeper water.

"I'm not a very good swimmer," Professor Fulton said.

"Let's break the search up," Alan said. "I'll look seaward of the outer reef. Kate can look between the two rows of coral, and you can stay here and keep track of where we both are. You can relay messages between us, while we're searching."

They all agreed with Alan's plan.

"Look in the deeper areas," Alan said to Kate. "I think, it's going to be nearly 30 feet to the opening."

"OK. I'll signal the professor if I find something. You do the same."

Alan agreed. He dove into the water and began taking long, easy overhand strokes toward the outer reef, doing the best he could to look like a graceful swimmer. As he did so, he realized he was trying to show off for Kate. Why was he doing that? Although a competent swimmer, Alan was not graceful.

Kate watched Alan swim toward the outer reef. She was not impressed. Over five years on swim team in high school and college, she could tell a good swimmer when she saw one. Alan wasn't. She smiled and donned her face mask. She would make quick work of the area between the reefs. He could very well need help on the outer reef, she thought.

———•———

The bottom contour was all wrong. Kate had inspected over 300 yards of bottom terrain between the inner and outer reefs. Over this entire region, the bottom flattened out to nearly horizontal before it reached 20 feet in depth. She found no vertical surfaces below that depth. She was sure the opening must be seaward of this area, somewhere beyond the outer reef.

Treading water, Kate tipped up her face mask and scanned the surf to seaward. She caught Alan's feet submerging as he dove. She made her way over the outer reef between rows of surf. Then diving just under the surface, she swam seaward and out of the surf zone.

Outside the outer line of coral, the water darkened to a deep blue and the bottom dropped precipitously. Live coral, tropical fish and all forms of sea life speckled the face of the reef. Perhaps 100 feet below her, several sharks moved slowly along the reef wall, which continued down past them and out of sight. The water visibility was better than anything Kate had ever experienced. To the west, she could see Alan making his way along the reef, perhaps 15 feet below the surface and nearly 100 yards away. As she watched, he rose to the surface, took a fresh breath, then dove again and continued along the reef. She followed his progress not noticing a large round black spot on the side of the reef until he was just over it. It must be the opening they were looking for, she thought.

As Kate watched, Alan swam past the spot, surfaced for another breath and then dove again, continuing along the reef. He had missed it! How had he missed it?

She took a few strokes on the surface then dove, covering the last 30 yards to Alan's location under water. She tapped him on the shoulder and motioned him to the surface.

"It's right behind you," she said, after a wave passed them and broke on the reef. "You missed it."

"I didn't see anything," he said.

Kate ducked her face mask below the water. The black spot was clearly visible. There was a blue fringe of light now visible around its perimeter.

"You can't see that?" she said. "It's right below us."

Alan dipped his face mask under the water as another wave broke over the top of them. He scanned the face of the reef. He could see sand, coral and sea life; he saw nothing that remotely looked like the tunnel opening. As he watched, Kate dove below him, swimming gracefully down the face of the reef, stopping at about 30 feet. She was, obviously, very comfortable in the water. Alan took a breath and submerged, swimming after her. Then, as he watched, she disappeared into the face of the reef! Alan clamored to the surface coughing. He had inhaled some seawater. Treading water for a moment to catch his breath, he scanned the face of the reef below him. There was no sign of Kate. Alan dove again, and at about 10-feet down, he saw Kate's hand protrude from the reef 20-feet below and beckoning him deeper. It looked surreal.

He swam toward Kate's extended hand. It was protruding out of a small patch of plant life and coral, along the vertical face of the reef. This area looked just like the rest of the reef, except for Kate's hand.

There was a slight current flow along the reef, and at about five feet above Kate's hand, he reached out to steady himself by grasping a protruding section of dead coral. His hand passed through the coral and into the face of the reef. As it did, Alan noticed a slight pull. He was being pulled into the invisible opening. The force grew as his entire arm disappeared behind the camouflage. He tried to hold himself back, but as more of his body passed through the camouflage barrier, the stronger the pull was. Moments later he literally fell into a dark tunnel, landing on top of Kate.

———————•———————

Kate broke Alan's fall. Otherwise, he would have landed head-first on the rock floor of the tunnel.

"Are you all right?" he said helping her to her feet.

"I'm OK," she said.

"That could have been more graceful," Alan said, laughing at himself.

"Lucky, you weren't here for my entrance," Kate said. "It wasn't all that graceful, either. Now, we know what it feels like when gravity takes over, unexpectedly," she added. "Is this the tunnel you and the professor were talking about?"

Alan looked around. The opening he had just fallen through looked the same as the one the professor had found. He looked in the opposite direction. The tunnel was dark, trailing off into blackness. The only light was that which came through the opening. He closed his eyes and waited for them to adjust to the near darkness, then eased his way deeper into the tunnel. Beyond where he stood the tunnel turned to the left and disappeared into blackness.

"Looks like it," he said returning to the barrier.

29. The Key

2000 03 April, 2007 Clipperton Atoll

Kate and Alan stood for a moment looking through the barrier at the blue of the water, the live coral growing along the face of the reef and tropical fish swimming in and out of the coral and marine plant life. They were both dripping wet and the cool air of the cave was beginning to be uncomfortable. They were starting to get cold.

"How did you find this opening?" Alan asked. "I must have gone right by it."

"I don't know how you missed it. It was in plain view."

Alan shook his head. "I sure didn't see it."

Kate shook her head. "Shall we get started?"

———•———

Alan led the way, moving slowly and keeping to the right side of the round tunnel. He figured that, as it was so dark, the only way to find the opening to the upper cavern was to feel along the wall of the tunnel until they reached it. They both remembered that the lantern, Kate and the lieutenant had in the cavern the first day, had been left behind and should be near where the shafts entered the chamber. They decided to go after the lights first. Then they would figure out what to do about the machine.

As they made their way deeper into the tunnel, their progress slowed in the total darkness. Glancing down, Kate noticed something glowing in the pocket of her jumper. She reached in and pulled out the pentagon-shaped stone she found in the wall of the old shack earlier that day. The stone was glowing––quite brightly–– in the darkness of the tunnel. It cast a blue light on the solid rock walls around them, once Kate had the object out of her pocket.

"You have a flashlight?" he said, before he saw the object.

He turned to see the blue-glowing stone in Kate's hand.

"What is that?"

"I don't know. I found it hidden in the old shack, but it wasn't glowing then. I have no idea what it is, but it looks like it must have something to do with the machine. Its color appears to be the same as the blue spheres."

"It also has the same blue glow as the machine, itself," he added.

Kate handed the object to Alan. He studied it for a few moments and then shrugged.

"I have no idea what it is either," he said.

Holding it out before them, they continued along the tunnel. The object provided enough light to make their progress along the wall much easier.

At about 100-feet in, they came to the opening at the back of the upper cavern. Alan could just make out the rubble that blocked the remainder of the tunnel, as they turned and stepped through the camouflage curtain. The narrow cavern, where Lieutenant Baker had been hurt that first day, was dark, as they carefully made their way around the rubble that partially blocked the opening. Reaching the opposite end of the cavern where the upper and lower shafts entered, Alan found the gas lantern Kate was using the day Lieutenant Baker had been injured. Alan picked it up and shook it gently. He could hear gasoline sloshing in the tank. The lantern had, apparently, gone out as the tank lost pressure. He worked the lantern's hand pump and re-pressurized the tank, as Kate used the light of the glowing object to find the matches she left near the lantern.

Moments later, the harsh, white light of the gas flame replaced the soft, blue glow from the object. Kate could see Alan clearly for the first time since they entered the tunnel. She realized by looking at him and then her own clothing, just how wet they were. Alan's wet hair lay flat on the top of his head. There was a drop of water on the end of his nose. She looked down. They were both standing in ever-growing puddles of water. She began to shiver.

"Are you cold?" She asked, her teeth beginning to chatter.

"Freezing," he replied. "Huddle up next to the lantern. It puts out quite a bit of heat. I'm going up the shaft to the cave entrance. I'll get the other light we left up there. I'll be right back."

Alan used the light from the pentagon-shaped stone to make his way up the shaft.

At the top, he could just make out rubble from Mr. Fox's demolition work, filling the area of the cave where the entrance had been. He found the large battery-powered searchlight, where it had been left, apparently undisturbed by the high explosive blast. He switched it on. Sergeant Thornton's backpack was sitting where it had been left, also undisturbed by the blast. He checked the contents: a few pitons, a carabiner, a hammer, a small flashlight, a notepad and pencils. Rolled in a tight ball at the bottom of the bag was a black wool sweater, a camouflage uniform shirt and a black stocking cap. Exactly what he wanted to find.

"Thank you, Sergeant Thornton," he said, as he pulled on the uniform shirt and hoisted the pack over his shoulder.

Before returning to the upper cavern, using the powerful searchlight, Alan inspected the area around where the cave entrance had been. As well as a great deal of rubble, which had spilled into the cave, there was an enormous rock that now blocked the opening. He traced the edges of this boulder around its periphery. There was no way. They would not be able to remove this giant boulder with the small quantity of explosives that were left. How could they restore the machine to operation with the cave entrance blocked? Alan stood for a moment shaking his head. With a growing sense of defeat, he eased his way back down the shaft.

As he reached the opening of the upper cavern, he could see Kate standing over the lantern. She had wrung out her clothing and dried her hair as best she could. She had continued to warm her hands over the lantern and was huddled as close to it as she could get. He hesitated for a moment, watching her as she knelt over the bright, gas light. She was beautiful in a way that seemed to come from deep inside, he thought. Why hadn't he noticed that before? She had been all business since they met, and stiff, maybe even overbearing. No, that was too harsh…abrupt. That was it; she had an abrupt manner.

But she had changed. He couldn't put his finger on when it happened. She just seemed more genuine, as if she had let down her reserve and become, beautiful. He entered the cavern and pulled the pack from his shoulder, handing her the sweater and cap. Kate's eyes glowed.

"Thank you," she said.

"Thank, Sergeant Thornton," Alan replied.

———•———

With the dry clothing, they were both more comfortable. Kate looked like a small child in her father's clothes with the sergeant's oversized sweater on her slender frame, but she was pleasantly warmer. They sat huddled next to the lantern for a few minutes, taking off the last of the chill.

"I got a good look at the cave-in blocking the entrance from this side." Alan said. "It doesn't look good. We're not going to be able to clear it with the explosives we have."

Kate was silent for a few moments.

"We'll have to redirect the spheres, so that they go through the tunnel then. We'll have to redirect them, so they go out the way we came in."

"How do we do that?"

"I don't know. But we have to try."

They sat in silence, warming themselves on the lantern for a few more moments.

"OK. Let's try then," Alan finally said.

They eased their way down the steep shaft to the lower chamber. This room was new to Kate, and she was struck by how alien the scene before her looked. The dim, blue glow of the walls and ceiling gave her an uneasy feeling. The partial rock covering of the glowing metallic surface projected an odd shadowy effect into the opening. It was unsettling. Moreover, the size of the machine struck her. It was larger than she had imagined. The cavern, perhaps 50-feet across, was, as best she could tell, enclosed by the machine. Floor to ceiling and wall to wall, blue-glowing surfaces showed through solid rock. The walls appeared to form a roughly triangular shaped chamber but with a complex curvature. In the center of the chamber, the ceiling dipped down to a pointed protrusion, somewhat like a stalactite. A bare section of the machine was void of any remnants of rock.

"There is what looks like a control room along the wall to the right," Alan said as they entered the chamber. "That's where Fox found the Cyrillic message."

"I can see it," Kate said. "Over in the corner."

"You can see…" Alan was interrupted by a high-pitched sound, something like that of a jet engine increasing in speed. It wasn't loud, but its sudden onset startled both of them.

As they watched, the blue glow of the cavern walls seemed to increase in intensity and a blue sphere formed in thin air just below the protrusion in the center of the ceiling. The sphere grew in size from just a spot to about five feet in diameter in a few seconds. Almost as soon as it formed, it darted past them and into the shaft, disappearing as it rounded the corner at the upper cavern. Moments later, there was a bright flash of light from the shaft. Alan took Kate's hand and moved along the wall of the chamber toward the control room. As he did, another sphere formed at the same place as the first one, repeating the scene they had just witnessed.

Finding the opening, Alan guided Kate into the control room

ahead of him. As he passed through the curtain himself, a third sphere formed. It grew to about half the size of the first two then just *blinked* out, disappearing where it had formed. A moment later, they both noticed the blue light from the walls of the chamber dim to the level it had been when they first entered. Inside the small room, Alan took a deep breath.

"Did we trigger that, or did we just happen to be here when the machine activated?" he asked.

"I don't know." Kate replied. "If the past is any indication, we just happened to be here."

She glanced at her watch. 9:07 p.m. "It doesn't make sense," she said.

The machine's previous activations had all been timed, so that they occurred when the location of the island lined up with the comet.

Kate had already determined that this position of the earth in its rotation about the poles occurred close to noon. It was too early for the machine to have activated.

Then she remembered what Professor Fulton had said.

"Alan, whatever we are going to do, we need to do it quickly. We don't have much time."

"So how do we go about redirecting the spheres?"

"I don't know. We'll have to figure it out."

"Should we go back and get help from the professor? He may be able to help you figure out how to fix this thing, so the spheres go out through the tunnel. I'm not going to be able to do much with this high-tech stuff." Looking at the machine's complex control panel, Alan felt way out of his depth. "Maybe we could get some equipment together, waterproof it and get it in here tomorrow morning, along with the professor and…"

"We don't have that much time, Alan," Kate said. "We don't have tomorrow. There has to be another way."

———————•———————

Kate seemed to be lost in thought, almost trance-like, staring at the *control panel* in the tiny room.

"Are you all right, Kate?"

No response.

"Kate?"

"Yes," she nearly shouted. "I'm sorry. Just thinking. I need to think for a minute, Alan." She continued staring at the panel. Alan looked through the curtain at the large chamber. It seemed to him that the machine's activity was over for the moment. He ventured back through the curtain and studied the opening for some minutes. The floor, walls and overhead were clean, almost dust free. He scanned the room with the searchlight. There were four bodies that he could see, all dressed in what looked like business suits, all wearing hats, like something out of a 1940's gangster movie. On the opposite side of the chamber, there was rubble lining the wall. It seemed to Alan that wherever there was rubble in the caverns around the machine, it was there because of some man-made event.

Leaving Kate to her thoughts and avoiding the area near the ceiling protrusion, Alan made his way back past the entrance shaft to the pile of rock on the opposite side of the room. As he got closer, he realized he had been handling similar rocks the entire day. Looking at it made his back ache.

Stepping around the rubble, he placed his hand on the wall to steady himself. There was nothing there. He tried to catch his balance before falling forward as his hand passed through the wall up to his elbow. He stepped forward and stumbled on the rubble, falling headlong through yet another camouflaged curtain into darkness.

"I've got to quit doing that," he said to himself.

Alan stood up and felt for the edge of the camouflaged opening. Finding it, he felt along its perimeter. It seemed to be nearly round and about the same diameter as the shafts and tunnels that, apparently, honeycombed Clipperton Rock. He turned the light into this new chamber and looked around. Before him was another chamber that looked similar to the one he had just left, except that it was pitch black. Alan scanned the walls with the searchlight. It was, indeed, very similar, a triangular shape with the same protrusion in the center of the ceiling. The major difference was that the walls were not glowing. There was a large area to the left of where he had entered that was filled with rubble. He stepped out into the room and glanced back at the opening. It was camouflaged and looked like the rest of the rock walls in the chamber. This opening was camouflaged in both directions.

Alan took a mental picture of the rubble around the opening, so that he could find it when he returned. Turning, he walked around more rubble and came out near the center of the chamber, where he scanned the walls with the searchlight.

There was a body partially buried a few feet in front of him. It had only become visible as he reached the center of the room. The body was dressed differently than the men in the other chamber; these clothes were of coarse cloth with rough stitching. Alan bent down and retrieved a small piece of folded paper that was protruding from a patch pocket of the man's vest. He unfolded it.

It appeared to be some kind of pay voucher for a *Mr. Hank Carter* of the *"British Pacific Island Company"* dated *July 2, 1907.* Alan looked at the body. He was certainly not a forensics expert, but it didn't look decomposed enough to be that old. Maybe entombed in this cavern, it had been preserved somehow. He noticed a faint blue glow coming from beneath the rubble next to the body. He removed a bit of the rock. In the man's left hand was a glowing stone, pentagon in shape.

As Alan picked it up the room became lighter. *The machine was turning on,* and he was kneeling directly under the ceiling protrusion, right at the spot where the spheres would form. He jumped, landing flat on the floor several feet from where he had been kneeling and then lay motionless for several moments.

He waited for it to happen, for the objects to form just above his feet. He waited....

Nothing happened.

Alan sat up and looked around the chamber. The passage that he had just come through was now visible. The blue light from the walls of the first chamber was shining through the round opening, partially illuminating the otherwise dark chamber he was in. He looked down at the blue glowing object in his hand. It looked exactly like the stone Kate had found in the old shack.

"What is this thing?" He asked himself.

Alan stood back up and scanned the room a few more times with the searchlight. There was nothing else of interest that he could see. He decided it was time to get back to the control room, where he had left Kate and see what she had worked out. Her last comment had been confusing. "We don't have tomorrow," she had said. Had she given up on getting the machine reactivated?

As he walked back to the now well-lit passageway between the two chambers, he attempted to assess their situation. The project didn't look promising. The shaft was blocked, the blue spheres could not get through. There was no way they were going to be able to clear the cave entrance in less than two days with the equipment they had. Any misgivings Kate had about getting the machine operational again were, probably, more than warranted. Their best bet now was to get out of these caverns. Then they needed to move the boat to the northwestern side of the reef, put every anchor he had out and batten down for the coming blow.

He put the glowing stone in his pocket and walked through the opening back into the first chamber, making his way around the pile of rubble. On the other side of the chamber, Kate was clearly visible, standing in the little control room. Alan watched, as she passed her hands over the control panel. With the five-sided stone in his possession, the camouflage of the control room entrance was gone.

"That's how she found the tunnel opening in the reef," he said to himself.

Alan made his way across the chamber, steering clear of the protrusion in the middle of the ceiling. As he walked by the shaft they had come down, the blue glow from the walls of the chamber went dark. Then moments later, it returned to the now familiar blue color. Alan realized he had stopped breathing. He took a breath, his eyes glued just below the point at the center of the ceiling where the spheres had formed before. He waited several moments. No spheres materialized. He worked his way along the wall to the control room and entered.

"I've found out what the glowing object is. I mean what it does," Kate said, as Alan stepped through the control room entry. "Look at this."

Alan watched, as Kate reached down and rubbed her hand over the smooth surface of the control panel. The surface immediately lit up with an array of lights, mostly blue but also other colors, all with different shapes. Kate moved her hand to the very bottom and center of the panel. She touched a pentagon shaped blue light on the panel surface. The smooth features of the panel changed, and the pentagon-shaped light began to rise out of the surface, continuing for about three-quarters of an inch. She grasped this raised section and pulled. It came free, still glowing blue. The section of panel Kate had removed looked exactly like the object Alan had just found in the other chamber and the one Kate had found in the ruins of the old shack. He could also see through the control room door that the walls in the larger chamber went dark.

Kate took the object she had found earlier out of her pocket and lining it up with the recess in the control panel, inserted it into the opening. It fit perfectly. Alan noticed that the walls in the outer chamber immediately began to glow again.

"I think it's a key," she said.

Before he could say anything, a screen on the control panel became illuminated, just above where Kate had inserted the key. A message appeared. As far as Alan could tell, it was the same Cyrillic Russian message that Fox had showed him earlier on the same screen. He could only identify a few of the words--*welcome, emergency, dirt* or *soil*, something like that. He couldn't make out what it said.

"Can you read this message?" Kate asked.

"Only a couple of words," Alan replied. "It's Russian…a greeting…or maybe a warning. I simply don't remember enough Russian to understand what the message is saying."

Kate became silent, continuing to stare at the control panel.

"I don't think we can fix it," Alan finally said.

"There has to be a way," Kate responded.

"The cave entrance is blocked. There is no way we can move that amount of rock in less than two days. I don't see any other way," he continued. "The spheres can't get out."

"There's still the tunnel we came in through," Kate said. "There must be a way to redirect them, so they go out that way."

"How?" Alan responded.

"I don't know. But there has to be a way." Kate paused, staring at the five-sided stone glowing in her hand.

"We are running out of time," she finally said in a low voice.

30. On Second Thought

1830 03 April, 2007 Clipperton Atoll

Professor Fulton stood in knee-deep water at the base of Clipperton Rock and watched the surf break over the outer line of coral where Kate and Alan had been diving. He watched for several minutes. They didn't return to the surface. He wasn't sure what to do.

———————•———————

It had been a long night for all of them. They had searched the reef late into the evening, both free diving and using Alan's scuba equipment. They found nothing. There was no sign of either Alan or Kate and no indication of any opening into the caverns. There were, however, plenty of sharks. And the longer they were in the water, the more sharks there were.

Early the next morning, Sergeant Thornton continued the search, while Lieutenant Baker patrolled just outside the surf line with the dinghy. While they were searching, Corporal Hansen and Professor Fulton set about clearing rubble from the cave opening. There was still no sign of Kate or Alan. They set the last of the explosives, cracking a few of the larger rocks and exposing the enormous boulder that Alan had seen from inside the cave. They were all disheartened.

They made several attempts to pry the massive stone out of the cave opening. Hard as they tried, they were unable to move it. Finally, the men relented.

Steven C. Golly

"We are not going to get through to the caverns," Professor Fulton said. He was the first to voice what everyone knew. They had been attempting to use some of the lumber that the professor and Kate had recovered from the old shack as leverage with the enormous rock. It wasn't working. The three of them sat down in the sand, staring at The Rock. Lieutenant Baker was still running the dinghy up and down the reef off the south end of the island, looking for Kate and Alan.

"We need to move the boat to a more protected anchorage," the professor continued.

The marine sergeant and corporal sat silently for a few minutes, not ready to quit, but knowing the task was futile.

"You're right, Sir," Sergeant Thornton finally said. "I'll signal the lieutenant to come and pick us up."

———————•———————

After returning to *Wind Gypsy*, there was a short discussion about how best to proceed. As the professor was the only one aboard with any sailing experience, he was elected captain. They all agreed that the best course of action was to move the boat north to an anchorage off the northwestern side of the island, where they would be provided better protection from the blast effects of the comet impact. There they would hunker down, as the sergeant called it, and wait out the effects of the calamity. They stowed the remainder of the supplies they had brought to the boat from the campsite and set about the task of dislodging the big storm anchor from the coral bottom. It took Sergeant Thornton several dives to unravel the anchor chain from the coral it had wedged itself into. After the chain was freed, he came back aboard with several coral cuts on his hands and feet.

The short trip to a good anchorage spot just off the northwestern reef had been uneventful. The men set three anchors; three were all they could find aboard *Wind Gypsy*. After the big anchor was set, the professor gave the marines the task of stowing the dinghy and motor and removing and stowing the sails. During this time, the professor secured all the remaining rigging. The topside chores complete, they all went through the boat's contents and stowed everything that could fall, shift or otherwise become a hazard, should the boat be rolled over by the wind and seas.

Lieutenant Baker had been monitoring the radios, since their return to the boat. Every channel on the sideband had talk of the comet. The most recent information indicated that it would impact the earth 300 miles off the coast of Peru at 11:23 a.m. local time the following morning. Nearly the entire Pacific shoreline of the western states had been evacuated. Honolulu, and in fact most of Oahu, as well as other islands in the Hawaiian chain, had been evacuated to the Big Island or to the mainland. Professor Fulton checked the boat's chronometer above the navigation station. Less than 13 hours to impact. He plotted the comet's impact point on Alan's chart and measured off the distance between it and Clipperton Island. The impact point would be 2,000 miles east southeast from their location and 30 degrees below the horizon at impact. Hopefully, the majority of the blast would pass over their heads, but he didn't know for sure. And he really had no way of estimating the size of the wave that would be formed. It could be enormous.

———————•———————

After they had completed all the preparations they could think of, Corporal Hansen put on some coffee and the other three men settled into the bench seats of the cockpit. Lieutenant Baker was starting to get around quite well now, mostly hopping on one leg, but making his way up and down the companionway without assistance.

The night was clear and moonless. The professor noted with some satisfaction that the boat was riding quite well at anchor in the light breeze that now blew over the port bow. The three men sat silently until Corporal Hansen poked his head out of the companionway and asked who wanted coffee. They all accepted, knowing it would be a long night.

A few minutes later, Corporal Hansen came up the companionway with four mugs. He sat down and began to pass them out. As the professor reached for the cup, a wave of nausea overcame him. The cup crashed on the cockpit floor, spreading shattered bits of porcelain mug and hot coffee all over the small floor area of the cockpit. The nausea passed almost as quickly as it had arrived.

"I'm sorry, I..." The professor didn't finish the sentence. By the looks on their faces, he could tell that they all had the same sensation.

"We all felt it, Doc," Sergeant Thornton finally responded. "It's the machine."

31. Effects

Alan and Kate stood in the small control room. Kate was deep in thought and Alan was beginning to wonder whether she was all right. She stood staring at the control panel, not saying anything, just as she had done earlier. Finally, she spoke.

"Two keys…why would there be two keys?" Then, not waiting for Alan's reply, "There has to be another control room down here, and maybe another sphere generator that isn't activated." Her excitement was palpable. "There must be another chamber."

"There is," Alan said. "I found the entrance a while ago." He pointed through the control room door to the far side of the triangular room. "It's over there, on the other side of the main chamber, but it's turned off, and…" Alan realized they probably had the means to turn it on. "…but I think the exit may be blocked."

"Let's check it out," Kate said, stepping through the control room entry and out into the generator chamber.

"Hurry," she said, looking back at him as he passed through the opening behind her.

Kate walked directly across the middle of the chamber and under the center ceiling protrusion. As she approached the far wall, she could see the dark circle of the opening into the adjoining room. Alan couldn't understand why she seemed so agitated. She had been so methodical up until now, like the scientist that she was. But now…

Easing around the periphery of the room, he walked past her, stepping over the rubble, where he had tripped earlier. He switched on the searchlight.

"This way," he said, then added, "Kate, this is a dangerous place. It's not a good idea to be in a hurry in this type of underground environment or around this machine."

"You don't understand," she said shaking her head. "We don't have much time."

Alan shined the searchlight on one of the bodies in the room that was close to Kate's feet.

"We need to be careful," he repeated.

Kate stared at the body. The clothing looked like something her father might wear. A shiver went up her spine. Alan was right. She needed to be more careful.

She had been working through a dilemma ever since the machine activated, shortly after they entered the chamber. As the second sphere formed, Kate had glanced at her watch. It read a little after nine o'clock. But every other time the machine had activated, it had been close to 11:45 a.m., the time when the earth's rotation resulted in the island lining up with the comet's position. She had racked her brain, trying to understand the time change. There shouldn't be a significant time change. When Alan asked her whether she thought they had caused the machine to activate, she realized that maybe there wasn't a time change. Maybe her watch was not keeping correct time, just as Professor Fulton had said happened to him that first day in the cave. His watch had lost time. It had to be that time was passing more slowly in the caverns and tunnel under Clipperton Rock than it was on the outside. The Fifth of April could very well occur in the next several hours. In fact, it may already be here, at least from their prospective in the caverns. They had to hurry but…She glanced up, and looking into Alan's eyes, she took a deep breath.

"You're right," she said, forcing herself to slow down.

———•———

Alan led the way into the second chamber. Kate followed with the lantern. In the lantern light, the chamber looked identical to the first chamber, roughly triangular with a central protrusion in the ceiling. Kate noticed, however, that this room was oriented differently. It seemed to be rotated to the right relative to the first, and there was a lot more rubble. Rubble filled the area in front of where the entrance shaft and the door of the control room should be located. Both openings were blocked, and the rubble looked impassable. She felt a twinge of defeat, and then her mind began to race again.

As Alan took the searchlight and passed over the rubble pile, Kate could see the body Alan had found earlier. He was dressed differently than the others.

"This cave-in occurred earlier than did the deaths of the men in the other chamber," Kate said, thinking out loud.

"1907," Alan replied. "This is, apparently, the remains of a Mister Hank Carter...from the British Pacific Island Company." He was reading from the pay stub he had retrieved earlier.

Kate remembered reading about that company in the data Phil Beckman had sent her, while she was aboard the ship.

"Guano miner," she said almost absentmindedly.

"And treasure hunters," Alan added, retrieving the object he had found in the dead man's pocket. He also had one of the machine keys."

Kate took the key from Alan's hand.

"Oh God," she said. "There's another control room."

————————•————————

It took them just a few minutes to find the passage to the next chamber. It was in the same relative location as the one Alan found in the first chamber, in the wall directly across from where the control room should be. This third chamber was also dark, but as the lantern light illuminated the walls, they could tell that it was just like the others. Kate noticed that it was also rotated relative to the second chamber, just as the second had been rotated relative to the first. A shaft left this chamber at a steep upward angle, exactly as in the first chamber. There was no rubble. They moved along the wall to the point where the door of the control room should be. There it was, clearly visible. As they entered, Kate noticed, immediately, that the key was missing from the control panel. She inserted the one she had retrieved from the shack.

The control panel lit up, just as the first one had done, as did the walls of the chamber outside the control room. Moments later, the same Cyrillic message appeared on the display screen.

They both turned their heads, looking through the control room door at the spot just below the ceiling protrusion in the large chamber. They waited. Five minutes passed, then 10 minutes, 15... nothing happened.

"Is there something that is supposed to be happening?" Alan finally asked.

Kate had been looking at her watch for the last several minutes, like she was timing something. As far as he could tell, nothing was happening that needed to be timed, in fact, he couldn't see anything happening at all.

"If my estimating is correct, not for another 10 minutes but..."

Before Kate could complete her sentence, the walls of the chamber grew brighter. Three blue spheres formed in rapid succession beneath the point in the ceiling and raced up the shaft. Kate and Alan stood in the control room for a few moments watching the walls of the generator chamber dim.

"I guess my timing was a little..."

Again, before she could finish, the walls brightened, and three more spheres formed and disappeared up the shaft. They both fell silent, watching as this process repeated itself three more times before stopping.

They waited for several minutes after the last spheres disappeared. Alan was the first to speak.

"Wow! That was impressive. Do we really have any clue what we are doing here?" There was a hint of nervousness in his sarcasm.

"I didn't expect those last four events," Kate said. "I don't know why they happened."

32. More Effects

"*Wind Gypsy, Wind Gypsy, Wind Gypsy.* This is Coast Guard Honolulu calling the sailing vessel *Wind Gypsy.* Over."

"That's us," Corporal Hansen nearly shouted.

They had finished cleaning up the broken cup and rinsing the spilled coffee out of the cockpit with buckets of seawater. The corporal retrieved the microphone and responded to the call; his voice was still quite loud.

"Coast Guard Honolulu, this is the vessel *Wind Gypsy.* Over."

"*Wind Gypsy,* this is Coast Guard Honolulu, ah, roger Skipper, we have traffic…wait. Out."

The wait, which was only a few minutes, seemed like an hour to Professor Fulton. Everyone sat silently.

"*Wind Gypsy,* this is Coast Guard Honolulu, Captain Bennett speaking, Skipper. May I speak to Miss Harris, please. Over."

Corporal Hansen passed the microphone to Lieutenant Baker, who passed it to Professor Fulton. The professor was the only remaining technical member of the research team.

"Captain Bennett, this is Robert Fulton. I'm sorry to have to tell you, but Miss Harris is missing, along with the owner of this boat, Mr. Peterson. I'm also sorry to say that Mr. Geoff Fox is dead. Over."

There was a long silence.

"Mr. Fulton, ah, the machine…the machine has stopped operating. Have you…has the team there done something to stop the machine? Over."

"Mr. Fox blocked the entrance to the cave with explosives, before he was killed in the last storm. Over."

"Can you clear it? Over."

Professor Fulton sighed, seeing a significant amount of irony in what Captain Bennett was saying.

"At least, we will not be thrown in the federal lockup for violating the Hellfire Protocol," he said to the others. He hadn't keyed the mike. "That is, if we live through the comet impact."

The professor wasn't sure how to answer Captain Bennett. Lieutenant Baker reached for the mike, and the professor passed it to him.

"Captain Bennett, this is Second Lieutenant Baker. We have been trying, Sir. No joy. It's blocked by a large boulder. We'll need heavy equipment to move it, Sir. Over."

Another long silence.

"Professor Fulton said Kate, Miss Harris, and the sailor were missing. Where are they missing Lieutenant? Over."

"They were looking for another entrance to the cave along the reef, Sir. They were in the water diving, and they never came up. I'm sorry Sir, but we think it was sharks."

Professor Fulton indicated he wanted to talk. Lieutenant Baker handed him the mike.

"This is Robert Fulton again, Captain. It is possible that they may have found another entrance into the caverns. I believe the machine just activated again a few minutes ago. They may have got it operational again. Over."

"Roger. I'll get back to you. Stay on this frequency. Out."

The conversation was over. The four men sat in the cockpit of the small boat and stared at each other.

Steven C. Golly

1230 05 April, Temporary PACOM Headquarters, Oahu, HI

Captain Richard Bennett hung up the phone, wrestling with the thought that he may have sent Kate Harris to her death on the tiny island. He pushed it out of his mind. Now was not the time.

The last few days were a blur. Keeping on top of the massive amount of data being generated by all of PACOM's sensor assets, most of which were pointed at the comet, required a staff of 50. He had eight.

That aside, Bennett now found himself engaged in something that was way above his pay grade. That afternoon Harry Thompson called from Keck Observatory. Harry had done some data reduction on the perturbations seen in the trajectory of "Comet Thompson-O'Conner." Harry was embarrassed about the naming of the comet; it was Bennett who had told him where to look for it.

That aside, the resolution of the Keck telescopes had allowed Harry to determine the impulse direction, strength and duration needed to cause the perturbations. The measurements were far more accurate than anything the military had done. The results were very unsettling. The comet's trajectory was being "disturbed" *exactly* at the same time as the anomalous events on Clipperton Atoll, if one included propagation delays. And the most startling thing, these disturbances were resulting in changes to the comet's trajectory, changes which decrease the likelihood of impact with the earth. There was only one conclusion Bennett could draw: The machine that Kate and the others had found on the island was causing the comet to be deflected away from the earth. The problem was that the impulses had stopped, the machine had stopped working, and a collision with the earth's atmosphere off the coast of Peru was still imminent.

Bennett knew there wasn't time to convince Washington that the order to stay clear of the machine needed to be rescinded. In fact, he was sure he would be unable to even get anyone's attention on the issue, given that everyone was focused on the impending global catastrophe. It would be even more impossible to convince them that assets needed to be expended to fix a probable alien device at this particular time. In fact, thinking about trying to convince anyone made him very uneasy.

"They'll put me in a rubber room," he said to himself.

That's when he had decided to contact Kate and have her team look into the problem with the machine, that is to say–– have her disobey the orders they had received from Washington.

"Guess, I prefer a courts marshal to a rubber room," he had said to himself.

He had no luck finding a navy communications facility willing to divert attention from disaster preparations, in order to set up a communications channel with the boat. Fortunately, he found an old friend in the Coast Guard that would.

Now, the news from the island was worse than bad. Kate and the sailor were missing, Fox was dead, and the machine was damaged.

But Fulton had suggested that the machine might have reactivated. He realized he should have asked him why he thought that to be the case. But then, he could determine that himself.

Bennett picked up the telephone receiver and started to dial. A petty officer came through the door of the little trailer that was now his office.

"We have a message from Kwajalein, Sir," the man said. "It's garbled, and we didn't get it all. Communications went down a few minutes ago."

The sailor handed a folder to Bennett.

```
OTTSZYUW RULSWCA0001 0870008-SSSS--RHMCSUU.
ZRN SSSSS
Z 2149Z 04 MARCH 2007
FM USAKA//00//
TO CDRUSPACOM//N56//
INFO USA//00/S3//
BT
S E C R E T //N00000//
SUBJ IMMINENT DAWN {S}
REF {a} CDRUSPACOM INST 5292
1. {C} SIGNIFICANT PERTURBATION TO COMET THOMP-
   SON-O'Conner OBSERVED COMMENCING 2128Z.
2. {S} PRELIMINARY ANALYSIS INDICATES EFFECT ON
   TRAJECTORY SZWIE AK PWJ9A J;WKQW
ERN W[;.
KPAER209DK S;3W90A4'
_

DKEP94DL
BT
```

"Well, it didn't take long to prove Professor Fulton was right," Bennett said.

"What's that, Sir?" the sailor asked.

"Oh, nothing. Sorry. Talking to myself," Bennett replied.

"Seems like a lot of people are doing that, Sir."

"Yes," Bennett said absentmindedly. He studied the message. Even though it was garbled, he knew what it meant. The machine was back in operation and affecting the comet's path. Bennett picked up the phone again.

"I need to speak to the admiral, right now."

———•———

Admiral Wells looked tired and irritated.

"I really don't have time for this, Bill. We've got a catastrophic disaster about to happen. There's been a major earthquake in California, and my communications just went down again. Can't you take care of your little group on, what is it, that little atoll without my help?"

Bennett hadn't heard about the earthquake.

"Admiral, I'm not convinced that the comet is going to impact the earth."

"That would make you the only person in the Pacific Theater with that opinion, Captain. What would you have me do?"

"I think the people at ALTAIR, on Kwajalein, might also agree with me, Admiral."

"I saw the message you are referring to, Bill. It was garbled. Do you know what they were trying to say?"

"Well, Sir, I'm betting they were trying to say that the comet's trajectory has shifted such that it will no longer collide with earth, but I'm not sure. What I am sure of is that the machine we found on Clipperton is not related to the Hellfire Program. I think Washington was wrong to shut our research team down. And I think CIA's attempt to destroy the machine was an incredibly bad decision."

Admiral Wells wondered how Captain Bennett knew about Langley's order to their man on the island.

"I don't know what the machine is, Sir, but as far as what it's doing, I can say that it's apparently not only causing the anomalies we saw in our satellite systems, but it's also deflecting the comet's trajectory every time it activates. And those deflections are moving the comet away from the earth. I think the last one occurred less than half an hour ago."

"I thought the anomalies stopped after Fox..." The admiral caught himself, before taking the discussion in a direction Bennett didn't have clearance for. "You're suggesting there has been another anomaly?"

"Yes, Sir. Kwajalein saw the effect on the comet trajectory, and we're now seeing the associated effect with our communication satellites."

Admiral Wells was finding himself getting impatient, something he had practiced not doing his entire career. The coming disaster was a logistics nightmare. There weren't enough ships, aircraft or ground vehicles to move everyone and everything that needed to be moved, in time to avoid anything other than major losses. He was down to hard choices. He really didn't have time for Captain Bennett's science project.

"Captain, you are going to have to deal with…"

At that moment, Admiral Palmer, PACOM Operations Boss entered the office, interrupting him in mid-sentence.

"Excuse me, Paul. I just received a call over the landline from Colonel Elder at the Maui Observatory. The satellite links are still down. Anyway, Elder said the comet trajectory had changed significantly. Same thing Kwajalein was saying, before we lost the satellite. Colonel Elder had the data. It looks like it's going to miss us."

Admiral Wells was staring into Bennett's eyes, as if searching for something in the back of the captain's head. He stood up from behind his desk and moved over to the little conference table at the corner of his office.

"Come and sit, gentlemen. Captain Bennett has a wild theory about that little item on Clipperton that he needs to share with you."

————————•————————

"Where I come from, machines don't operate without some kind of oversight. Are you suggesting that oversight is from aliens?"

The gruff, no nonsense PACOM Operations boss was having a harder time with Bennett's story than had Admiral Wells.

"I don't know, Sir, but I think for the near future, oversight of the machine needs to come from us."

"I concur with Captain Bennett."

Admiral Wells had been listening to the debate between his operations and technical officers for more than an hour. He had used his pragmatic, if somewhat abrasive operations officer as devil's advocate to Bennett's seemingly far-fetched theories. The conversation had been interrupted several times with messages about the comet. They now had good confirmation that it would miss earth.

Meanwhile, data from the California earthquake had it at over 7.0 on the Richter scale. There had also been a big earthquake in Indonesia, over 7.5. The good news was they were already prepared for the tsunamis that were being predicted.

"We need to get some assets down to that island ASAP, Frank," Admiral Wells continued. "For starters, a carrier task group and an amphibious group. We need the capability to put forces on the ground."

"Then we'll need to deal with the French, Sir," The Operations Officer said.

Admiral Wells picked up the phone.

"Get me a line to the consulate's office. Buzz me when you get through," he said into the receiver.

"I believe we should get the research team off the island as soon as possible and do a thorough debrief. We need to know everything we can about what we're dealing with," Bennett said.

"I concur. Get a chopper down there, and get those people off the island Frank." Admiral Wells stood up, signaling an end to the meeting.

"If you gents don't mind, I'm going to need to talk to my bosses at the Joint Chiefs."

———————•———————

1430 05 April, Eastern Pacific Ocean

Two hours later, Bennett found himself aboard a helicopter bound for Clipperton Atoll. There was a large tanker aircraft flying off to their port side. They would in-flight refuel once on the way south and twice on the way back, he had been informed. He missed the southbound refueling. Captain Bennett slept most of the way to the island.

Steven C. Golly

33. Triangulation

1030 05 April, 2007 Clipperton Atoll

Kate and Alan both sat down on the floor of the control room next to the glowing panel. They were enjoying the heat from the gas lantern, which had taken the chill out of the air in the little space. Kate was still shivering. Now, it wasn't from the cold but from adrenaline.

"Do you think this means it worked?" Alan finally spoke.

"I don't know. I don't know where the spheres went. The spheres that were generated in the first chamber went up the other shaft just like these did, but we know they didn't get past the cave-in. We don't know whether these spheres encountered a similar barrier. I think we'll have to look." Kate glanced through the control room entrance to the mouth of the shaft that the spheres had disappeared through.

"Do you think it's stopped for a while?" Alan asked. "I'd like to see where that shaft leads,…check whether it's open."

"I think, it will be a couple of hours before it activates again." Kate replied. "But I'm making some assumptions. I'm not sure why so many events just occurred. Maybe the machine is making up for the ones that were missed?"

"Why do you think it will reactivate in two hours? I thought it only turned on when the island was lined up with the comet. That won't happen for another 24 hours, right?"

"I'm sure time is progressing 10 to 12 times faster in these caves than it is outside Alan."

"Are you serious?"

"Yes."

They decided, it was a good idea to check the path of the spheres, generated by this new section of the machine. Following the shaft up and out of the generator chamber, they reached a junction with a nearly level tunnel. The shaft intersected with this tunnel at, what appeared to be, a 90-degree angle. Both the shaft and the tunnel had the same 10-foot-diameter, circular cross section they had seen earlier. Like the other shafts and tunnels, these also had smooth but contoured surfaces. They stood for a moment at the junction of the shaft and tunnel, catching their breath after the climb. Not quite level, the tunnel rose slightly in either direction from the junction. They turned left and followed the tunnel about 80 feet, to where it opened into a small chamber. There were two tunnels leaving the chamber, one at nearly 90 degrees to the right, the other at somewhat less of an angle to the left. As they stepped into the chamber, Kate noticed that they passed through one of the camouflage curtains. Glancing back, the tunnel had disappeared, and she was facing what looked like a solid rock wall. It looked exactly like the rest of the shaft and tunnel walls.

About 80 feet past the small cavern, they came to a barrier. On the other side, the tunnel continued. It was, however, obviously flooded. The barrier had the same appearance as the underwater opening they had used to enter the caverns, except for one thing. On the outside of this barrier, an underwater tunnel continued on in darkness, rather than opening up onto the island's reef.

At this point, Alan was starting to lose his sense of direction. He took Sergeant Thornton's pack off and retrieved the pencil and pad of paper he had found earlier. While Kate inspected the barrier and tunnel, he sketched a layout of the underground caverns, tunnels and shafts, trying to get a sense of which direction the tunnel before them ran. When he was finished, he got Kate's attention and showed her the drawing.

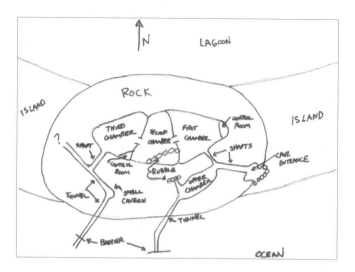

Kate studied Alan's sketch, which seemed very confusing. She noticed that the tunnel they had just come through was hidden by the camouflaged curtain at the small cavern behind them. These were the first camouflaged openings she had seen since they had entered the cave that first day on the island, and she found them disorienting. She turned back to Alan's sketch. It wasn't right. He had the orientation of the shafts and chambers wrong.

"I think it's a pentagon," she said, "rather than just a string of chambers."

"You think what's a pentagon. I don't understand?"

"The generator rooms, I think these chambers form a pentagon." Kate pointed to what Alan had marked as the first, second and third chambers on his drawing.

She took his pencil. Alan watched as she drew two regular pentagons, one inside the other. She spent as much time erasing as she did drawing Alan noted. Miss Harris is very much a perfectionist, he thought.

Kate filled in more details to her sketch. Then she showed it to Alan.

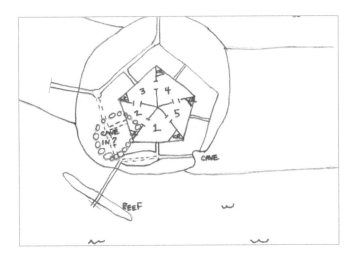

Alan studied the sketch.

"You think there are two more generator chambers and control rooms we haven't seen?" He asked, after a few moments.

"Yes, and if the orientation is right, this tunnel we are in must run a long way under the south reef of the island before coming out into the ocean." She was pointing at the location of the second barrier on her sketch. "I don't think we'll be able to tell whether it's open all the way to the surface."

"What do you want to do?" Alan was still studying Kate's sketch.

Kate checked her watch.

"We had better get out of this shaft. It's nearly time for another event," she said.

They started back down the tunnel. As they approached the small cavern, which now looked to Kate as if it were a solid rock wall, Alan said, "If your sketch is right, then this other tunnel must lead to the cave-in that you're showing here." He pointed to the area marked cave-in on Kate's sketch.

"What other tunnel?" Kate said, sounding confused.

"Oh, that's right. You can't see it," Alan said.

"See what?"

Alan reached into his pocket and brought out the penta-gon-shaped stone, handing it to Kate. As soon as it left his hand, the two openings out of the little cavern disappeared. He was looking at solid rock walls on all sides.

Kate gasped, as two dark openings instantly appeared in front of her on the solid rock walls of the little cavern. Then she realized why it was so easy for her to find the tunnel entrance in the reef, the black spot that Alan had passed right by without seeing. She held the key.

"I've got an idea," Alan said. He took Kate's hand in his, holding the key clasped between them. The tunnel openings became immediately visible to him again.

"Can you see them?" he asked.

"Yes." Kate smiled.

"You're a good person to have around when one is lost in caverns," she said, still smiling.

Alan smiled back.

"Not that good," he said. "It looks like you were right on, and I was off by 90 degrees on my orientation," he continued, comparing the two sketches.

"I've been told I have a pretty good sense of direction," Kate said. "And if my sense of timing is right, we don't have much time before the next event." She nudged Alan along, directing him down the shaft they had come up earlier.

Back in the small control room Kate studied her watch. It had been two hours and 10 minutes since the last series of events. It was time. As if on cue, the control panel came to life at the same time as the walls of the generator chamber became brighter. They noticed the faint high-pitched noise start up again. Then, as before, over the period of the next 10 minutes, five groups of three spheres each formed below the protrusion in the chamber ceiling and rushed out of sight up the shaft.

"If those worked," Alan said, "I'm guessing, the weather is going to get very nasty outside."

Before he had finished his sentence, the control panel went dark except for the blue pentagon shape region around the key that Kate had inserted earlier. Then, as they watched, the walls of the generator room went dark.

Kate sat down in the little room again, still studying her watch. Two minutes passed, then five.

"I didn't feel anything," she finally said.

"Feel what?" Alan looked at her with a curious expression.

"The comet strike should have happened. I didn't feel anything. Did you feel anything?"

"No," Alan said.

Kate closed her eyes and started shivering again. Alan took Sergeant Thornton's uniform top off and draped it around Kate's shoulders, moving the lantern closer to her.

"Wait here and warm up," he said. "I'm going to check out the other passages on your drawing."

Kate wanted to protest, but she was too cold and exhausted to do so. The heat from the lantern felt good. The little room was warming up again. She leaned her head back against the wall and rested. It was over and, as far as she could tell, they had been successful. But would they feel the blast of the shock wave inside these caves below The Rock? Would there be a large enough earthquake for them to feel here on the island, if the comet had not been deflected? The only way to find out was to go back to the surface. They needed to do that…in just a few minutes,…She just needed to get a little warmer.…

A few moments later, Kate fell asleep in the little control room of the alien machine.

---·---

She was right about the configuration of the machine's chambers and control rooms. Alan found the entrance to the fourth room, in the same relative location as the passage between the second and third rooms. The key was also missing from the control panel. Apparently, the keys had been a hot item for the guano miners.

One could only guess how they found the machine; they were probably exploring the natural caves back near the turn of the century. Looking for treasure, no doubt. Alan made his way to the passage between the fourth and fifth chambers. He passed his hand through the opening and was about to step through, himself, when he sensed something was wrong. He pulled his hand back. It was wet. The fifth chamber was flooded.

Alan checked the exits out of both the third and fourth chambers. These shafts lead to, what appeared to be, long, flooded tunnels, the flooding blocked by the same barrier as they had seen in the other tunnels. It appeared that the only way out was the way they had entered.

He made his way back to the number three control room. It was warm and almost comfortable inside, although the lantern had run out of gas and gone out. Kate was sleeping where he had left her, leaning against the wall. He put his hand on her shoulder, and she opened her eyes.

"We should get out of here, before the weather gets bad outside," he said.

———————•———————

They backtracked through the second and first chambers and up the shaft to the upper cavern, where the lieutenant had been hurt so many days ago. Alan led the way with the searchlight in his left hand and Kate's hand in his right. All of the lower chambers were now dark. The machine had, apparently, shut itself off. At the upper cavern, Alan took off the sergeant's pack and left it at the junction of the two shafts. Then they passed through the opening at the back of the long cavern, into the tunnel they had used earlier. They could see the turquoise blue of sunlight shining through the waters of the reef, at the end of the tunnel.

At the barrier, they stopped for a moment to don the face masks they had left there earlier. A school of tropical fish swam by. Moments later, they stepped through the opening into the warm water of the Pacific. They were still holding hands.

34. Bon Voyage

Captain Bennett entered the new temporary SCIF area (Sensitive Compartmented Information Facility) that had been set up for his program. This was only the second time in his career that he needed to go through a guard post that verified his ID and signature, then have his ID scanned in order to enter his office. The last time he did this was when he worked on a classified satellite program several years earlier.

The government was moving quickly after the discovery of the machine's effects on the comet. The USS *Enterprise* Carrier Task Group was enroute to Clipperton Island. It would arrive in three days. Additionally, an amphibious task group was to be identified for deployment to the island, as soon as one could be made available, following the earthquake disaster operations in California and Indonesia. Debriefing of the research team survivors was going well, and they would have a new team on the island within five days, weather permitting.

Bennett feared it wouldn't be soon enough for Kate and the sailor, Alan Peterson. There was no sign of them, when he arrived on the island four days earlier. The marines and Professor Fulton had spotted the helicopter, when it arrived, and came ashore in the small rubber boat. Before leaving the island, they inspected the cave entrance that Fox had blocked with explosives. They also did a flyover of the reef where Professor Fulton had last seen Kate. No sign of Kate or Alan Peterson.

Captain Bennett entered his new office and sat down. There was a large folder on his desk. He had requested satellite imaging of the island and particularly the base of Clipperton Rock to be done nearly continuously. The machine had wreaked havoc on a good percentage of US satellite imaging assets, during its last two activations. Cheyenne Mountain was still trying to regain control of several of the NRO satellites that had been affected. The good news was this new program had nearly top priority for satellite tasking, at least until the military arrived on island.

He slid a large stack of images out of the folder. He first looked at the weather satellite image of the region around the island taken earlier that morning. The 0530 DMSP satellite picture showed formation of several storm cells over the Eastern Pacific Region. In fact, storm cells had formed along the entire length of the equatorial region of the Pacific, the region known as the Inter-Tropical Convergence Zone. These storms appeared to correspond with the sites where the machine had activated. He glanced at the report that was stapled to the DMSP image. The weather in the area around Clipperton Island was *unsettled*, the report claimed.

The limited satellite data, they had been able to collect during the last two activations of the machine, was revealing. In each instance, a sequence of five events had occurred. Each of these events was characterized by three objects appearing at the base of Clipperton Rock, 500 yards to the south and west of the original location where they were sighted, when the anomalies first occurred. In each of these 10 total events, three objects fanned out from the point of origin in the waters of Clipperton Rock, to form an equilateral triangle approximately 100 miles on each side. At the termination of the objects' trajectories, the center of the triangle they formed corresponded to the geographical position of the comet at the exact instant of time. Each event was separated by 20 minutes, making the location of the triangle centers five degrees in longitude apart from each other. The event centers were all on the track of the comet. There was no question about it now. The machine had saved the earth from a cataclysmic collision with the comet.

Bennett flipped through the rest of the satellite images on his desk. They were all of the area around the island and The Rock, of various resolutions. At the bottom of the stack was an image of the sailboat off the northwest reef of the island. It was a pretty boat, he remembered. What was the name again? *Wind Gypsy*. That was it, as he recalled. He was about to put the entire stack back into the folder, when he noticed something peculiar about this last image.

He looked again. The boat's sails were up. *Wind Gypsy* wasn't at anchor, she was underway.

———•———

"I have the new images you requested, Sir." The petty officer placed another large folder on his desk. Bennett noticed the man was smiling.

"Thanks, Parker. I didn't expect them that quickly."

"We have top priority, Sir." Parker said, still smiling as he left the room.

In the folder were more satellite images of the sailing vessel *Wind Gypsy*, annotated with its location at the time each one was taken. They varied in resolution and azimuth angle. The last one was highly oblique, looking at the stern of the boat. The location indicated that the boat was nearly 120 miles south southwest of Clipperton Island. Bennett studied the image. He could see a woman and a man in the cockpit of the boat. He took his magnifying glass out of his desk drawer and brought the two people into focus. Captain Bennett smiled. There was no mistake about it. It was Kate and the sailor Alan Peterson.

They were kissing.

The End

Steven C. Golly

EPILOGUE

0800 18 May 2008 Clipperton Island

Rear Admiral Select Richard Bennett put his new orders down on his desk and looked out the window of his office. The ragged peak of Clipperton Rock dominated his view. He had enjoyed his tour on the island. The Oversight Program would, probably, be the last assignment, where he could come to know everyone that worked for him this well. And he did know every one of the 230 people on Clipperton very well. They were all good folks.

"The Pentagon will not be as much fun," he said to himself, as his phone brought him away from his thoughts.

"Lieutenant Baker, Sir. I have the report on that Mexican fisherman from last night. Oh, and I thought you might like to know that our friends in the French frigate are on their way here, again."

"Thanks, Tom. Let's talk about it at the 1100 staff meeting."

"Aye, aye, Skipper." First Lieutenant Baker hung up the phone.

The lieutenant had recovered completely from his wounds, and Bennett had been fortunate to have him assigned as security officer for the island. In fact, he was lucky to have the entire original contingent of marines working for him. Lieutenant Baker and Master Sergeant Thornton now ran his security department, and Sergeant Hansen was assigned to the communications department. He liked them all, particularly Sergeant Thornton's enthusiasm and down-home common sense.

The research team had made a tremendous amount of progress in the last year. All of the associated shafts and tunnels around the machine had been cleared, thanks to Alan Peterson and his crew. There was excellent progress toward understanding the science of the machine control system, thanks in part to the support of Professor Fulton at the University of Hawaii and Phil Beckman's systems organization. Phil was a good choice for the chief engineer's job, and Bennett was glad Kate had recommended him. But most important was the progress to date in solving the power puzzle. They were getting close.

Up until two weeks earlier, there had been no explanation as to what powered the machine. There were lots of theories coming out of Kate's research team, but none of them had panned out. That was when Alan's crew cut through to the central shaft.

Kate's original sketches of the layout under Clipperton Rock had been right on. The machine consisted of five large generator chambers with their associated control rooms arranged in a pentagon shape. The maze of shafts and tunnels, she had sketched in that first encounter, had proved to be a very accurate depiction of what they found. However, what they also found was a central hub. The triangular shaped generator chambers did not extend all the way to the center of the pentagon. After this observation was confirmed by the survey team, they began looking for a means to enter this central chamber. They couldn't find it, until just two weeks ago. Then they got lucky.

That was when one of Alan's exploratory tunnels, being dug below the machine, intersected the central shaft. This shaft ran vertically downward. It was twice as large as the other shafts and tunnels that surrounded the machine. There was a central conduit five feet in diameter running down the middle of the shaft, made of the same metallic material as the machine walls. To date, they hadn't found the bottom of the central shaft. It appeared to extend down through the earth's mantle.

Originally, the speculation was that the machine used the earth's magma as a thermal energy source, but that theory was dismissed, when this most recent event occurred. Actually, Bennett now knew there were two events. Yesterday's phone call from Harry Thompson was the clincher. Thompson's casual statement about the recent SETI sighting had Bennett wondering. He confirmed his suspicion with a call to the NASA research group at Moffett Field, California. The ongoing Search for Extra-Terrestrial Intelligence had detected a signal. It had the same characteristics as the old WOW signal detected back in the 1960s. Bennett checked the timing, and his hunch was right. The new SETI signal was received just before the machine turned on. It seems "ET" was sending radio signals to the machine...in Russian. But why Russian? Bennett's old ham radio buddy at the ALTAIR radar had a crazy theory that was starting to make sense. ET was using radio signals to control the machine. The oldest high-power radio signals on earth were from the Russian transmitters in Moscow almost 100 years ago. Coincidence?

The phone rang again. It was Phil Beckman.

"Good morning, Captain Bennett. Or should I be calling you Admiral Bennett?"

"It's still Captain, Phil. Have you heard back from the Naval Observatory?"

"Yes, Sir. John Martin called me at three o'clock this morning. You would think that a guy whose job it was to keep global time would know what time it was," Phil joked. "John said there was, in fact, a shift in the South Atlantic Anomaly that occurred at the same time as the machine came on, at least to within the timing accuracy they can achieve with SAA measurements."

"So, we are fairly sure, then, that the power source is magnetic?"

"It sure is looking like it, Sir. It definitely appears that there is a fluctuation in the earth's magnetic field, and we are detecting what appears to be an associated current flow in the machine's central arm."

"Good work, Phil. Of course, you know with this you have earned another chance to brief our congressional friends. You might as well get started on your presentation. Bennett was only half joking, but they both laughed.

———•———

The morning staff meeting was finishing up, and people were leaving Bennett's office. There had been little change in the machine's activity, since the four keyed control panels lit up three days earlier. The generator chamber walls were still dark. There were no Cyrillic messages on the control screens.

The Mexican fisherman, who attempted to land on the northern end of the island the previous night, turned out to be just that--a Mexican fisherman. They had originally thought otherwise. Meanwhile, a French naval vessel, a La Fayette Class frigate, was enroute to the island on what was, no doubt, another intelligence gathering mission. Enough of the mock, guano-mining charade would be activated to keep their attention away from the research work. Bennett smiled at how the research facility had been constructed to look like a phosphate processing plant. So far, the charade seemed to be working, even though the French must know the American effort on the island wasn't about guano.

Bennett's phone rang again.

"It's activating."

It was Phil Beckman. He sounded excited.

"Control room four lit up just a few moments ago. It's turning on, Captain, and the control room message, Sir,...it's in English."

"Is it the same message, Phil?"

Captain Bennett opened his desk drawer and removed the translation of the original Cyrillic message that agent Fox had made a year before.

"Yes, Sir, direct translation. Sir, we need to get the men out of the shafts."

"DO IT!"

Bennett's tone was more of a shout. He had the report before him.

> **Original:**
>
> добро пожаловать в определенный артикль
> осевое проверка комната
> там крайний непредвиденный
> твой мир великий опасность
> безотлагательный действие необходимый
>
> **Translation:**
>
> Welcome to the "Definite Article
> Axial" control room.
> There is an extreme unexpected event.
> Your world is in great danger.
> Immediate action necessary.

Captain Bennett replaced the file in his desk and started to get up from his chair when Sergeant Hansen poked his head in the doorway.

"You have an off-island phone call, Sir, from Miss Harris…I mean Mrs. Peterson, Sir. I'm connecting you now."

Bennett sat back down.

"Hi, Kate. Ah, thanks for getting back to me. I had a heck of a time catching up with you two. I ah, I've…"

"It's our honeymoon, boss. You're not supposed to be catching up with us."

"It's activating, Kate."

There was a long pause.

"We thought that might be the case, Richard. Our key just began to glow."

"What are you doing taking that key off island?"

"We have a sentimental attachment." Kate's thoughts went back to when she and Alan first determined what the key was for.

Alan came into the bedroom and gave Kate a kiss on the back of her neck. She indicated it was Bennett on the phone.

"Has it activated?" he asked.

Kate nodded her head.

Bennett was explaining how he thought it would be a good idea if they cut their honeymoon short and returned to the island.

Then a loud siren noise came over the phone.

"Is that the alarm, Richard?" Kate shouted into the phone.

"Yes." Bennett shouted back. "It looks like…"

The phone line went dead.

GLOSSARY

Military Terminology

USPACOM	United States Pacific Command. Organization responsible for all US
(PACOM)	Military forces in the Pacific Region.
CINCPACFLT	Commander and Chief, Pacific Fleet. Commander of the
(PACFLT)	organization responsible for all US Naval forces in the Pacific Region.
INTELSAT	International Telecommunications Satellite Organization: provider of satellite communications systems for the government.
DMSP	Defense Meteorological Satellite Program: A constellation of military weather satellites.
TYCO	A fictional, government, imaging satellite constellation.
RYNO	Another fictional, government, imaging satellite constellation.
Zulu Time	Military term for the international time standard, also known as Greenwich Mean Time (GMT)
NAVCAMS	Naval Communications Station

Astronomy/Technical

Right Ascension	A measure of angular distance of a celestial body in the east-west direction.
Declination	A measure of angular distance of a celestial body in the north-south direction.

| IR, IR image | Infrared, infrared image. Light in the non-visible spectrum. Commonly used for "night vision" devices. |
| Azimuth | Compass direction |

Ship/Boat Terminology

Boomkin	A small platform at the stern of a boat
Anemometer	Instrument for measuring wind speed and direction
Port	To the left—left side of vessel.
Starboard	To the right—right side of vessel.
Bow	Front of vessel—forward.
Stern	Back of vessel—aft.

Made in the USA
Middletown, DE
19 February 2022

61551086R00169